THE WRITING ON THE WALL: A HORROR TRIBUTE TO IRON MAIDEN

JYL GLENN & JOSEPH MURNANE

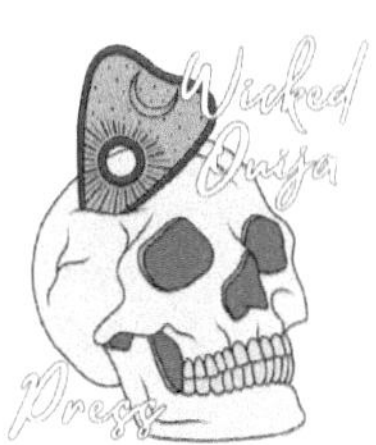

To Iron Maiden, every member past and present, and to the fans who keep the fire alive.
Up the irons—forever.

Set List

FOREWORD
THE STORIES HIDDEN IN IRON MAIDEN'S MUSIC

BY THOMAS R. CLARK

There's something to be said about good art. It endures. Part of the reason it endures is people can find multiple interpretations and meanings within the art. And Iron (fucking) Maiden? They're fucking art. And this volume you hold? It's filled with art inspired by them. For fifty years the band has entertained the masses, flying across the world and declaring "Up the irons!" And now as we near their twilight, it's only appropriate for this anthology to come out and pay homage to the band.

Many of Iron Maiden's songs are inspired by history, classic literature, movies, and television programming. From Samuel Taylor Coleridge to Edgar Allan Poe and Frank Herbert. There's television in the form of The Prisoner, movies like Children of the Damned (which in turn was inspired by the classic sci-fi horror novel The Midwich Cuckoos) and The Quest for Fire, the fictional-ized caveman adventure. And speaking of history, Iron Maiden are experts. Whether it's the plight of American

Indians, Norse raiders, the Crimean War, WWII (a subject often visited by the band), or epics about infamous warlords like Genghis Khan, listening to Iron Maiden does something other than entertain you, it educates you.

I was *today-years-old* when I finally put two and fucking two together regarding a pair of albums I've listened to in tandem for decades: Iron Maiden's first releases, the self-titled album, and their sophomore effort, Killers. Both albums feature the band's original line up, including vocalist Paul Di'Anno and drummer Clive Burr (both have since passed away). The songs on these albums are very different from the songs that followed on The Number of the Beast and after. And today? I finally realized they are (possibly?) a two-part conceptual story. A supernatural rock opera if I dare say. Or maybe Tommy, the serial-killer punk version.

"You're high, Tom!" Says the intrepid reader. That may be so, but it doesn't change the facts, and the first two Iron Maiden Steve Harris penned albums may indeed tell a story, whether or not it was intentional remains to be seen. I wouldn't be so brash as to think it was. Steve wrote songs and each had their own inspirations. This is full of serial killing, wannabe vampires, and drug-inspired dreams. Hammer movies, library books, hookers, and hallucinogenic substances make up the rest.

We can postulate the first two Iron Maiden albums tell the story of Eddie (What else would his name be?), a serial killer who fancies himself to be a vampire (The theme of retaining your youth is prevalent through the songs on both albums). Eddie believes he can stay young forever through his murders, by torturing his victims. He likes taking them down on city streets. His weapon of choice is a hatchet. Then he takes them back to his lair... for some private fun and ritual torture.

Let's look at the track listings on the two albums (keeping in mind some of these songs are re-imagined in this volume!), and go into more depth with each. Much of it is cursory. I'm providing only a bit of logic and interpretation of the songs. I'm sure more connections in the story can be built from what I present.

Iron Maiden, with the cover boasting Eddie under a street light. This is how Eddie perceives himself to be, a strung-out, drug-addicted teenager, emaciated and wraithlike. Prowler opens the album, and with it, we get our cold open. We don't know Eddie is a killer, yet. But we do know he likes to stalk women and girls at night. His dreams are filled with fantasies, fueled by the drugs he takes, and Remember Tomorrow exemplifies this. The album's anthem is Running Free, it is Eddie's ballad of liberation and leads to his first kill.

As it turns out, Eddie is a *huge* fan of Hammer horror films. In the epic Phantom of the Opera, Eddie sees his next victim through the eyes of a Hammer Horror character. He's turned on by the screams of his victims and it alludes to Eddie's secret torture room with its last verse, which is told from his victim's POV. Transylvania keeps us in Hammer-land, as Eddie visualizes himself as the Prince of Darkness, Count Dracula himself.

Strange World tells of Eddie's drug-induced dream state. The police are on his trail in Sanctuary But he hides out with his girlfriend, Charlotte the Harlot a local prostitute. She can't believe he would do these things. Then he tries to kill her in his torture room, which features, you guessed it, an Iron Maiden, among other devices of torture. Think SAW but he's having a grand old time administrating the pain. The album ends, open-ended...

Killers, the cover to which features Eddie using his ax, doesn't fuck around bringing us back into things. It opens with another dream sequence, Eddie on the run as the Ides of March loom over him. He's a Wrathchild, on the run from English authorities. He lands in France, and can't stop his murdering ways. "Murders in the Rue Morgue" He kills in a much-publicized case he again sees through the eyes of Hammer Horror film, and goes on the lam again. He starts to feel regret in Another Life wherein he fights with the urge to kill. But his mania has made him think he's a God, as evident with Genghis Khan.

—Thomas R. Clark

Bruce Smith discovered the boots in his grandfather's attic on a Tuesday that felt like the end of the world. Rain hammered against the dormer windows with biblical fury, and the old house groaned around him like a dying beast. He'd been putting off this task for months since the funeral.

As he sorted through decades of accumulated memories, deciding what deserved preservation and what belonged to the fire, the boots sat alone in a corner, separate from the other military memorabilia that told the story of Colonel William Smith's distinguished service.

These weren't regulation issue. Hand-crafted from supple crimson leather that seemed to absorb rather than reflect the dim attic light, they bore intricate Celtic knotwork burned into their surface. The silver buckles were tarnished black, and strange symbols were etched into the metal.

Bruce lifted one boot, surprised by its weight. The

leather pulsed warm despite the attic's chill, and he caught a scent that made his stomach clench. A familiar smell, something between copper and roses, sweet and metallic.

Inside, yellowed parchment bore his grandfather's careful script:

"Found these in a bombed cathedral outside Normandy, 1944. The priest who gave them to me said they once belonged to a Celtic warrior-king who refused to kneel before the Romans. He died standing, sword in hand, boots on his feet. The priest warned me they carry a price, but I was young and foolish. I wore them only once. Never again. Some gifts from the dead should remain ungiven. —W.S."

Below that, in shakier handwriting added years later: *"For Bruce, should he choose to understand what it means to die with honor. But may God forgive me if he does."*

The thunder outside seemed to echo his grandfather's words, and Bruce felt something shift in the air around him as if reality itself was holding its breath. He should've left boots there. Should've burned them with the rest of the questionable artifacts. Instead, he found himself removing his sneakers.

The boots slid on as if they'd been crafted for his feet alone. The moment his weight settled into them, the world exploded into sensation. The attic vanished, replaced by a windswept moor beneath a sky the color of old, dried blood.

He stood on a hilltop, surrounded by the clash of steel and the screams of dying men. The Battle of

Culloden raged around him, and he was no longer Bruce Smith, suburban insurance adjuster. He was now Alasdair MacBride, clan chieftain, and the English were cutting his people down like wheat.

A bayonet thrust deep into his ribs. Pain knifed white-hot through his chest as he staggered backward, tartan soaking crimson in the Scottish mud. Blood frothed from his lips, and his vision blurred, but his feet remained planted firm. He raised his claymore one final time, defying the English bastards who had slaughtered his clan. The world darkened around him, but even as death claimed him, he stood upright, boots rooted in the blood-soaked earth. He died standing, as warriors should. With his boots on.

Bruce gasped, finding himself back in the attic, hand clutched to his chest where phantom pain still throbbed. The boots hummed with warmth around his feet, and he could swear he heard distant pipes playing a lament. He clawed at the buckles, desperate to remove them, but they wouldn't budge. The silver had fused somehow, become part of the leather, part of him.

"What the hell?" he began, but the words died as the attic faded again.

This time he was Jacques Montclair, crouching in a muddy, bloody trench as German shells screamed overhead. The Great War had been raging for three years, and the rats were getting bolder, nibbling at the edges of sanity. Out of the trench, he sprinted across no man's land, dodging craters and corpses, his rifle clutched tight. He made it perhaps twenty yards before the bullets found him, stitching a line across his chest. The impact spun him around, but he didn't fall. Even as his life poured out onto the scorched earth, he remained upright, boots planted firm, rifle raised in defiance against the Hun.

He died standing. In his boots.

Back in the attic, Bruce slumped against a dusty trunk, understanding beginning to dawn like a cold sunrise. The boots didn't just carry the memories of their previous wearers. They trapped them, cycling through their deaths like a cosmic record player with a broken needle. Each death was real, each agony genuine, but the boots wouldn't let him stay dead. They had a purpose, a hunger that fed on noble deaths and standing stones. And him.

He tried everything. Knives couldn't cut the leather, fire couldn't burn it, and no amount of force could remove the boots. They had become part of him, or perhaps he had become part of them. The deaths came faster now, each more violent than the last. He couldn't, no, *wouldn't* scream.

He was now Titus Aurelius, Roman centurion, standing alone as barbarian hordes overran his position. Spears pierced his body, but his feet never left the ground. Blood streamed down his armor as he hacked at the screaming warriors with his gladius. A war axe split his skull, but he remained upright even as his heart stopped beating. He died standing. In his boots.

He was next William Marshal, knight errant, an underdog in a tournament that had become a blood sport. Lances shattered against his armor, sending shock waves through his bones. Swords found the gaps in his plate, slicing deep into flesh. But he remained mounted, remained upright, his horse's hooves stamping the earth as enemies surrounded him. They dragged him from his horse, but even on his knees, he fought. Even bleeding out in the mud, he swung his sword until his arm could no longer lift it. He died standing in spirit, if not in body. In his boots.

He was Miyamoto Yoshitsune, samurai lord, facing a hundred enemies with only his katana and his honor. They came at him like a crimson tide, screaming their battle cries. He danced among them, his blade singing as it carved through flesh and bone. They cut him down by inches. A thousand cuts, they called it. But his spirit never wavered, his stance never broke. Blood painted the cherry blossoms red as he fell forward, but even in death, his feet remained planted. He died standing. In his boots.

Days blurred into weeks, weeks into months. Bruce lost track of time, of self, of everything except the endless cycle of noble deaths. He was every warrior who had ever faced long odds with courage, every soldier who had chosen honor over survival, every man who had decided that some things were worth dying for.

The visions grew more intense, more brutal and often. He lived entire lifetimes in the space of heartbeats. He was a Spartan at Thermopylae, holding the pass against Persians. He was a Viking berserker, foam flecking his lips as he carved through Saxon shield walls. He was a Union soldier at Gettysburg, standing firm as

Confederate artillery tore his regiment apart. He was an RAF pilot, diving his Spitfire into a formation of German bombers over London, his fuel tank burning but his determination unwavering. Bailing out and killed by German soldiers when he wouldn't be taken prisoner on the ground.

Each death taught him something new about courage, about sacrifice, about the weight of standing firm when everything inside screamed at him to run. The boots were reshaping him, forging his soul in the crucible of a thousand heroic endings.

But understanding came slowly, like dawn through heavy clouds. The boots weren't cursed. They were a test. Each death added another layer to his soul, another strand to the tapestry of courage being woven within him. He was being prepared for something, shaped.

The pattern finally broke on a Thursday that felt like resurrection.

He was what he thought was himself again, Bruce Smith, standing in a convenience store as three armed men burst through the door.

The bell jingled cheerfully, an absurd counterpoint to the violence about to unfold. The cashier, barely out of high school, cowered behind the counter. An elderly woman in the corner clutched her purse and whimpered prayers. This wasn't ancient Scotland or the trenches of France. This was his world, his time, his choice. Right *now*.

The gunmen hadn't noticed him in the back aisle, hidden behind a display of energy drinks. He could've stayed hidden, could've waited for them to leave. But the boots thrummed with power, with the accumulated courage of a thousand heroes, and Bruce felt their strength flowing through him.

He stepped forward, his movements fluid and confident. The boots shrieked against the linoleum floor.

"Hey," he called out, voice steady despite the fear clawing at his throat. "You want something, take it from me."

The gunmen spun, weapons tracking toward him. The leader, a thin man with wild eyes and shaking hands, pointed his pistol at Bruce's chest. "Get back, old man! This ain't your business!"

"It is now," Bruce replied, taking another step forward. He could feel the weight of every warrior who'd ever worn these boots, their courage flowing into him like a river of fire. "Let them go. You want money? I've got money. You want a hostage? Take me."

The second gunman, younger and more nervous, swung his rifle toward the cowering cashier. "Stay back or the kid gets it!"

Bruce moved without conscious thought, muscle memory from a hundred battles guiding his actions. He dove to the side as the first shot rang out, the bullet sparking off a shelf of canned goods. Rolling behind the counter, he came up swinging a metal door stopper like a club. It caught the young gunman in the temple, dropping him instantly.

The leader's second shot took Bruce in the shoulder, spinning him around and sending him crashing into a display of lottery tickets. Pain exploded through his body, but he pushed himself upright. The boots kept him standing, kept him moving, even as blood soaked his shirt.

"You crazy old fool!" the leader screamed, his voice cracking with panic. "I'll kill you!"

"You can try," Bruce said, advancing steadily. He felt no fear now, only the calm certainty that comes with absolute purpose. "But I'm not going down easy."

The third gunman, who had been silent until now, raised his weapon. Bruce saw the barrel swing toward him, saw the finger tighten on the trigger, and knew he wouldn't reach the man in time. But he didn't stop moving. The boots carried him forward, each step a defiant rejection of death.

The shot rang out, but it wasn't the gunman's weapon that fired. The elderly woman, who had been cowering in the corner, had picked up the fallen gunman's pistol with shaking hands. Her shot went wide, but it was enough to spoil the third man's aim. His bullet went high, shattering a beer cooler behind Bruce's head.

Bruce tackled the leader, driving him to the ground. They wrestled for the gun, rolling across the floor in a tangle of limbs. The weapon discharged again, the bullet punching through the ceiling. Bruce felt his strength failing, blood loss making his movements sluggish. But the boots wouldn't let him quit. They demanded he stand, demanded he fight, demanded he protect the innocent.

He managed to get his hands on the pistol, but the leader

drove a knee into his wounded shoulder. Bruce screamed, his grip loosening. The gun skittered across the floor, coming to rest near the third gunman, who was struggling to rise from where the elderly woman's shot had grazed his leg.

Time slowed to a crawl. Bruce saw the man reaching for the weapon, saw the deadly calculation in his eyes. The cashier was frozen in terror, the elderly woman had collapsed from shock, and Bruce was too far away to stop what was about to happen.

But he didn't give up. Even as his vision blurred and his strength failed, he lunged forward. The boots carried him across the floor in a desperate dive, his hand closing around the gun just as the wounded gunman's fingers brushed the grip.

The final shot was muffled against Bruce's chest as he wrestled the weapon away. Pain ripped through his torso, but he managed to roll away, the gun clutched in his hands. The leader was getting to his feet, murder in his eyes, but Bruce swung the pistol toward him.

"Stop," he commanded, his voice barely a whisper but carrying the authority of every warrior who'd ever stood their ground. "It's over."

Sirens wailed in the distance, growing louder. The leader looked at his fallen comrades, at the gun in Bruce's steady hands, at the determination in his eyes, and raised his hands in surrender.

As police cars screeched into the parking lot, Bruce felt the boots' grip loosen. He'd learned their lesson, proven himself worthy of their gift. He had faced his death, his *real* death with courage and honor, and in doing so, had saved lives.

But this time, death didn't come to claim him.

The paramedics worked frantically to stop the bleeding, their voices urgent but distant. Bruce felt himself fading, but not into death. But into something else. A peace he'd never known, a satisfaction that came from knowing he had stood when standing mattered most.

He awoke three days later in a hospital bed, the boots gone from his feet but their lessons carved into his soul. The doctors called his recovery remarkable. The bullets had missed vital organs by millimeters, and his blood loss, while severe, hadn't been fatal. But Bruce knew the truth. The boots had protected him one final time, ensuring he lived to tell their story.

On the nightstand beside his bed lay a new piece of parchment, written in his own hand though he had no memory of writing it:

"The boots choose their own successor, seeking those who need to learn what it means to stand firm in the face of darkness. I learned. I stood. I am ready to pass on the lesson. —B.S."

A week later, Bruce returned to his grandfather's attic. The boots sat in their corner, the crimson leather now faded to brown, the silver buckles tarnished to pewter. The strange symbols were gone, their power spent. But Bruce could feel them stirring, reaching out, searching for their next student.

He wrapped them carefully in an old military blanket and placed them back in their corner. Someday, someone else would find them. Someone who needed to learn what courage meant, what it cost, and why some things were worth dying for.

As he descended from the attic, Bruce carried with him the memories of a thousand noble deaths. But more importantly, he carried the knowledge that he'd finally learned to live. Truly live. By learning how to die with honor.

The boots waited in their corner, patient as gravestones, ready for their next student. Outside, a storm passed, and the sun was beginning to shine through the clouds. Bruce walked into the light with steady steps, his feet bare but his soul armored in the accumulated courage of heroes.

He'd died a thousand deaths and lived to tell about it.

Behind him, the attic grew quiet, but in the corner where shadows gathered, the boots began to glow with a faint crimson light. They were already reaching out, searching for their next wearer, their next student in the art of dying well.

The cycle would continue, as it always had, as it always would. Because some lessons could only be learned through death, and some gifts from the dead were too important to let fade away.

The boots waited, patient and eternal, for their next student to arrive.

**

Sarah Smith climbed the attic stairs with heavy feet, twenty-three years old and already weary of the world. Her father had been gone for six months now. A heart attack at fifty-five, the doctors said, though she suspected the real cause was a lifetime of carrying other people's burdens. Bruce had always been the one to step forward when others stepped back, the man who'd intervened in that convenience store robbery five years ago and somehow walked away when he should've died.

She'd inherited the house, the debts, and the overwhelming task of sorting through a lifetime of memories. The insurance money covered the funeral costs, barely. Everything else would have to go.

The attic felt different today, charged with an energy that made her skin crawl. Dust motes danced in the afternoon light filtering through grimy windows, and somewhere in the shadows, something waited. She'd been avoiding this room for weeks, but the estate sale was tomorrow. Time to face whatever secrets her father had kept hidden up here.

The boots drew her attention immediately. They sat in the far corner, wrapped in a military blanket that had seen better decades. Unlike everything else in the attic, they seemed to pulse with life, as if blood still flowed through their crimson leather veins. Sarah unwrapped them carefully, surprised by their weight and warmth.

A piece of parchment fell from the wrapping. Her father's handwriting, but shaky, as if written during his final illness:

"For Sarah, who has forgotten what it means to stand for something. The boots will teach you, as they taught me. But remember—courage isn't the absence of fear. It's standing up when your knees are shaking, when your heart

is breaking, when the whole world tells you to sit down and be quiet. Some battles can only be fought by those willing to die for what's right. — Dad"

Below that, in different ink: *"P.S. - Don't let them win, sweetheart. You're stronger than you know."*

Sarah's hands trembled as she held the boots. Her father had always believed she was destined for something greater than her dead-end job at the call center, more than the string of failed relationships and mounting credit card debt that defined her existence. But she'd stopped believing in herself years ago, worn down by a world that seemed determined to crush anyone who dared to dream.

The boots hummed against her palms, and for a moment, she could swear she heard distant battle cries echoing from their depths. Her father's voice whispered through the shadows: *Stand up, Sarah. The world needs warriors now more than ever.*

With shaking hands, she began to unlace her sneakers.

D ark. Endless. Cold.

Those were the first words that came to me when I saw the pool.

The same words I would use to describe my own heart and soul. A lot has changed in a year. The fire that took everything that mattered from me. My breakdown. My move from New Jersey to this ancient, depressing house in Wilmington, North Carolina.

But perhaps none so dramatic as my discovery of the pool.

That is why I've begun this journal. The one Doctor Adams suggested months ago. There are things happening, strange things, things I cannot yet fathom, and I feel I should keep a record of them. Not out of fear of what I might become, but rather what other peoples' interpretations of those changes might be. I can't take the chance of someone like Adams, or Jazelle, or Jane, my agent, thinking I've suffered another mental collapse, as my sister so bluntly put it. No, this journal will detail everything that I've discovered, every change I've experienced, up to now, and then moving forward.

Just in case.

Anyone reading this is most likely aware of the events that led to my being here.

The fire that night, the one that stole my beloved Monique and our unborn son. Even now I cannot write about it, think about it, without lapsing into tears. The pain of losing them is worse than any burn I could've suffered. If I could only go back in time and trade places with her, let her be safe on a stalled subway train and me in bed when the fire broke out in the apartment downstairs...

But I can't think like that. Adams has told me over and over that there's no place for 'what if' in a tragedy. Jazelle agrees with him, but what do they know, him in his stuffy office and my sister ensconced in her perfect life in Westchester? After I was released from the institution, I pretended to agree with them, just to shut them up. And to convince them I was sane enough to move as far from the place where my life ended as possible.

I chose Wilmington at random, but lately I've wondered if anything is random at all. I'd hate to think there's a grand scheme to everything, because that would mean some immortal being decided it was okay to sacrifice Monique and our baby just so I'd end up here.

The house itself is a centuries-old, two-story

Georgian-style brick building the locals call 'the Nickie House,' despite there being no record of anyone named Nickie ever owning it. It's not in the greatest of shapes, but the roof doesn't leak and there's no rats in the walls. It sits at the end of a street surrounded by dozens of live oak trees that keep it in perpetual shade.

As soon as I saw it, I knew it was 'the one.'

According to Marsha, my annoyingly cheerful real estate agent, it's supposedly haunted. I took that with a grain of salt; after all, half of Wilmington claims to be haunted.

Now I'm not so sure.

I spent the first few days moving in my meager belongings and setting up my studio in what used to be the dining room. The house came fully furnished, which is a blessing, since I had little more than a box of clothes and some toiletries that I'd bought after I got released and I was staying at Jazelle's. Even my art equipment was new, bought with the insurance money. Luckily, my portfolio had been backed up to the ether.

The same ether where—

No, I must stop thinking that way. Like Adams keeps saying, this is a new beginning.

The dining room came with a large, scarred wooden table. On it went my computers, drawing tablets, and a small printer. Next to it I set up my large-scale printer and a scanner. Two ancient French doors with faded stained-glass panels open onto the patio, which is over-grown with weeds. Beyond that is a long, narrow yard enclosed by a ten-foot cement wall that is cracked in several places. At the back of the yard is a run-down, wooden shed that looks like it will collapse in the next hurricane. When I commented on the shiny, oversized padlock on the shed doors, Marsha informed me that inside it is a well of some kind, but it's considered a hazard so for legal purposes the real estate agency locked it.

"Gotta keep the neighborhood kids out, or they'll find a way to get themselves in trouble. Maybe even drown. Can't have that."

I asked her about the well's history, but she just shrugged and said that was before her time. Her interest was more in me signing the final papers, to which I obliged as much to send her on her way as to take possession of the house.

Then I went inside, without a second thought for the shed or the well.

Those came later.

The first nightmare that I can remember happened about a month after I moved in.

Looking back, I think they were probably occurring before that, maybe as soon as the first few nights, because from day one my sleep here has always been unsettled. But I attributed it to a combination of living in a new place and still being in mourning, a background ache that is always with me whether I am awake or not. And God knows I've had more nightmares than I can count over the past year.

The difference was, this time it didn't involve the fire. And I didn't wake terrified and sweating, my teeth clenched around a scream.

Some less frightening and more disturbing occurred.

I was in a place of total darkness. In the distance were round, pale objects. I couldn't tell what they were, their details so vague as to be non-existent. And the shapes wavered, like puffs of fog in the slightest of breezes. I heard whispers, faint murmurings that allowed no understanding of actual words, but I could tell they were voices, not natural sounds. There was a sense of urgency associated with them and I wanted to move closer, but something prevented me from doing so, blocked my way. The emptiness around me grew colder. I tried again to move forward and this time my face connected hard with the invisible force and the entities disappeared.

I woke in my studio, my hands pressed against the glass doors.

When I stepped back, warm wetness dripped over my lip and I tasted the metallic tang of my own blood.

In my apparent somnambulistic state, I'd walked face-first into the door and bloodied my nose.

It happened again the next night. And the night after that.

After the fourth such occasion, it came to me that perhaps my subconscious was trying to tell me something. That the unsettling dreams were, in fact, a message rather than some supernatural aspect of the house. So before retiring, I left the studio doors slightly ajar.

And woke to find myself standing in front of the

shed, my hand on the rusted handle, the pleading dream voices fading in my mind.

That must be it, I told myself. A curiosity I hadn't been aware of, the Mystery of the Hidden Well. Thank you, Martha from River Realty, for sowing the seed of interest in the fertile soil of my imagination.

There was no opening the door, however, because of the heavy lock that secured it. Exploring that mystery would need to wait until morning.

Sleep eluded me the rest of the night, as did any attempts at work. My brain remained preoccupied with the shed and what might lay beyond those doors. I was also taken aback by my apparent unconscious obsession with such a mundane object. Staring at the glass doors from my workstation, I wondered if it was the first sign of another mental breakdown. Should I contact Adams? He'd said to stay in touch, something I'd not done at all since moving into Nickie House. Not with him, not with Jazelle. Oh, I answered their texts with brief ones of my own, more to ease their minds that I hadn't regressed in my recovery than any desire to speak to them. But initiating contact? No.

The mind works in strange ways, and during the long hours as I waited for dawn, it took me down many an unexpected, and sometimes disturbing, path. Was the house actually haunted? That would explain the voices— if they were not figments of my imagination. And what of my sleepwalking? Something I'd never done in my life. Another sign of mental degradation? Or possession?

When first light broke, I immediately took my

hammer and a screwdriver and headed out to the shed, the morning dew cold on my bare feet. Had anyone entered the yard at that point they'd surely believe me a lunatic. Dressed in t-shirt and boxers, hair uncombed, and attacking a lock in manic fashion.

The metal was new and heavy gauge; there was no breaking it. After a few strikes with the hammer I gave up and turned my attention to the hasp. This too was recent enough that the steel still shined. The handles, however, were decades old and screwed into boards that had probably been pieced together before I was born. Once I remembered the old adage of work smarter, not harder, it took only a minute to pry both handles from the soft wood and fling the doors open.

There before me lay the pool.

And nothing has been the same since.

As I write this, it's been a week since I opened that door. A week in which I have finished ten—yes, ten!—paintings. Never have I experienced such productivity. Each evening after dinner, with the house and yard deep in shadow of the coming night, I sit down at the tablet and pick up my stylus. Within minutes, I am lost in my art. It's as if I'm accessing a part of my imagination I could never reach before, that I've unlocked a treasure trove of new images and ideas. And how they flow! From my inner eye through my hand and into the computer. Time ceases to exist and there is only whatever world I've been transported to. Fantastical, macabre lands filled with alien creatures and dark forests.

And at some point deep into the night, I wake from this mental astral projection and I'm in the shed.

Each time is the same as the first. I stand before the dark, impenetrable water. The real estate agent called it a pool, but it is really neither that nor a well, but rather something in between. Roughly square in shape and about six feet on each side, it takes up most of the interior, with just enough room to walk around it. From what I have seen, it is a natural feature, not man-made. The sides, what little of them show above the Stygian liquid, appear to be gray stone. Decades, or perhaps centuries, of people standing at the edge have compacted the earth into something as hard as cement. There is no mechanism for drawing water; no bucket even for dipping into it.

A faint odor, barely noticeable, drifts up. Not sulfur like the local swamps, nor copper-metallic, like the sphagnum bogs back home in Jersey. More like the sharp, slightly sweet, bleachy smell that happens after a thunder and lightning storm, when the air contains a heavy concentration of ozone.

No algae grows on the surface or the walls, at least as far down as I can reach my hand. Something I've only done once, because the water is colder than December snow, so bitterly frigid that I immediately withdrew my arm with a gasp. When I dipped a glass into it, the water was a pure ebon in color and I couldn't even see through it. I thought about what kinds of minerals there must be to taint it that shade, and in what concentrations. Surely I would not be drinking any of it!

Pristine, yet poisoned. Unable to nurture life.

Truly, it reflects that which is inside me these days, much as the surface mirrors my face when I visit in daylight.

More than once, I have found myself wondering if anyone has died in those waters. It's easy to imagine some child or drunk falling in and succumbing to the cold before they can climb out. Martha did say the shed was built as a safety precaution.

Are you a place of death? I wanted to ask on that first day I entered. *Do we have that in common as well?* But much like my sister and my shrink, I kept those kinds of questions to myself. Like them, I didn't want—or wasn't ready—to know the truth.

Despite these dark musings, I truly believe this is where I am meant to be.

How else to explain why it draws me so, each and every night?

The first nocturnal visit gave me a terrible fright.

I opened my eyes and nearly fell into the water.

For the briefest of moments, I swore a face stared up at me from below that glass-smooth surface, a visage so blurred I couldn't tell if it was a man or woman, young or old. Dark smudges gave the impression of wide eyes and an open mouth, as if caught mid-scream.

Then I blinked and all I saw was my own pale reflection.

The glow of my computer screens behind me, combined with the few stars visible above, provided just enough light so that I could barely see the outline of the pool and my own limbs.

How long had I been standing there, that my eyes had adjusted to the dark? I had no recollection of leaving the house.

My last memory was of working on an idea I'd been toying with for several days, right after washing the dinner dishes. A forest scene with some hellish creatures peering out from between the trees, their forms just barely visible. I'd been frustrated by my inability to transfer the mood I wanted into the image on my screen. And then...

Nothing. An empty space in my memory.

When my first shock faded, I realized I'd most likely fallen asleep. The more I thought about it, the more sense it made. There were vague impressions of a dream, a dark place. I wasn't alone. There'd been a voice, or perhaps voices. Whispers. And a smell like a mountain stream in the winter, crisp and metallic.

I'd never sleepwalked before, not that I know of. The idea of it made me nervous. What if I'd fallen in and drowned? Or walked through those glass doors and cut myself so badly I bled out on my studio floor?

Death had never been a phobia of mine. Not until the fire. Now I dwell on it to the point of obsession. I decided then that I'd be sure to lock the doors each night. Relief and anxiety battled each other as I went back inside.

Where I found another unsettling surprise.

My forest scene now contained a large, black pond. One I couldn't remember drawing.

An indistinct, grayish face stared up from the center of it.

Its mouth silently screamed at me.

Since that night, my productivity has known no bounds. I've said that before, I know. I'm repeating myself. I can't help it. A manic energy fills me each night, as if the setting sun flips a switch and turns on some previously untapped internal power source. I no longer fear my visits to the shed, despite that they always seem preceded by a blackout state in which I leave my desk and go outside. On one occasion I apparently crossed the lawn in a ferocious rainstorm with no recollection of doing so, waking up inside the shed with my clothes and body soaked.

Each return to consciousness is accompanied by the same visage looking up at me. As the nights have progressed, the image has grown incrementally clearer. It is definitely a face, although blurred beyond identification. It appears to reside several feet down, like an undersea moon, with black craters for the eyes and mouth. I've not yet seen any sign of ears or nose. The spectral visage wavers constantly, as if strong currents lie beneath the glasslike surface of the pool. The mouth moves in time to the whispers in my head, which remain frustratingly incomprehensible. Although they, too, grow clearer.

At some point, I blink, and the unnatural presence is gone.

It's not just my artistic imagination working better, my conscious mind thinking clearer. My dreams have become more vivid. Blurred faces float in a starless void, each one reminiscent of the thing in the pool. Their voices murmur faintly.

"—*ussss.*"

"—*joy....*"

"—*come...*"

"—*nee...*"

The impenetrable darkness creeps in from all sides until it engulfs the whisperers. And that is when I wake by the pool.

After each episode, I return to the house, all my previous energy gone, and fall into bed, where I sleep for several hours without any dreams. I wake to late morning sun streaming in around the edges of the curtains, the sheets tangled around me or sometimes thrown off the bed completely.

The sun seems to sap my strength now that I've developed my nocturnal habits. I move through the day listless and dull. The stifling heat keeps me inside except for the most necessary of trips to the market. Sometimes I doze on the couch, other times I force myself to check emails and phone messages. They are all the same. Jazelle. Doctor Adams. Bill collectors. The former I ignore, the latter I don't worry about. Because as dusk returns, so too does my newfound energy, and soon I'm back at the computer, finishing pieces faster than I ever did in New Jersey. The only struggle is to make sure I devote some time to my commissioned works, when all I want to do is work on the incredible ideas my brain keeps delivering.

Soon bills will be nothing I have to worry about. I've shown some of my new work to Jane, who believes there's a real market for what she calls "modern grotesquerie."

"Art de la mort," she said. "The art of death."

Once I have enough pieces finished, she's going to arrange a showing. Or perhaps even a tour.

Who would've guessed that tragedy and relocation would result in success?

I see them more clearly now. The faces. The ones in the pool and the ones in my dreams. Although I cannot really call them dreams any longer. They are more like experiences. So vibrant they seem like real life. There are sensations now. A deep chill that sinks into my bones, as if the void truly is somewhere in space. The wet, metallic odor is always present. And there is a feeling, something I can't yet describe. Not fear, more of an unease, although that word doesn't do it justice. The closest I can come is queer, in the sense that writers like Lovecraft or Poe would've used it. Like those moments in life where chill moves down your back but you don't know why, or you wake up anxious from a dream you can't recall.

Perhaps some people would call these nightmares, but I can't, because I welcome them.

Because sometimes the voices . . . they sound like Monique. Not all of them. But I can hear her, among them, calling to me.

I know these occurrences are tied to the shed, and

what lies within. The empty void in my dreams mirrors the impenetrable depths of the pool. The spirits—for I believe now that's what they are—speak to me in both places. The sentences grow with each passing day.

"Come. Be with us. Need you. Help."

As of yet, they cannot tell me what they want. I've taken to visiting the shed even in the day, when my strength allows. The cool dampness is a welcome respite from the insufferable Wilmington heat.

I believe the pool is my muse.

How else to explain its presence in all my paintings and drawings? The black square, with the specters barely visible below the surface. Woods, fields, mountains, even suburban neighborhoods. No matter the setting, the pool is there. Sometimes in the foreground, others tucked away, hiding in plain sight, peering out from behind a corner or dimly visible in the shade.

I've told no one this; they would think I'm crazy. Not Jazelle, not my agent, certainly not Doctor Adams. They've all been pestering me, leaving messages, sending texts and emails. I ignore them all. I can't let them interfere with my work, and when I'm not working I'm too tired to even look for my phone.

There's no telling how long this font of imagination will continue to flow. I must harness it while I can.

Everything else can wait.

If only they wouldn't interrupt me so damn much!

Putting my thoughts to paper has been harder lately. Sometimes I don't even have the strength to lift the pen. Other times it's as if my thoughts simply aren't there. I've been spending more and more time by the pool. Hours each day. Listening. Talking.

I can hear them clearly now. Awake, and in my nightmares. The faces.

They tell me things. Show me things.

Today I emerged from one of my spells to find I was sitting at the edge, my feet submerged in the icy water. When I drew them out, they were pale and wrinkled as a corpse's. The dead-looking skin went halfway to my knees. Hours later, it hasn't changed.

My fingers look the same, although I don't remember putting them in the water. Perhaps yesterday, or the day before? Time no longer flows straight; it whirls around and around. I'm not sure what

Wait. Someone's at the door.

They have her. Martha, my real estate agent. It was her at the door. Yesterday? I think so.

She said I haven't paid my rent in two months. Impossible, of course. I haven't even been here that long. She showed me the date on her phone but I didn't believe her. That would mean I've lost

No. She said that I needed to clean the house, too. That it was a pigsty. I told her it wasn't my fault, it was the faces, the spirits of the pool. They occupy so much of my time. She laughed, and I told her I could prove it. She just had to follow me to the shed.

When she saw the broken door she threatened to call the police but I urged her to look.

We stepped inside and there they were. Waiting for us. For me. They whispered, told me what to do.

It only took one hard push.

There was no scream, no splash. She disappeared the moment she touched the water, almost as if pulled in from below.

After she was gone, they spoke to me again.

"More. More."

I ran from the shed. But I can't run from them. I hear them all the time now. Awake. Asleep. It doesn't matter. They terrorize me in my dreams with their ghostly images. The things they ask me to do...

Each time I wake, I'm back there. In the shed. Hands or legs in the water. My limbs are shrunken, my muscles wasting away. They're draining me.

There's only one way to stop it. But I can't do that. Not now. My work . . . it's so beautiful. I'm painting them now. The faces. Over and over. Jane saw them. She told me I should seek help, that there's something wrong with me, she could never sell them.

She won't return my calls.

I can't stop. I must paint them all. There's a new one now. It looks like someone I know. Or perhaps used to know. A woman? I think I remember her being here.

They are my muse, and it is my hand that brings them back, calls them up. More and more, so many of them down there!

So many. So hungry.

And I think... I think Monique might be there with them.

I know what I must do now. It's all so clear.

It's not just me they want.

I have to bring them all.

They're coming, I tell them. Soon.

I made the calls. Jazelle. Adams. Jane.

They'll know it's not me. I'm not crazy.

The faces are real. The pool is real.

They'll see. I'll take them there.

And then we'll be together. Monique. Our baby. Our family and friends. All of us.

Forever.

The house didn't look any different; that would've made it easier.

No, it still loomed—two stories of rotting gray clapboard and vacant windows, as if waiting for her. The porch groaned under her weight just like it used to, and the front door stuck at the same warped angle, like it remembered how to resist her.

She hadn't been back since she was eighteen, since the night she fled, while her mother screamed nonsense about the devil into the dark after her.

They said she and her sister ran away. That was the official story. The one the church helped circulate. The one the cops didn't question too hard.

But Ruth knew better. She stepped into the entryway, greeted by that old, almost-clean smell—Pine-Sol, mildew, and the faint, sour tang of fear. Everything was just as she remembered it. Father's coat still hung by the door. Mother's ceramic angel collection stared blindly from their crooked shelf.

And at the end of the hallway: the door to the prayer closet.

Closed. Of course.

The air felt heavier the closer she got.

Ruth learned early that silence was a form of worship.

Her mother didn't like questions, and her father didn't like noise. If you spoke too much, you were prideful. If you questioned anything, you were ungrateful. The Lord loved a quiet woman, her mother said—and so Ruth practiced stillness like it was scripture.

Grace never quite learned.

She was three years younger, born pink and wide-eyed with a tangle of curls and too much voice. She asked why angels needed wings if they didn't fly anymore. She stuck raisins in the heating vent and said they were offerings to God's mice. She was sunshine in a place that only grew mold.

Ruth adored her. Protected her. Sometimes even envied her. Grace didn't understand yet that their house had rules carved in stone and punishment nailed to the wall.

Ruth caught the first punishment. She'd whispered to Grace that she didn't think God listened to kids, not really. Grace laughed, the way kids laugh—quick, bright, gone. But Father had been standing behind the door.

That was the first time she saw the inside of the prayer closet. It was just a linen cupboard, barely wide enough to kneel in. Her mother called it "cleansing solitude." Her father called it "correction."

Later, in whispers, Grace asked what it was like. "Like being swallowed whole," Ruth said. "Like you're in God's mouth. And He's not chewing, but He's not letting you out either."

🤘 🤘 🤘

By the time Ruth was eleven and Grace eight, the punishments had escalated.

No more television, not even religious cartoons. No radio. No school.

"The Lord will provide your lessons," their mother said.

And no doctors. Not even when Grace's asthma flared up and she wheezed so hard she turned red. Their mother called it "a spiritual affliction."

"The Devil chokes children who disobey," she'd mutter while boiling water with eucalyptus oil instead of getting an inhaler.

When Grace caught a cold that turned into a cough that turned into a wheeze, their mother said it was because she'd let pride enter her lungs. She locked her in the prayer closet with a bottle of water and a tiny Bible.

Ruth tried to open the door once, but it wouldn't budge. She could hear her sister breathing through the slats, small and rapid.

She stayed pressed against the wood all night, whispering verses just loud enough to keep Grace awake.

"You're not bad," Ruth had told her. "Your lungs just don't work right."

"Then why does God keep breaking me?" Grace had whispered back.

The day they shaved Grace's head was the day Ruth knew she'd leave. Ruth had just turned sixteen.

Grace had flirted with a boy from church by smiling too long. Their mother called it Jezebel behavior. Father held her down while their mother cut and buzzed and prayed.

Ruth waited until nightfall, crept into their shared room, and helped sweep the hair into a shoebox. Grace didn't cry.

Not until Ruth said, "You're still beautiful."

"They said beauty is wicked," Grace whispered.

"Then we'll both be wicked," Ruth said.

They made a pact. One day, they'd run. Together.

But Ruth ran first.

It was a Tuesday. Grace and Ruth liked Tuesdays because Father worked the late shift, and Mother spent more time in prayer—long, silent hours behind the locked bedroom door, whispering scripture like it was a spell. She called it her private communion.

Sometimes on Tuesdays, they got away with whispering in their room. Ruth would even read to Grace from the hidden book under her mattress—*Pride and Prejudice,* the one their cousin had given her in secret for her seventeenth birthday last year.

But not that Tuesday.

It happened to be Grace's fifteenth birthday, and she wasn't feeling well again. Ruth had been quietly reading to Grace when their mother burst into their room.

"Secular garbage!" she hissed. "You want stories? Read the ones God gave you."

She'd stormed down the hall with the book in hand.

But Ruth had followed—quiet, barefoot, unseen.

From the shadows of the hallway, she saw her mother shove the book into the coat closet by the front door, behind her sewing baskets on the top shelf.

Ruth had hurried back to their room before their mother could catch her. Grace was sick again. She'd been coughing through the night, the wheeze in her chest sounding worse than usual. Her lips looked pale. Her shoulders stayed high with each breath.

They'd asked to skip Bible study. Their mother said no.

"You girls want stories? I'll give you the Lord's stories."

Grace rolled her eyes when she started reading from Proverbs—and that was all it took.

"Disrespect," Mother had snapped, grabbing Grace by the wrist. "A mockery of His Word."

Ruth had followed them into the hallway, trying to stay calm.

"Mother, she's not mocking anything," she pleaded. "She's not feeling well. She hasn't slept—she's struggling to breathe."

"Are you questioning God's judgment?" her mother asked.

That was the game: if you protested, you became the wicked one. If you stayed silent, you were complicit.

Ruth stood frozen as the door shut behind her sister.

The latch clicked.

Dinner was silent.

Ruth picked at her meatloaf until it turned cold, listening for any sound from the hallway. Grace hadn't made a noise since the door closed. No prayers. No coughing. No banging. Silence.

Their mother sat opposite her, hands folded neatly on her napkin, as if there weren't a sick child locked in a closet at the end of the hall. She chewed with mechanical precision and closed her eyes when she swallowed, like it brought her closer to God.

At exactly 7:06 p.m., the first thump came.

It was quiet—like a fist, gently bumping the inside of the door. A minute passed. Then another. Another thump.

Their mother didn't flinch. Just reached for the butter.

Then she turned, sharply, her voice rising without warning.

"I don't hear you praying, Grace!"

The words echoed down the hallway. Cold. Sharp. Performed.

Ruth froze mid-bite.

"If you've got the strength to roll your eyes, you've got the strength to speak His name," her mother snapped, still not leaving her seat. "Don't think silence will spare you. He sees you in your quiet."

Silence followed. Heavy and wet.

Their mother turned back to her plate as if nothing had happened.

"May I be excused?" Ruth asked, voice trembling.

"You may go to your room and reflect," her mother said. "You've grown too attached to sin. And don't let me catch you whispering to her through the vent."

"It's not sin to love your sister."

"She's disobedient. And prideful," her mother snapped. "And so are you. You think the Devil waits for convenience? You think his temptations don't come when the body is weak?"

"She's not sinning. She's sick," Ruth said, more forcefully now. "She's been wheezing all day, she didn't sleep—"

Ruth's throat clenched. Her father didn't speak. He never did during punishments. Just kept eating, eyes on his plate like a man trying not to get in the way of God's will.

"You punish her for everything," Ruth whispered.

Her mother's eyes flared, and Father—stoic as ever—stood without a word.

Her mother set down her fork with a soft *clink*.

"Go. To. Your. Room."

She went.

But not because she was afraid of her parents.

Because she was afraid of what she might do if she stayed.

🤘 🤘 🤘

In her bedroom, Ruth lay stiff on top of the blanket, shoes still on, eyes fixed on the ceiling. The air was thick and still, the way it got before a summer storm—except there was no storm, just silence. Thick as syrup. Wrong.

She knelt by the floor vent and listened. For a long time, there was nothing. Then came the sound she was waiting for—and dreading. A thump. Then another. Then a wheeze.

Not a cry, not a voice—just that sick, rasping inhale. The one Grace got when her lungs got tight and her chest started to hollow out. Ruth had memorized that sound. Had lain awake for years listening to it while their parents pretended it was the Devil and not disease.

It kept going. Soft thuds, like Grace was trying to knock but didn't have the strength. In between them: short, dry, stark breaths. Too fast. Too shallow.

Ruth pressed her mouth to the vent.

"Grace?" she whispered.

No answer.

But the wheezing continued.

Every so often, a thump would interrupt it—slower now. More space between. Hours passed like that. Ruth sat with her arms around her knees, rocking slightly in the dark, whispering Grace's name through the floor.

At one point, she thought she heard her praying. Or trying to.

A broken, breathless whisper.

"H-hallowed... be... thy... n-name..."

But it faded.

Around midnight, the wheezing stopped.

So did the knocking.

And that was worse.

She waited.

She waited even longer after that.

For a cough. A breath. A whisper. For footsteps outside her door. But the hallway stayed silent.

When the grandfather clock in the living room struck two, she knew they were asleep. She crept from her room barefoot, careful not to let the floorboards speak. In the hallway, she paused.

The prayer closet door was there, just steps away. Closed. Still.

She didn't go to it.

She couldn't.

She turned and went back to her room.

She opened her closet and pulled out her old backpack. It still smelled like mildew and old crayons. She tucked in a toothbrush, as many outfits as she could fit, and her few personal items. Then she paused.

The book.

Ruth had never forgotten where it was hidden, but this was the first time she had been brave enough to go get it.

Now, with the house still and her parents asleep, she crept down the hallway and eased open the coat closet door. She reached up high, careful to not knock anything off shelves. It was still there.

The cover was bent. The corners soft. But it was still intact. It wasn't her favorite book because of the story— it was her favorite because it was the first thing anyone ever gave her that her mother hadn't approved of. It had *joy* in it. It had *choice* in it.

She held it for a long moment before sliding it into the backpack like something sacred.

Father's Sunday jacket hung on the peg by the front door, just like always. She slipped a hand into the inner pocket and pulled out his envelope—folded thick with bills for the tithe jar. She took four tens and two fives, then put it back exactly how she found it.

She made her way to the kitchen and grabbed the magnetic notepad her mother used for the grocery list from the refrigerator. She tore off the current grocery list and let it flutter to the floor. Her hand trembled as she wrote the note:

You call yourselves holy, but you lock up a sick child and call it love. You starve her of air and call it discipline. You think this is God's will? God isn't in that closet. I don't think God was ever here. I'm done being afraid of you. I hope someday everyone knows what you did.

She folded it in half and placed it on the kitchen table like it was a gravestone.

Then she opened the back door and walked out of that house for the last time.

She didn't run at first.

She walked through the yard and around to the street like a ghost, dew soaking her jeans. The moon was just a crescent. Her breath hurt in her chest like she was the one with asthma now.

And then—

"Ruth!"

The scream. Far away. High-pitched. Raw.

"You will not escape His judgment!"

Her stomach dropped.

"The way of the wicked shall perish!"

She stopped in the middle of the street, her back to the house. The scream had come from behind her—loud, jagged, unmistakable.

"Ruth! He will burn away your lies, Ruth Gideon!"

It wasn't pleading. It was angry. Commanding. It was her mother's voice.

Not a voice calling for her out of concern, but for obedience. For submission.

She didn't turn around. She stood trembling under the moonlight, the backpack digging into her shoulder, her fists clenched at her sides.

Her mother's voice cut through the dark like a blade, ringing off the rooftops, sharp and shrill and righteous.

"You're walking into the arms of the Devil! Do you hear me? He will not save you! TURN BACK, NOW!"

Go back, the voice in her head whispered.

But another, louder one followed. *If you do, you won't leave again. Not alive.*

She whispered Grace's name once. Just once. It vanished into the dark like breath on cold glass.

Then she ran down the street. Past the church. Past the neighborhood houses that watched like witnesses. She didn't stop until she reached the edge of the highway, headlights smearing past like Vaseline on a windshield. Where the world no longer smelled like mold and fear and God.

She clutched the straps of her backpack tighter, feeling the soft corner of the book press against her spine like a reminder, or maybe a question.

I should've opened the door.

Then she turned toward the road and walked.

Sixteen years later, the house looked almost exactly the same.

The paint had faded to the color of old bones. The porch sagged deeper than she remembered. The windows were still dark, still blind. The air smelled like cut grass, dry rot, and memory.

Ruth stood at the edge of the driveway, keys in hand.

She hadn't said yes right away when the lawyer called. He'd said the words plainly, like they meant nothing: *Your parents have passed. The estate is yours.*

Estate. As if this place had ever been anything but a trap.

She almost told him to burn it.

Instead, she'd taken the key. And now she was here, staring at the house where her sister died. Or was buried.

Everyone had believed the story. *Grace ran away.*

That's what her parents told the church, the neighbors, the police.

"They both left in the night. We prayed for them, but some children are just lost to the world."

Ruth had gone to the sheriff's office the morning after she escaped.

She told them Grace was sick. That she'd been locked in a closet. That she hadn't left with her.

But the story changed by the time the officers knocked on the Gideons' door. Her parents had already reported both daughters missing.

"They left together," her father said calmly. "Ruth must've made up the rest."

The sheriff believed them. The church believed them. Everyone believed them.

Ruth was eighteen. Grace was fifteen. Impressionable. Lost to the "bad influence" of her big sister.

No one questioned a righteous family like the Gideons. No charges were ever pressed, not against Ruth for taking her sister, and not against her parents for Grace's death.

After that, Ruth got as far away from home as she possibly could.

She didn't know what she hoped to find by coming back here. Answers. Maybe guilt. Maybe bones. Maybe nothing.

Maybe Grace's ghost.

She stepped up onto the porch. The boards creaked beneath her boots, just like they used to under bare feet in the middle of the night. Her hand hesitated at the door.

It still stuck—just a little—before giving way.

The air inside was cooler than expected, and stale.

The kind of stale that meant the windows hadn't been opened in years.

Ruth stepped over the threshold and into her past.

The floor groaned. The light was dim and yellowed, bleeding in through warped curtains. Dust hung in the air like something waiting to settle.

Everything was still there.

The framed verses on the walls.

The ceramic angels on their crooked shelf.

The small wooden cross above the hallway arch, slightly tilted.

The only thing missing was the noise. No sermons. No prayer recitations. No stifled coughing behind a closet door.

Just silence.

I should've opened the door.

The words came back, uninvited. They echoed between her ribs.

Ruth moved slowly, her fingers brushing along the chipped wood of the hallway trim as she passed.

And there it was.

At the end of the hall. The same door. The same brass handle. The same warped frame.

The prayer closet.

Closed.

Waiting.

Ruth stared at it for a long time, her hand resting lightly on the frame. The brass knob was cold—colder than the air around it. The wood shimmered in the half-light, warped with age and something else, like it was holding its breath.

Her stomach clenched.

She turned away.

Not yet.

She moved down the hall and opened the door to their old bedroom.

But... it didn't look the way it should have.

The furniture was wrong. Older. Sparse. A narrow bed with a thin quilt. A plain wooden dresser. A single Bible on the nightstand, its cover cracked.

She stepped inside slowly, her footsteps muffled on the thin rug.

The wallpaper was peeling. The closet door hung slightly open, empty. The air smelled like dust and eucalyptus. And something else.

Like absence.

Her eyes scanned the room. No clothing. No personal items. No second bed.

It's like they tried to erase her.

She crossed to the nightstand.

And stopped.

The book was there.

Pride and Prejudice.

The same one she'd taken when she left. The same worn corners. The same tape on the spine.

But she remembered packing it. She remembered holding it as she ran. It sat on her bookshelf at home.

So why was it here?

She picked it up. Opened it.

Her throat tightened.

Inside, written in faint, looping pencil, was her own name, just as she had written it all those years ago. Identical to the copy she had taken with her when she left.

She stared at her name until the letters blurred, then set the book down carefully, like it might break, and stepped back into the hall.

The air felt denser now. Like the house was closing in around her. Like something was holding its breath.

At the end of the hall, the prayer closet waited.

You know nothing is there. Let's get this over with.

She moved toward the closet.

Her feet dragged, each step slower than the one before, like dread was pulling at her ankles.

She stopped in front of the door.

The brass knob was still cold. Still waiting.

She took a breath.

Then opened it.

The door swung inward on silent hinges.

And there she was.

Curled on the floor. Knees to chest. Head bowed. Wheezing. Hair matted and damp. Skin pale and thin and wrong.

"Grace?" Ruth whispered.

The girl looked up and it was her own eyes gazing back at her.

The world went black.

Darkness unfolded around her. Then she heard a voice. *Grace.* Soft. Gentle. Inside her head. A voice she hadn't heard in years—except she had, every day.

Her own voice.

Then something else. A deep ache in her chest, clawing for breath.

The wheezing filled the space like an alarm. Too loud. Too familiar.

She blinked.

A sliver of light spilled in from beneath the door. The brass knob. The warped wood grain. Inches from her face.

She was in the prayer closet. Panic bloomed.

She reached out, scraping her hands along the inside of the door. Fingertips found familiar grooves—marks she knew. She had made them.

She pressed her palm flat against the wood. Tried to steady her breath and quiet the wheezing.

She gasped for her sister again. "Grace!"

Then she heard footsteps. Heavy and deliberate.

Then the lock turned and the door creaked open. Light flooded the space—yellow, warm, wrong.

Her mother stood above her.

Expression blank. As if she'd opened the pantry and found something rotten.

"I hear you asking for Grace. But God only grants grace to the faithful—and the faithful pray."

Ruth squinted hard against the light. Her voice came out cracked and raw.

"Where's my sister?" she whispered. "How did I get here?"

Her mother sighed. Turned away slightly, as if already done with her "Not this sister business again. You've got the devil in you. Sounds like someone needs to pray harder."

Ruth opened her mouth to speak again but nothing came out. Her throat closed around the truth.

Grace. She had made her up to have someone to talk to in the dark. Someone to love her

and to suffer with her.

"Now, start over like a good girl," her mother commanded. "Or wait and see what happens when your father gets home."

Ruth hung her head and began as tears rolled from her cheeks and hit the floor. "Our Father, who art in Heaven. Hallowed be thy name..."

No, there was no Grace in this house.

There never had been.

R hiannon lay in bed unable to sleep. It was 11:30 P.M. and it always took her at least two or three nights to get comfortable enough to sleep easily in a different bed. By the time she was relaxed enough to get any real rest, the trip was usually over. It's one of the reasons she had been dreading this weekend trip. She was grateful it wasn't camping. Her friends went camping all the time and how anyone enjoyed sleeping on the ground, with all the bugs and dirt, in the forest, was beyond her. Trees were pretty from a distance, but being in the forest made her feel claustrophobic and it awakened a primal fear deep within her. A weekend in an Airbnb with a group of people wasn't exactly her idea of fun either, but at least there was indoor plumbing and electricity.

There was a forest that rimmed the back of the property which made her uncomfortable, but there was a defined tree line and plenty of garden space between it and the house. Everyone else had agreed this Airbnb in the small town of Land O' Lakes would make for a relaxing little getaway. She was inclined to disagree, but didn't want to make waves and didn't have any suggestions to offer herself, so she kept quiet. If she was honest with herself, she couldn't think of any kind of vacation that sounded fun these days. In fact, she couldn't think of much of anything that sounded like fun.

Lately, the only things that seemed to make her happy were her cat, her books, and coffee. Some days even those things didn't work. She knew that she needed to stop isolating herself from people, though. It wasn't healthy and it certainly wasn't helping. So, despite her lack of enthusiasm for the trip, she was there. She was lucky anyone still wanted her to come along. She turned down so many invitations, she was always surprised to wake up and find she hadn't been removed from the group chat. She wouldn't blame them if they decided to stop including her. They didn't know her well yet, and her loner behavior was probably a bit strange to such a tight knit group.

Rhiannon met her group of friends a few months prior while she was working part time at a small coffee shop near the university. They were the only customers and she was the only barista that morning. When she delivered their second round of coffees, they'd struck up a conversation with her. They were there to go over the details of an upcoming weekend vacation and asked her opinion on some things. Over the following months, they became regulars and Rhiannon got to know them a bit. She learned that Leah and her boyfriend Todd met on campus at the university where they both worked. Leah taught zoology and Todd taught biology. They met when Leah's office was temporarily relocated next door to Todd's. Leah had a middle school aged daughter from before she met Todd, and he seemed to truly care about both of them.

She learned that Brad and his husband Chad adopted infant twin boys, a few years ago, after a lengthy and expensive process. The details of how hard they worked to adopt their children was both heartbreaking and inspiring. Chad was a freelance advertiser and Brad worked as a financial advisor for a national bank and they'd met when Chad needed financial advice. She didn't really know much else about them, and she'd shared very little with them about herself.

That was because connecting with people had always been hard for her. The deep scar that traced down her right cheek had shown her early on how cruel people could be. She had been made to feel like an outsider, so she leaned into it. It was sort of a self-fulfilling prophecy, if you think about it. Rhiannon knew that she should be over it by now. That people could be cruel, but she was far too old to still be so concerned with other people's opinions. Yet, she had built the walls around her with bricks made of pain and sorrow, and materials that strongly hold fast. Tearing them down was difficult, but she was doing it one brick at a time.

Leah had been asking her for weeks to come on this

trip and Rhiannon had relented at the last minute, the night before. The whole group had been going on and on all week about what she was going to miss out on: all the food they were going to eat and the activities they were going to do and how much fun the weekend was going to be. Maybe she watched too many movies, but Rhiannon had expected to be up until the early hours of Saturday morning. Which is why she had been a bit surprised to find herself in bed this early on the first night. There was a comfortable lounge in the basement that everyone relaxed into after dinner. They turned on a nature documentary narrated by David Attenborough at Todd's request and went over the plan for the following day.

Everyone would get up around 6:30 AM so they would all have time to get ready, eat breakfast, and be out the door by 8:30 AM. There were some local shops they wanted to check out in the town square, and Leah had heard about a pumpkin festival happening that afternoon, not far from the house. Seeing as they had all weekend to hang out, Leah was the one to suggest they call it an early night so everyone could be more energized for the following day. Everyone seemed grateful for the suggestion, and Rhiannon didn't want to put up a fuss.

Around 10:00 PM, Chad nudged Brad and asked him if he was interested in hitting the sack, waggling his eyebrows suggestively. Brad had giggled and turned a lovely shade of pink. And then they raced each other up

the stairs to their room on the second floor. Leah and Todd had taken the master bedroom on the first floor, as it was their idea to stay there. They'd taken care of all the arrangements and even drove everyone up in Todd's van, so everyone agreed that they should get the master bedroom. At the sound of the door to the boys' room closing upstairs, Leah yawned and said she thought they ought to head to bed themselves. Todd was still engrossed in the documentary and made no sign of moving. Leah smacked his leg to get his attention. When he tore his eyes from the colony of penguins featured on the screen and saw Leah's scowl, he nodded and stood up, turning off the TV.

Rhiannon, feeling as though she was overstaying her welcome, quickly said goodnight and went up to her room. The television in the lounge was the only one in the house, so she couldn't watch TV until she was sleepy like she sometimes did at home. The Wi-Fi didn't work at all, and she'd forgotten her kindle charger at home. With nothing to do to entertain herself, she'd been laying here for the last hour and a half, thinking.

She rolled over and faced the window, hoping the change of position would put an end to her chattering brain and lead to sleep. From her angle in the bed, she could see through the open window to the brilliant night sky. She'd forgotten to close both the window and the curtains and was instantly captivated by all the stars. Since she didn't leave the city very much, she never got used to the lack of light pollution. At home, the night sky was obscured by the haze of city lights. But out here, she was mesmerized by the sparkling black velvet sky and the bright glow of the moon. The moon was shining directly on her face, and she knew she'd never get to sleep at this rate.

With a sigh, she flipped the comforter off her and began to swing her legs off the bed. As she slowly began to lower her feet toward the ground, she heard a loud creak from beneath her bed. Her heart stopped. Panic shot through her and she pulled her feet back onto the mattress with a yelp. She leaned over to the bedside table and snapped the lamp on. She sat there, motionless, watching the floor by her bed.

Eyes wide, waiting for something to move. After a few moments, when nothing happened, she relaxed a bit. She knew turning the lights on made everything fine. But she was still rattled. She couldn't believe she'd almost forgotten and stepped out of bed in the dark. After a few deep breaths, her heart rate began to slow down, and her rational mind returned to her. No matter how old she got, and no matter how silly it seemed, she refused to step out of bed with the lights off. She knew in her logical mind that the only danger of getting out of bed with the lights off was tripping over something unseen on the floor. But fear isn't always logical. It didn't stop her from being annoyed with herself, though. She was a fully grown adult who was still afraid of the dark.

Bathed in the safety of light, Rhiannon stepped out of bed, onto the cold wooden floor and moved to close the window and the curtains. She stood at the window breathing in the cool night air and enjoying the silence.

The darkness was harder to get used to than the silence. She loved the quiet, and noise was one of the only things that she deeply disliked about the city. It was always loud back home. Deciding that she'd sleep better with the fresh air, she left the window open and reached to pull the curtain closed. As the curtain inched closer to the other side of the window, she thought she saw something move in the garden below. She paused, searching the ground for what it might have been. The garden, and the forest beyond it, was still. It must have been a wild animal. She shuddered, uncomfortable at the thought of something slinking around in the dark. She stared into the empty garden for a bit longer, trying to satisfy her anxious mind. When nothing else moved, she reached up to finish pulling the curtain closed, and that's when she saw it.

A creature had appeared at the edge of the forest, just beyond the garden. It was like a person, but it was abnormally tall and impossibly thin. The creature kept within the shadows of the trees, just out of reach of the moonlight, making it impossible to discern any other details of who or what it might be. The creature didn't move, and neither did she. She stared down at it, feeling goose flesh ripple across her body. Despite her inability to make out any of its features, Rhiannon was confident it saw her and was staring right back at her. A shiver crawled down her spine and she took a small step back from the window, not taking her eyes off it.

Suddenly, it bent sideways at an impossible angle and let out a groan. Its arms and legs began snapping and cracking and creating joints where none existed before. Its body began to double in size while its neck stretched farther away from the body and the head bobbled like a Jack-in-the-box. Bones stretched and broke through the skin and elongated into more limbs, as she watched. The creature shook and chittered as it violently contorted itself like a dying spider.

In the still of the night, the snapping of bones echoed in Rhiannon's ears. Then it stopped shaking and silence fell over the yard. She waited, terrified to move, terrified to breathe, terrified of what might happen next. Suddenly, the now eight-legged creature skittered forward, toward the garden and the house, at an impossible speed. As it scrabbled across the yard, it emitted a high-pitched squeal Rhiannon was sure the whole neighborhood would have heard, if there had been neighbors to hear. Then it hit the side of the house with a thud and Rhiannon shrieked, dropping to the floor.

She remained on the floor for a few moments, hoping to hear any movement the creature made. Silence lingered around her, and she knew she'd have to get up and look. Rhiannon carefully stood up and, eyes closed, stepped closer to the window again. She took a moment to summon her dwindling courage and then looked down. The creature was clinging to the side of the house, staring up at her with milky white eyes. Now that its face was fully visible, Rhiannon wished more than ever that she'd skipped this trip. She was staring down at a mask made from a human man. It was tied primitively around the head of the creature with thick twine. The creature's cloudy white eyes stared through the holes that had once held the eyes of an elderly man. The crude marks around the edges of the "mask" suggested the removal process wasn't done with much thought toward the finished product. And that certainly didn't bode well for whoever the victim had been.

She screamed and the human mask strained to keep the creature's true visage concealed as it widened its mouth and bellowed back at her. Its open jaws revealed a dark hole, rimmed with jagged yellow teeth and rows of serrated suction cups extending all the way down the figure's throat. A thick brown sludge dripped from its gaping mouth.

It began slowly climbing the wall toward her and Rhiannon scrambled backward. All rational thought abandoned her for the second time that evening, as anxiety gave way to panic, and she dove under the bed. She crouched there, breathing heavily, listening to the slow scraping sound of a nightmare climbing ever closer. The sound of raspy breathing and snarling reached Rhiannon's ears as the creature drew in line with the window. She realized she left the window open at the same moment the creature climbed effortlessly into the room. Rhiannon squeezed her eyes shut, praying she'd just disappear. If she had closed and locked the window, it wouldn't have been able to get in and maybe it would have gone away. Or it would have at least bought her a little time to get the hell out of there. She knew she had made a huge mistake. She'd had an opportunity to run down the hall, but in her terror, she'd trapped herself under the bed and whatever it was going to get her.

The creature dropped onto the floor beside the bed with a soft thud. It took a small step to steady itself and the sound of claws scraping softly against the wood grain shot lightning bolts of panic to Rhiannon's brain. The creature was now whispering what sounded like gibberish and she watched, horrified, as the dark sludge landed with sporadic plops on the floor. Slowly, the figure began to move around the bed. Rhiannon guessed it was surveying the room, looking for her, and she prayed it would see the open door and think she went down the hall. She listened for someone coming to help her, but didn't hear anyone else in the house moving around. Surely the sounds this abomination had made would have woken them up. Or if not that, then her shouting should have done it. Yet the house was silent except for the low mumble of gibberish coming from the creature.

Desperation bloomed within the roiling panic in her stomach. Anxious questions spun in a frenzy in her mind. Why isn't anyone coming? Where are they? What if they'd already been attacked while they slept? What if they were hurt in their own rooms and needed her help? She had to get out of here and she had to get out of here fast.

She took a shaky breath and scanned the floor around her, hoping to find something she could use as a weapon. She swept her eyes back and forth from where she was sitting to the end of the bed in front of her. As her eyes reached the far side of the bed, having found nothing of any use, a drop of sludge hit the floor and Rhiannon looked up to find the creature staring at her, grinning. It screeched and tried to scrabble underneath the bed to grab her. Rhiannon screamed and backed up against the wall. It managed to wedge its upper half under the bed, and it snapped its jaws as it swiped its claws at her, trying to grab a piece of her. She wished she had more space to move into but now she truly was trapped.

The creature continued to swipe at her but couldn't reach her. Frustrated, it moved to pull itself back out but appeared to be stuck. She watched the creature attempt to shove itself backward and out from under the bed, but the bed did not yield, and the creature remained in place. Understanding that this would likely be her only chance, Rhiannon scrambled out from under the bed, just missing the wildly flailing claws of the now irate creature.

She darted into the hall and slammed the door behind her. She didn't expect the bed to keep the creature trapped for long, and she had no idea if a door would stop it. But Rhiannon figured any little thing she could do to slow it down wouldn't be a bad thing. She sprinted down the hall and barged into Brad and Chad's room, terrified of what she might find.

Empty.

The room was completely empty.

She snapped on the light frantically scanning the room for her injured friends. Nothing in the room was disturbed. The bed didn't even appear slept in. Rhiannon heard the thing in her room let out a frustrated yowl, as it continued its struggle to extract itself from under the bed. She needed to keep moving. Maybe they'd changed their minds about going to bed, had gone back to the lounge, and had fallen asleep watching TV. She considered that the basement might be somewhat soundproof. It was a nice enough home for it and that could explain why no one else seemed concerned with all the noise. She stepped back into the hall and heard a loud crash as the creature freed itself from the bed. It slammed up against the door and Rhiannon squealed as she ran for the stairs.

The sound of it pummeling the door followed her to the first floor and she hurried to Todd and Leah's room. Bursting through the open door she found the master suite empty as well. The room was equally as undisturbed as the boys had been. They must all be in the basement. How could she have been so stupid? They obviously had pretended to all go to bed early so they could hang out for a while, without her.

Rhiannon felt a familiar pang of disappointment and embarrassment as she realized they probably regretted bringing her along. She really was too much of a loner to have friends like these. The first cracks of the splintering wood echoed from the second floor and brought her out of her spiraling thoughts. The creature was making headway with her door, and it wouldn't be long until it reached her. Even if they never wanted to see her again, she needed to get her friends out of that house.

She hurried over to the stairs leading to the lounge and shouted for everyone to get out of the house. When no response came, she decided that she was going to have to go down there and get them. The last thing she wanted to do was get herself trapped down there, but her friends needed her. They could be asleep, or hurt, or worse. She glanced over her shoulder at the stairs to the second floor and took a shaky breath. She couldn't see beyond the middle of the staircase from this angle, but she could hear the creature still fighting the door. If they were fast, they might beat the creature to the van. Todd had left the keys in the center console in the front seat, so they would just need to get up the stairs and down the hall to the front door. Steeling herself she descended into the basement to find her friends.

Rhiannon reached the bottom of the stairs, flipped on the light and there was, again, no sign of anyone. The room was dark, and neat. The remnants of their evening had been cleared away and the room had been straightened up. If she hadn't been there herself, she'd have argued the room looked like it hadn't been used at all.

The house was empty.

Where the fuck was everyone? What the fuck was that thing breaking down her door? What the FUCK was happening?

Rhiannon turned and moved quickly up the stairs, taking them two at a time. She reached the landing on the first floor as the creature broke through into the hallway on the second floor. She gasped and raced to the front door which stood opposite the stairwell to the second floor. She arrived at the front door as the creature appeared at the top of the stairs. Rhiannon looked up and they locked eyes and screamed in unison. But while Rhiannon screamed in terror, the creature's scream was one of fury. Rhiannon grappled with the doorknob as her sweaty hands failed to secure a lasting grip. The creature launched itself down the stairs at her and, feeling her narrow escape slipping through her fingers, she found purchase on the knob and flung the door open. She ran out into the night and was knocked forward onto the ground as something heavy hit her in the back.

With her face buried in the dirt, sharp claws dug into her skin through her clothes. She felt a sting in the nape of her neck and a bolt of white lighting exploded in her head. Rhiannon lifted her head and had time to register two things before everything went dark. The creature had caught her. And there was no car in the driveway.

Her eyes fluttered open and she watched trees slowly moving past her as she was pulled, by her foot, through the forest. Her shirt had ridden up and she moaned as the fresh lacerations on her back were assaulted with sticks and stones. Her arms, limply trailing above her head, scraped the ground as she was compelled through the dirt. She was dragged over a sizable flat stone with a sharp edge that left a long gash down her left cheek. Rhiannon had a fleeting thought that it would match the one on her other cheek and then she passed out.

She came to little by little, and as the stars came clearly into view, she realized she was staring straight up at the night sky. The stars seemed to shine brighter than before, and the moon was near blinding. Her head was pounding, her stomach was churning, and her back was a symphony of pain. She tried to wipe her eyes but couldn't move her arm. She tried to sit up but could only lift her head. Panic shot through her heart and her mind was suddenly clear. Rhiannon raised her head and surveyed her situation. She was laying on a cold concrete slab that was speckled with dark stains that worried her. What worried her more, though, was that her arms and legs were splayed out and restrained at the wrists and ankles with thick rope. She pulled on the restraints willing them to release her, but they held fast. It hit her like a slap to the face. She was trapped. She, Rhiannon Washington, was tied to a concrete slab in the forest after being attacked by a creature that looked like a crab wearing a mask made from a human man's face. Horror crept back to the forefront of her mind as she remembered the creature.

She quickly scanned the area around her thinking it might be waiting to pounce. What she saw, instead, were walls of decaying stones. She let her eyes drift all the way up the wall, to the sky, and realized she was in a deep hole. As she looked more closely, she spotted tunnels in the walls on either side of her. Tears flooded her eyes as she let her head fall back to the concrete. How had she found herself in this nightmare? This wasn't supposed to be possible in real life. This had to be a bad dream. And yet, she could feel the cold slab beneath her throbbing head and the lacerations on her back were singing. The tears spilled over and ran in streams down her face, pooling in her ears. Terror at the inability to get up—to run and save herself—washed over her and she began to scream.

"HELP!" Rhiannon shrieked, "Somebody help me!"

Her voice echoed off the walls around her, but then settled into silence. Complete and utter silence was all that existed around her. She couldn't hear anything at the bottom of that hole. No wind rustling the leaves, or animals moving in the brush. From where Rhiannon lay, there was nothing but the pounding of her heart in her ears.

"Please!" She cried. "Someone! Anyone! Can anyone hear me?"

Silence.

Overwhelmed and exhausted, she succumbed to utter hysteria and began to laugh. She cackled as tears continued to flow down her cheeks. When she finally stopped to take a breath, she heard noise in the tunnels around her. Someone or something was coming, and she braced herself to come face to face with the creature again, when Brad and Chad stepped from the tunnel on her right.

"Hey, Rhiannon!" Brad said excitedly as he moved closer to the slab. Chad elbowed him in the ribs and Brad dropped his smile in favor of a grave expression.

"Oh, thank God, Brad! Chad!" Rhiannon gasped "I thought I was going to die alone down here." Her fear turned to relief at the sight of her friends, and she jiggled her right arm at them. "Little help? I don't know what's going on, but we must get out of here. Now." Brad and Chad exchanged a look and made no move to help her.

"Seriously you guys, I need your help. I was attacked by a monster that came out of the forest." She said, realizing how insane it sounded when she said it out loud. "It scratched me or something and knocked me out. Then it must have dragged me down here and tied me up."

The boys continued to stare at her.

"Please believe me. I know how it sounds but it's true. It looked like a man at first and then it morphed into this crab-like monster. It was horrible! It was wearing this old man's face like a mask." She shuddered remembering the milky eyes of the creature boring into her.

The boys remained silent and still.

"Why are you looking at me like that? Please come help me." Rhiannon pleaded with them.

Chad frowned and turned to Brad, "Shit. I feel bad now. I told you we shouldn't have come down here."

"Oh, come on, don't pretend you care enough to feel that bad." Brad scoffed. "This was always the plan, and you were more excited about this than I was."

"What the HELL are you talking about?" Rhiannon snapped; desperation replaced by fury at their baffling behavior. "You aren't hearing me! We need to get out of here NOW and I can't move without your help."

"Stop yelling." Leah commanded, as she and Todd moved into the space on her left. "No one is helping you go anywhere. You are exactly where you're supposed to be."

"Leah? Todd? What the hell is going on here?" Rhiannon begged.

Todd looked across Rhiannon's body to Brad and Chad, dismissing Rhiannon as if the slab she was splayed out on was empty.

"Why the fuck are you two down here?" Todd asked, irritation tinging every syllable. "I warned you to stay up top until it was over."

"We wanted to see the slab up close!" Brad said quietly.

Chad glanced at Brad. "No," He corrected. "YOU wanted to see the slab up close."

Brad rolled his eyes and started to respond when Todd cut them both off.

"I DON'T CARE who wanted to come down here!" He hissed. "You could have come look at it afterward."

"But it will be all gross by then, we wanted to get a picture of it before -" Brad began.

Todd exploded. "A PICTURE?!" He bellowed. "You want tangible EVIDENCE of what's happening here? How could you possibly be that stupid?"

"I - I - I just thought it would be cool to have a picture of it." Brad stammered.

"Shut up." Leah said. "We don't have time for this now. None of us should be down here. It will be back soon. And if we don't want to get caught in the melee we need to be up there." She pointed to the ledge at the top of the hole.

"If these fucking idiots get me killed, I swear to god." Todd muttered.

Turning to Rhiannon, Leah smiled.

"Rhiannon," Leah began "I know you're very confused and I empathize with that. Well, no. I don't. But I tried to empathize. I really did. It's just that, well, you landed in my lap and this experience is too important for me to pass up. You should be very proud to be here, Rhiannon. You are doing a magnificent thing."

"What experience? What am I doing? What are you talking about?" Rhiannon asked, wide eyed.

"You are here to provide nourishment and strength to one of the Movers." Leah explained.

"Movers?" Rhiannon interjected. "What the fuck are 'Movers'?"

Leah continued, as if Rhiannon hadn't spoken. "It will come and take from you what it needs to nourish itself and build its strength. Its hibernation period is coming, and it needs to feed all it can before it goes back underground for thirteen more years."

"What the fuck is a Mover, Leah?" Rhiannon demanded.

"I was getting there!" Leah spat. In a flash, she reached out and slapped Rhiannon. "Don't push me, stupid bitch. I've been waiting a long time to witness this, and you are getting on my nerves. I should leave you to find out on your own." Leah sighed and composed herself to proceed with her monologue. "A Mover is the local name for a cryptid species that is part man and part crab that have been rumored to live under this forest for millennia. They are massive in size." she glanced at Rhiannon and smiled. "Though I don't need to tell you that."

"An ancient crab man. Great." Rhiannon muttered.

"They're thought to be extremely intelligent and social creatures, though those who claim to have seen it around here have only reported seeing one. They're also incredibly fast and venomous. One bite can cause a human being to slip into a state of unconsciousness for hours." Leah continued. "At which point the Mover relocates the prey to their nest and begins feeding."

Knowing how Leah could get about this subject if someone didn't reign her in, Todd interjected. "It didn't bite you like we expected it to, though. It scratched you and took off." "So we had to bring you down here ourselves." Chad added.

"And we tied you up in case the venom wore off too fast." Brad finished.

Leah glared at them all. "She doesn't need to know everything." She hissed.

She turned back to Rhiannon, smiling as if they were just catching up over a cup of coffee at the coffee shop. "Anyway, this is the coolest part! They eat the flesh as well as drink the blood and then they use the face of their prey as a form of camouflage." She gushed. "How cool is that?"

"So cool." Rhiannon dully.

"Most cryptozoologists don't believe they ever existed. And those that acknowledge their existence believe the folklore is exaggerated and what did exist died out thousands of years ago."

"But not you." Rhiannon muttered, glaring at Leah.

"Exactly!" Leah grinned. "I had faith that these beautiful, fascinating creatures exist, and I was going to find them and witness them for myself."

"So, Leah told us about the Movers and we realized this was year thirteen and they'd be surfacing in the fall. Fall in the Great Lakes region? We just couldn't say no!" Brad chimed in.

"We just needed bait." Todd said, leering at her.

"But why are you all helping her?" Rhiannon asked. "Why do you care about these creatures so much?"

"It's not about the creatures, for us, Rhiannon." Brad explained. "We want to watch you die." He stared at her without expression. Rhiannon searched his face for a sign of regret, of empathy, for a sign of humanity at all. She found none. She looked to Chad, who seemed the most empathetic of all of them, but he would not look at her.

"Please, Chad." Rhiannon pleaded. "Please don't let them leave me here to die."

"Please don't let them leave me here to die!" Todd mocked.

Leah rolled her eyes. "ANYWAY!" She said, louder than she planned to, and they all heard a click deep in the tunnel behind Todd. "Shit. Now we absolutely must go. Look, you get it. I've been waiting a long time to see these incredible creatures, and I needed someone as bait. Truthfully, I picked you out of convenience. It's nothing personal. Right place, right time, for me. Wrong place, wrong time, for you, I'm afraid." She shrugged.

Leah and Todd crossed quickly behind her to join Brad and Chad in their tunnel.

"Let's move!" Todd said as they stepped into the darkness. Before disappearing completely, he leaned back to look at Rhiannon. "Do me a favor and scream as much as you can. It'll really help me get off later. Thanks, doll." He winked and disappeared.

The sound of clicking grew louder to her left and the footfalls of her former friends diminished on her right, as they left her behind. The Mover was coming, and she was going to die if she didn't do something. The pain in her back and her head forgotten, Rhiannon frantically pulled at her restraints. The rope bit into her skin as she tugged with all her strength. The clicking grew louder and then the sound spread out and seemed to be coming from all around her. From somewhere deep in the tunnel on her right, Leah screamed. Rhiannon stopped struggling with her restraints and smiled. She supposed her former friends hadn't made it out in time, after all. A moment passed and then all four of them were all screaming. Rhiannon was pulled from her momentary reverie as the clicking on her left grew closer. She renewed her effort to free herself, pulling with all her might. Hope that she could free herself was dwindling and she began crying again and pleading with her god to help her. The pain in her wrists was immense and she was reminded of the degloving scene in Gerald's Game. She imagined the rope biting through her flesh and slowly tearing the skin from the muscle as she pulled. Still, Rhiannon kept at it. Then, a small snap from the rope on her left hand signaled that she was making headway.

With renewed vigor, she strained even harder, and the rope finally gave way. Her left hand was free. She knew she was running out of time and reached over to untie her other hand. As she released her right hand and sat up, the Mover entered the room from the tunnel on her left. Rhiannon turned and was again face to face with the creature that attacked her. The face of the old man was still tied around its head and those milky white eyes bore into her. It reached out with one of its claws and tried to caress the gash on her cheek that was still dripping a small amount of blood. Rhiannon pulled her head away and whimpered. The Mover then used its claws to remove its mask. The face behind the old man's face was more horrifying than Rhiannon could have predicted. There was no skin on the face. Instead, muscle and bone were visible but covered with a gelatinous substance. It stepped closer, smiling at her. It opened its mouth and exposed the jagged yellow teeth and rows of serrated suction cups, and the dark sludge began to flow. Horrified, Rhiannon finally registered that the brown sludge was the creature's saliva. It was hungry and it was drooling over its food. She screamed and the creature bellowed back. And then it was upon her.

Epilogue

Brandon thought this family trip was stupid. He was

14 years old, which he felt was old enough to be allowed to stay at home alone for the weekend. He wasn't a child anymore and they should stop treating him like one. They refused to see reason, though, and had dragged him to this stupid house in the middle of nowhere. No internet, and they wouldn't let him turn on the TV in the basement. Mom kept insisting that "they could watch TV at home." and they "hadn't come here to watch TV.". She was being ridiculous. Mom had planned so many activities for them this weekend that he wasn't worried about watching TV during the day. Even though he wanted to be at home playing Call of Duty with his friends, he couldn't help being a little excited about the pumpkin festival Mom had told him about. He loved pumpkins and he'd been promised that they could carve one while they were here. Brandon was too old for trick or treating, but he still liked dressing up and decorating for Halloween.

After his mother beat him in their third game of cribbage, he'd said his goodnights to his parents and his little sister went up to his room to read. Lydia had been given the room at the top of the stairs, closest to Mom and Dad. Brandon had refused to share the room with her, and had taken the one down the hall so he could have his own space. He'd brought along some comic books to read until he was sleepy, but it was 11:30 now and he was still wide awake. And he was going through them quickly. Maybe there was a comic bookstore in the town square and his parents would let him check it out. He'd heard Lydia call down the stairs to say goodnight to their parents about an hour ago, and then he'd heard the faint sound of his parents' door closing a short while later. The house was silent now and he felt a low hum of unease. He never liked being the last one awake. If something happened, it would be up to him to take charge, and he hated that thought. He shivered and looked up, noticing the open window.

Brandon rose and crossed the room to close the window. He looked out at the sparkling night sky and something moved in the garden below. He caught the movement in his peripheral vision and his eyes snapped down. He scanned the garden and, seeing nothing, reached to grab the window and pull it closed. At the last second, his eyes landed on a grotesque eight-legged creature, the size of a human, clinging to the wall just below his window. Brandon screamed and slammed the window shut, pushing back from the window. Slowly, a human face rose into view. It was the face of a young woman with a long vertical scar down each cheek. But the eyes. The eyes were milky white orbs shining through holes that used to hold the eyes of the young woman. Brandon realized the face was merely a mask and watched as brown sludge dripped from the mouth of the woman. He stared into the creature's eyes and felt how deeply it hated him. It raised a limb and slammed it against the window. Brandon shrieked and the creature bellowed back. And as the window shattered inward, windows in each bedroom shattered as well. And then the house echoed with screams.

# STRANGE WORLD

BY KILLIAN H. GORE

My dearest Elizabeth,

I hope you are well. I am sorry I haven't written to you sooner, but being quite some distance apart in an entirely different land it has been rather challenging. I don't wish to shock you, but I feel... I'm not quite sure how to word it without causing offense... I suppose the best way to articulate it is that I feel content here. I don't mean that to sound as if I don't desire to have you here with me, because I do Elizabeth, my love, and I truly believe you would feel content here too, you would absolutely love it!

You must relent, there's something missing from our lives in England, not between you and I, rather I refer to the country itself. Everything is so placid and ordered and downright dull, whereas here there is a sense of excitement in the air, an electricity that's almost palpable. Why, I swear I have even observed vivid blue sparks of light emanating from the very grounds I walk upon. It's so magical! Magic and mystery literally burst and spurt abundantly in liberation from the earth below.

Adverse to my joyous disposition, I must vent the nightmare I incurred last night, the nightmare that has compelled me to finally put pen to paper and write to you. Believe me when I say that I intended to correspond sooner, but my days have been filled with endless distraction. Every time I sat down in the library to write, the day would turn to night, dinner would be served, wine would be consumed, the sweetest and most vibrant red wine I have ever supped, and a haze would fall upon the world, a dreamlike state, all encompassing, a beautiful and welcoming warmth bathing the bleakness away.

What bleakness, you may ask? I don't wish to add a dash of doom and gloom, but my lodgings aren't exactly to my taste, nor do I think they would be to yours either. Were you to come and live out here, and I so wish you would give it serious consideration Elizabeth, we would settle in a more picturesque abode, a place where the majestic mountains peer down upon us, lush forests would surround us, and crystal-clear lakes would lie at our doorstep. I know such landscapes exist in our homeland too, but not in the oppressive smog of London. Oh, Elizabeth, I feel for your temperament, entombed in that environment right now, I dare not even picture it. In fact, come away with me Elizabeth right away, I'll enclose details of how to get here. Throw caution into the wind and join me, my dear!

You could sell our belongings, not everything, of course, just the items you'd be unable to bring. Keep anything of value, obviously all your jewelry should be kept, but sell the pots and pans and cutlery and plates and anything else you think would sell at market. My good friend George Godwin will be able to assist you and will lend you space on his market stall. His address is in my black notebook in the top drawer of my desk (could you make sure you bring this too?). George is a good fellow, and he doesn't live too far away, I believe he's on High Street North, but I can't recall the number, it's written in the book, look to the back pages where I have written several other contacts. Seek him out and he'll be more than happy to help for he has never let me down in the past.

The nightmare, though. Oh, the nightmare. Why must I tell you? Why must I dampen the atmosphere after my jubilant invitation? I don't know, I have no answer, it vexes me, and I feel I must vent the madness, perhaps that will help to dispel it. Yes, chronicling the nightmare will aid me in making my peace with it, the ink bleeding onto the page and draining the life from the images, imprisoning them onto parchment. Don't touch the letters, my dear, don't risk infecting yourself with the diabolical fluids. If you have, perhaps accidentally, brushed your fingers against the ink, please wash your hands thoroughly before continuing. I know this request may sound strange, but please do as I say.

The nightmare brought me to a location I was not familiar with, a compendium of stairs and corridors and locked doors. Each window I peered from displayed endless stretches of wall above and below. The view before me was vast, yet cloaked in darkness and I sensed a beautiful expanse with distant hills and shadows of valleys and gorges of velvety blackness. The fraught landscape felt like it existed in perpetual nighttime, its only illumination being the brilliant, persistent moonlight. The oppression of my predicament instilled in me a sensation of imprisonment, trapped within the stone bricks, unable to traverse into the extravagant landscape beyond the dense walls. I ran and ran through these dank and complex corridors, the monotony of them compelling me to question if I was in motion at all.

But then... a bottle, that's when everything settled, my running ceased and I realized I had, after all, been moving, I was sitting upon a cold chair. Was it a chair? Maybe a large, carved slab of rock? And the bottle was there, on a table, perhaps. Forgive my recollection of the details. I'm struggling as the light fades from the day. When I sat down to write the sun was blazing vibrantly through the window, all I see now is a dull grey, reminding me of London, reminding me of you. A large rock? What am I thinking? Oh dear. Perhaps it's the candlelight. I took a break for a moment to light it using a strand of wood from the fireplace. There was a lady here, I think, who lit the fire as I wrote. Or a man, perhaps, in a dark cloak. Someone must have birthed the flames into life, I can't fathom who in detail.

There was a lady in the nightmare too, she was at the table, and she poured me a drink from the bottle. The liquid was more gelatinous than wine and was colored blood-red. I became aware of its viscosity when the bottle fell from the table, breaking into an impossible number of pieces as it hit the stone floor with a shriek. The lady looked at me and smiled, but there was a malevolence in her beatific gesture. The blood splattered chaotically all around the dining area, liberally spraying us both and transforming us into garish demons.

Through her glistening, red face, her teeth were as white as the snow on the mountaintops in the moonlight and the more I stared upon them, the more I felt myself high in the hills in a relentless blizzard. The liquid from the fallen bottle now formed a pool that cut through the snow. Around the edges of this crimson lake were luscious green grasses that waved in a rhythmical, trance-inducing manner and I found myself falling deeper into unconsciousness. I should have felt relaxed, but I was not alone in the red waters. Sharp, triangular blades pierced the surface, they flashed into sight then disappeared just as fast, biting through the jagged fluid, biting at me, snapping, ferocious chomps tearing into me... and down into the ocean I slipped, deeper and deeper.

Within the blood red sea I swam through were angels... no, not angels, although they were visually angelic. They were, it transpired, the creatures that had fed on me in the water, the blades I had observed belonged to them. They were the hazardous incisors of the ladies dancing under the surface, grabbing at my vulnerable flesh and pulling me down into the inhospitable world where I could no longer breathe the oxygen my body craved. Down in the murky depths all I could inhale was blood and I felt the viscous fluids ravage my insides, pulsing in places it didn't belong.

"Edward, wake up, wake up," my client's voice pulled me out of the nightmare.

"Where? What? Where am I?" I felt delirious when I awoke, unsure of my location and who the man was at the side of my bed.

"It's all okay, Edward," my host said.

I looked up at him as he loomed over my bed. He was quite the imposing sight with his entirely black attire, perpetually dressed for a funeral. His strong, aquiline features and domed forehead together with his heavy moustache and eyebrows cut a daunting appearance. But despite his gloomy disposition, he was a decent enough gentleman. Always polite, always a gracious host.

"I trust you will forgive me, but I have much work to do in private this evening. You will, I hope, find all things as you wish," and in a flash he was gone, culminating in my pacing to the library to distract myself with the many tomes about my homeland, desperate to feel comforted by them. Although, with you here, my dear, I wouldn't require books to conjure sensations of contentment. You would be everything I desire.

A noise outside the window urged me to peer out into the night and I realized I must still be in my slumber for I thought I observed someone, or some *thing*, watching me with keen eyes. They were the eyes of a predator, hunting me. When will this nightmare end, I thought to myself. I felt so fully encumbered by it, like I was coated in a tacky fabric that I couldn't free myself from, a dreadful web. I wanted so badly to return to waking life, to daylight, to normality, but everywhere, in every crevice, unreality clung to the very air I breathed and wouldn't relent. Even now, as I write these words, I am unsure what is real, what is imagined and what is dreamt. This is why I feel it's a stouter urge than to merely *want* you here, Elizabeth, I *require* you here to liberate me from whatever nightmarish fever has swallowed me into its belly.

From the moment I arrived, I had the sensation that something was "off," so to speak. This was not true of my journey here, you must understand, for that was rather pleasurable. It only began once I arrived at my client's grand home, far too grand for me. There was something about the vast building that suggested a labyrinth, not the jovial type that one might find in a country park, but a grey and oppressive maze devoid of fun and frolic, a maze that felt inescapable. I had been instructed not to wander too far from my room, library and the dining area and I had, for the most part, stuck to that rule. I'm not even sure if I have strayed in waking life or if it has only been in the nightmare.

You may observe that I still refer to nightmare in the singular, rather than in the plural, this is because it has felt more like one long nightmare than a compilation. You must not fear, though, for I will leave my current lodgings and not turn back once I have finished this letter and had it mailed. My business with my client will shortly have concluded as we don't have many more matters to discuss. He appears quite content with the work that I have undertaken for him. It is more the nightmare that has troubled my time here but with you by my side, the nightmare will dissipate into obscurity.

I have thought back to my initial travels and recalled I primarily stayed at the Golden Krone Hotel in Bistritz, a delightful, thoroughly old-fashioned establishment, which I am certain you will love too. I will journey back there and await your arrival. I have enclosed a detailed map showing you exactly how to get to the hotel and I know that you will not disappoint me. I can already feel it in my blood that you are compelled to journey here, so I will count the days until you arrive. Should you not find me there, it may be on account of unfinished business at the castle, so I will also include details of how to get here too. I will see you very shortly, Elizabeth.

Oh so very shortly, my dear.

Your dearest Edward,
May 30th, 1876, Castle Dracula, Transylvania

O ut of the dozen software engineering interns in the 2019 Seattle cohort of my household name Big Tech employer—I won't say which—only three of us were girls.

By girls, I mean women, of course. We knew we were adults and that it was important that no one else called us girls, but we didn't quite have the hang of calling ourselves women. Women were our mothers. Professors and mentors maybe (when we were lucky). We were working on it, though. We were working on a lot of things.

Nova was the baby of the trio, and here I go infantilizing us again, but it was notable that she had just turned nineteen. She had graduated high school early and started at Stanford when she was only sixteen. When we met, I was immediately envious of her genius. Six years later, I look back and think about it differently, because wow, she was the only Black intern that year—and she had to be a literal child prodigy to get hired.

I would never have admitted this out loud, but I felt way under-qualified next to Nova in the same internship. My life may have started out rough, but by high school, you could say I basically lucked into one opportunity after another, just by asking for what I wanted and doing what the right people told me to do. I lucked right into a full ride at Georgia Tech and paid internship offers everywhere I applied. There was no way I deserved to be there as much as Nova, and her brilliance made me feel—in my deepest, darkest, most insecure place—like a cheater.

Anjali was twenty-one like me, but she didn't drink, so between that and Nova being underage, no happy hours for us that summer. We girl-women had to stick together. Instead, we established ourselves as regulars at a boba place that, for every dine-in order, would lend you a "conversation deck" for your visit—like playing cards, each card with an icebreaker question that we would drill way too far into, many layers under the broken ice.

We hadn't yet curated our personal canons of punchy anecdotes that we would later craft to make our desired impressions on the right audiences. We were still telling all our stories, verbose and messy, as openly as we could. We might embellish, but only in service to greater truth. Our earnestness still intact, we yearned to know and be known, to drink deeply from every exchange. We made no distinction yet between work friends and real friends. We believed with our whole young hearts the three of us would end up as more than just LinkedIn connections after the summer was over.

So that's where we were—the boba place—after work that Thursday when I drew the day's first and only conversation card. The question: *What was the stupidest thing you ever got in trouble for as a child?*

They both looked at me first, which I found funny and weird. College had taught me I was not special, just another dime-a-dozen white kid from the South. But for some reason I was a novelty to these two, and they never got tired of my stories. Maybe it was the red hair (this is a thing), or my free spirit laissez-faire single mom, or my small hometown where kids actually roamed free and had adventures and learned certain things the hard way, even in the late aughts when the era of that was supposedly over.

"Marybeth," said Nova at the same time that Anjali said "I want to hear Marybeth's."

"I have to think about it," I said. My childhood was kind of a blur before high school. I thought everyone was, to be honest, until I met these two.

"My parents were too nice," said Anjali. "I didn't get in trouble, exactly, but I would disappoint them, and that was devastating. I think I got in trouble once for saying a swear that I didn't even know was a swear. And I'm still not over it."

"Which swear?" asked Nova.

Anjali laughed. "I don't even remember."

"Everything I got in trouble for was stupid," Nova said. "Every single thing. I'm a legal adult but I'm in trouble right now for not texting my parents when I got home last night."

They looked at me again.

"All right, so. Y'all remember how my mom and her mom escaped a cult." Oh yeah, so, there was that quirky backstory that was the entry point to most of my tales. Maybe that was the allure. For me, it was just ugly wallpaper.

They nodded, rapt.

"The thing about that is, they left in the middle of the night, without saying goodbye to anyone, because that's how you escape a cult, you know. They left behind everyone they ever knew. That was the end of their family, and my mom was just a kid at the time.

"So, many years later when my mom's first cousin also escaped, it was a really big deal for my mom. I was a baby so I don't remember this part, but I guess the cousin lived with us for a short time. I think she ended up at a shelter first, and a social worker found my grandma. And that's how she came to stay with us."

"Wow," Anjali and Nova said in unison.

"Ruth—that was her name—she was pregnant, and she wouldn't talk. Like literally she wouldn't hardly say a word. Especially any questions they asked her about the baby, who the father was, she would shut down. Looking back, it's so obvious that she was completely traumatized. But at the time ... well ... then one day, she just disappeared."

"Oh my God," said Anjali.

"No idea where this is going, but I'm hooked," said Nova.

"So fast-forward a lot of time, we don't hear anything from Ruth. Then one day my mom gets a call from her. She was living in a cabin in the mountains in Georgia and she had a daughter named Mercy who was almost my same age, and she wanted to thank my mom for taking her in all those years ago and—oh—the weird part, although I guess this isn't too unusual for cult survivors, is that even though she'd left the cult, she then adopted a totally different extreme religion, and was raising her daughter super religious. It was a kind of Pentecostalism if you're familiar with that."

"Kind of," said Anjali, who had traveled the world and seen a lot.

"Not really," said Nova, who had yet to leave the West Coast.

"So of course, she also wanted to know if my mom and I had accepted Jesus Christ as our personal Lord and Savior."

"Oof," said Anjali.

"They don't cut their hair in this religion, so their hair is super long. I mean, the women, not the men. I guess the men can do whatever. Also the women and girls have to cover their arms and legs, and they can't wear pants. So they wear these long-ass skirts down to their ankles."

The two of them were slack-jawed. I was telling them about an alien planet.

"Also they don't have any tech. I mean the mom

probably had a phone for calls and safety, but no iPads, no internet, not even a TV. No streaming, no music except church music."

"I think I would ... unalive," said Nova.

"So my mom—who, remember, is excited to have any family at all—is all like, great, I got my cousin back, she's doing okay, she has a daughter—some kind of cousin to Marybeth, second or third or once removed or however that works—the point is, the daughters should meet. Me and Mercy.

"Mercy's mom, being religious and strict and all, didn't let her go anywhere, though, so my mom's like, I have a great idea—it's summer—you should go stay with Mercy and her mom for a week."

"In the cabin," Anjali said. "In the woods. The cabin in the woods. Is this a horror story? Because I am scared for you already."

I laughed. "Yeah, I know how it sounds. Like, yes, this is my mom's first cousin, but also they barely know each other. The religion thing is weird. And the place is way up in the southern Blue Ridge Mountains, pretty far from the nearest town, very woodsy, but at the same time it's a popular place to go for recreation. So there are hikers and cabins to rent in the area. Mercy and Ruth's cabin was very private though, surrounded by trees, just a short walk from a beautiful little lake. Remote, but it definitely didn't *look* like a horror story about to happen—"

"So it is a horror story," said Anjali. "Confirmed."

I smiled. "Well, my mom drops me off and it looks—

at least from the outside—like it's going to be a vacation. I'm actually pretty excited, even though I know there's no internet.

"The first thing I notice inside is religious stuff everywhere. A cross over every doorway. A picture of Jesus in every room. You get the idea. And of course there's Ruth —I called her Aunt Ruth—and Mercy, who was twelve. She had never cut her hair her entire life, never seen television or been to a movie, and not only that but it turns out she never goes *anywhere*, except to church in town. She was being homeschooled with a curriculum that they got through the church. I mean, they physically picked up the books and worksheets and things from the church. No internet, remember.

"And Mercy is mostly okay with things, because she's never known any other way of being. She gets to run wild in the woods, climb trees, build forts. When she gets tired of running around outside, she's happy sewing and doing crafts, reading everything she can get her hands on between church and home, practicing the guitar and stuff. There's just one thing that really bothers her.

"See, Mercy's a whiz at math, and she's finished the entire homeschool math curriculum, through high school trigonometry, which was the most advanced level there was in this church program. There wasn't even a calculus course. Go figure. So the church and Aunt Ruth, they're like, you're done with math, congratulations. And she's like, I'm actually not done with math, see—I know there is more to learn. I should be able to take college math classes. And they're like, nope, college is the Devil's playground, and you won't ever need any more math than that."

"What?" Anjali cried in disbelief.

"That is messed up," said Nova.

"In fact, that's how Mercy finds out that there never was any plan for her to go to college at all."

"Oh, poor Mercy," said Anjali.

"I would run away," Nova said.

"Mhm. So here I am, thirteen, terrible at math. It's the summer before high school, and I want to be the older, smarter one, but my twelve-year-old cousin has already learned ahead of me all the math I'm ever going to learn in high school as far as I know. I'm envious of her. But she's envious of me, because at least I already know I'll go to college for something or other. I don't know what yet, but my mom—who was lax about everything else—raised me with the idea that college was not optional."

"*You* were terrible at math?" Nova was incredulous, which pleased me more than a little.

I shrugged. "I guess, at the time, yeah. Anyway, Aunt Ruth seems like . . . surprisingly chill at first. She's like, yeah you kids have fun, run around, do whatever. Just these two rules: Don't swim in the lake, and be home by dark."

"Hold on," said Anjali, "because I'm also stuck on the math thing. How did you turn that around so fast in high school? I thought you were a mathlete like in *Mean Girls.*"

"'The limit does not exist,'" Nova quoted from the movie, one finger in the air.

"Yeah. I don't know. My education up to then was not the best. But back to the story, at first I figured there must be something wrong with the lake, like flesh-eating bacteria, or it's on someone's private property. But there aren't any signs, and we always see a few other people swimming there, and it's so hot in the middle of the day. So I start to bug Mercy about it. Like, why doesn't your mom want us to swim in the lake?

"And she's like, because there's no bottom. And I'm like, excuse me, *what*? She's like, yeah, it's a bottomless lake, and so the Devil can swim right up out of Hell and take you."

"Oh my God," said Nova. "This, from the girl who was good at math?"

"Yeah, but remember she was homeschooled. She might have believed the world was flat. I don't know. She didn't even have any reason to question what her mom said before that summer, but now the seed was planted because she was pissed off about not being allowed to learn calculus or go to college. So I got her thinking about how it was physically impossible that the lake was bottomless. And that scientists knew what the Earth was filled with, and there was no Hell down there."

"Did she believe you?" Anjali asked.

"I don't know. She would get really quiet when I bugged her too much about it. But I was also having an okay time just being a feral child in the woods with her. It was just a pain that she had to dress like a pilgrim, because it was so damn hot in the daytime. Her whole face was pink from sunrise to sunset. And the long skirt got in the way of jumping over stuff and climbing. And I swear, it was getting hotter and hotter every afternoon.

"So finally, it was the last full day I was going to be there. Aunt Ruth had to go into town to do a church thing for several hours, so it was the perfect time. I was so determined we were going to swim that I put my bathing suit on under my clothes that day.

"We went out as soon as her mom left, maybe two or three in the afternoon, and we headed the direction of the lake, which was a normal thing for us. We went by there every day. In fact if you keep walking around this, like, elbow of the lake, you eventually come to a small public access dock with a tiny bait shop and they have a couple arcade games in there which of course Mercy had never played until I arrived with a whole roll of quarters. So we had done that a few times. In fact, I think that's what she thought we were going to do that afternoon, but I grabbed her by the arm of her ridiculous long-sleeve shirt and dragged her off the trail right where there was a little tiny beach, where we'd seen some other kids swimming.

"She's like, what are you doing, let's go play the arcade games, let's go buy a Coke, but I'm like 'Nope, we're going swimming. You do know how to swim, right?' And she did. I made sure she really did, before y'all blame me—"

"Oh my God," said Anjali. "Did she die?"

"Are you confessing to something?" asked Nova.

"Obviously she didn't die, y'all," I said. "If she did, this would be a story about the most tragic thing I ever got in trouble for, not the stupidest.

"So anyway, I had to really convince her. I made her admit that she knew it was impossible for the lake to be bottomless. But I think she was still scared it was, you know, because imagine being told your entire life the Devil was down there, while your so-called science education is literally based on the Bible."

"Wild," said Nova.

"And it would've been fine, I'm pretty sure, if these two boys hadn't come along."

"Oh no," said Anjali.

"I know," I said. "They were older boys, high school age, and to us at the time that was cool, right?"

"Ew," Nova said.

Anjali rolled her eyes.

"Yeah. So these were local boys—they knew who Mercy was—they kind of teased her for being afraid of the lake. And eventually we convinced her. Of course, she did not have her bathing suit on—if she even had one—and she was not going to strip down to her underwear with these boys there. So we wade into the water a little ways, and she's fully decked out in her modest clothes, long denim skirt down to her ankles—"

"That sounds really heavy," said Nova. They both looked very concerned, even though I'd promised she wasn't going to die.

"It was. Have you ever picked up a pair of soaking wet jeans? Like that, but times five."

"How do you know what it weighs?" Anjali asked. "Did you try it on?"

"Just a guess," I said. "So, we're wading in up to our waists now and I'm saying stuff like, 'See those buoys out there? They're always in the same places because they're anchored to the bottom of the lake.' And then the boys are all, 'Watch out for the sharks,' of course. Then one of the boys said, 'Race you to the buoy' which was so silly, because how are you going to race someone swimming in a prairie skirt? But they raced each other, and because they were high school boys and I was dumb, I was like, come on, Mercy, let's go follow them out to the buoy.

"And we did, and it was farther than it looked, and it was hard for her to swim in that skirt. But we caught up to the boys, and then at least we could hold on to the buoy so it wasn't so bad for her. And after that we basically passed the time just talking to those boys, and splashed and dunked each other, and then somebody got the idea to play marco polo. It wouldn't be tiring, because we could just go from one buoy to the next and rest as long as we were quiet.

"It was my turn—I was it—and I suddenly realized I was calling 'marco' and only the boys were answering."

The two girls—women—gasped.

"So I immediately open my eyes and I only see the boys. I shout for Mercy, and I'm spinning every which way to look for her head on the water. Also the sun is beginning to set."

"Oh no!" Anjali covered her eyes.

"And I was like, 'Guys, help! Help me look for

Mercy!' But those stupid boys ... they just ... froze. Completely paralyzed out of panic, or whatever. I realize it's all up to me, and start diving, swimming around, holding my breath as long as I can. But I'm starting to panic myself because the visibility is terrible. I just see this murky green everywhere. By the third time I come up for air the boys are nowhere to be found, and I'm pretty sure my cousin is dead and it's my fault."

"No. What?" Nova said. "The boys just took off?"

"Yeah. So y'all, I take the deepest breath of my life and I do one last dive. I'm not religious at all, but just in case, I send out silent prayer to whoever might be listening, and I swear to you, after the little prayer is prayed, I see some bubbles right in front of my face and so I swim straight down, feeling out in front of me with my arms. And sure enough, my fingers rake through Mercy's stupid long hair and she grabs onto my arm. It scares me so bad I yell out half my air right then.

"She has almost given up the struggle. Her hair is tangled on something. This is why divers carry knives, right? So I'm yanking on her hair, she's yanking on my arm ... it might've been funny if we could actually breathe. But I finally find whatever her hair is caught on, and there's no time to think...."

I was out of breath now just talking about it, just remembering what I saw and what happened next. That press of the depths, that squeeze of no-time-to-think transposed from the lake into the boba shop that glowed and hummed here and now around me. Such cheery contrast to the cold fingers wrapped around my heart.

Such a vivid filter over the deep algal gloom where part of me would be suspended forever.

I shouldn't have begun this story without thinking of what I would do when it arrived here. And I'd known on some level, always, I wasn't ever really going to tell it. I was just a twelve-year-old swiping my finger through a candle flame, knowing I would not dare stop long enough to burn.

"Don't you *dare* stop there," Anjali said, eyes wide.

This wasn't the right story for these girls—and they did seem like girls now. Everyone seems young once you've been touched by an unfathomable, ancient thing. I wanted them to know what was there—because it could be out there anywhere—but they were just girls. What kind of monster was I? But then, they were grown women—who was I to think I knew better than they did? No, the truth was I needed them to hear my sin so that they could absolve me. And *that* disgusting entitlement was wound like ribbons into my very DNA.

It's how I ended up here, one finger wagging—*nuh-uh, no-no*—through a dancing flame.

I was the wrong storyteller.

"Hello," said Nova, tapping on the red-orange table. A color good for restaurants because supposedly it made people hungry. Leaves of the red oaks in a North Georgia October. The ponytail of a distant cousin who came to stay a while.

I sipped my boba, and chose my next words carefully. "Whatever thing it was that had her caught, it felt slimy and like … I'm sure it was a root or a tree branch or something, but I swear, it felt like a hand with fingers. Long, gnarled fingers with long nails like claws."

Nova and Anjali covered their mouths and made quiet screaming sounds.

"Anyway, I'm sure you've guessed that just in the nick of time, I rip Mercy's hair from the ... the grip of the thing ... and drag her up to the surface. We hold on to the buoys until she can cough out everything and cry and catch her breath. It's getting dark now and I'm worried she won't be able to swim to the shore. I considered leaving her at the buoy and going to find Aunt Ruth, but that doesn't sound like the best idea either.

"So finally when we're sure she is strong enough, we go for it. I stay right next to her the whole way, and I'm so glad when our feet kick the bottom again that I start crying myself. We are both crying. By then, I hear Aunt Ruth's voice yelling for us. 'Mercy! Marybeth!' Remember, her second rule was to be home by dark. We've broken both of the only rules.

"We shout back to her, sobbing, and she storms out of the woods, and she is thoroughly, otherworldly *pissed*. Not just pissed, though. I realize as we slosh onto the beach and fall on our hands and knees, and she comes running up on us, that she is absolutely *terrified*. And she starts hitting us."

"Shut up," said Anjali.

"Hitting both of us, for real, like wildly. Pounding us with her fists, and yelling, crying. 'You have the Devil in you, don't you? Answer me! You have the Devil in you!'

She kept screaming that over and over as she whupped us.

"So yeah, the stupidest thing I ever got in trouble for was swimming in a lake that my mom's cousin believed was a bottomless portal to Hell. And I don't even think that Ruth ever even knew what actually happened—that we ... that Mercy almost died."

"That's..." Nova shook her head.

I felt like I might have gone too far. I was the first of us to tell a story that contained physical violence—although I would not be the last—and I worried I had crossed more than one line.

"What happened next?" said Anjali.

"Well, Aunt Ruth called my mom to come get me immediately, which meant she had to drive there, way up in the mountains, in the dark. Mercy never spoke another word the whole time I was there. She just sat there at the sewing table with her back to me.

"Then once Aunt Ruth went to her bedroom and closed the door, Mercy jumped up and ran into the bathroom with the sewing scissors in her hand."

"I can't," said Nova.

"No, it's not like that. But I mean, I didn't know what she was ... I probably should have stopped her. But you have to understand, I had never even been spanked as a child, and I was pretty traumatized from this unhinged adult beating me up. So anyway, Mercy cut all her hair off. I was kind of proud of her for that."

The two of them breathed a sigh of relief.

"And since her mom now hated me and *my* mom was furious at her mom for beating me and making her drive up there in the dark, that was the last time Mercy and I ever saw each other. I don't even know what ever happened with her after that. My mom and I never talked about it. We act like it never happened. Like they never existed. So who knows? Maybe she still lives in those woods with her mom." I shrugged.

"Nooo! We have to find out!" Nova was already on the case, tapping on her phone. "What's her last name?"

"Wilson," I said.

Anjali was looking over Nova's shoulder. "There are too many Mercy Wilsons," she said.

"She has an unusual middle name," I said. "Beulah. B-E-U-L-A-H."

"Mercy Beulah Wilson," Nova said as she tapped. Then, "Oh my God."

"What?" I leaned forward.

"'Ruth Ann Wilson of Fannin County, Georgia, was found stabbed to death in her home on March 16, 2018...'"

"Oh, poor Ruth." It surprised me how fast the lump formed in my throat.

"Police were tipped off when a vacationing family discovered Wilson's daughter Mercy Beulah Wilson, nineteen, also of Fannin County, walking along a mountain road, covered in blood. Mercy Wilson confessed to stabbing her mother to death with scissors, but was not found competent to stand trial. She is currently receiving care at an inpatient psychiatric facility in Atlanta, where a judge has ordered she remain until such time it is determined she is able to understand the charges against her." Nova turned the phone around and showed me the mugshot.

Her head was completely shaved. Her face looked how I remembered it. Or maybe this face slipped into the old memory's place. I searched the eyes for any glint of the gentle girl I'd known for six days and assumed I'd know forever, but I found nothing. It had been years since the last time her voice had come into my head as I lay still and quiet under my covers, praying it away.

I shook my head. "Poor Marybeth."

"Poor Marybeth?" said Nova.

"You mean 'poor *Mercy*,'" Anjali said.

"Yes," I said. "Poor Mercy. Sorry. I thought that's what I said."

Anjali placed her hand on my forearm, squeezed gently, and let go.

We spent a thoughtful moment swallowing sugary milk tea. I shuffled our conversation card back into the deck, to give my hands something to do.

Nova was still reading. "It says here she only had a sixth-grade education."

I looked up at Nova. She continued looking at her phone.

"Just think," Anjali mused, "if only the lake were really bottomless, and the Devil were really down there. Maybe she could have made a deal with him. Like, to get a better education."

Nova nodded, eyes lifting from her phone, meeting my gaze. "Probably would've been worth it. She could have lived another life."

After three messy divorces and a personal bankruptcy, David Richardson still refused to entertain the idea that he had a problem with addiction. The junkies sprawled on the sidewalk in front of the ramshackle hotels downtown were addicts. So were the suit-clad speed freaks who spent their evenings with business partners doing endless bumps of coke in the bathroom of the local gentleman's lounge. David was just an ordinary guy who enjoyed placing the occasional bet. He considered it a harmless vice, something to counteract the dull monotony of his day-to-day life.

David was supported in his views by his partner-in-crime and enabler, Mickey Bates. Mickey was a stocky fellow with a ruddy face, a severely receding hairline, and a wardrobe that consisted primarily of second-hand khakis and flannel button-ups. Friends since high school, the pair shared the same cynical worldview and slacker attitude, convinced that they didn't owe the world anything. Their shared opinion was that for those unlucky enough to be born into a family of modest means, getting ahead required careful scheming and an understanding of how to game the system. Otherwise, you'd spend your life under someone's thumb, whether it be your employer, your spouse, or your god.

Gambling came naturally to David and Mickey. Both men understood enough about probabilities to place reasonably informed bets on anything from horse racing to boxing matches. And both possessed that essential quality common to every committed gambler: a short memory. David could lose $500 in ten minutes in an online poker game and wake up the next morning fresh as a daisy, ready for another trip to the bookies. Mickey could fritter away a chunk of his meagre savings on an over-under and forget about it within an hour.

The town of Mundy, where David and Mickey had grown up and continued to reside, was an ugly expanse of crumbling tenements and massive factories. Pulp was Mundy's claim to fame, and a handful of belching mills peppered the flat, Midwestern landscape, blanketing the town in putrid clouds of eggy stench. David and Mickey hated the mills. They represented everything the men despised about modern, neoliberal society: the exploitation of workers, the fetishization of the global economy, the cavalier destruction of the natural environment. At age eighteen, David and Mickey had made a pact that neither of them would ever take a job in the pulp industry. Each had given the other permission to use violence to prevent this eventuality, if it came down to it.

And so, with few other prospects, they had turned to gambling. For David, his betting career had begun the summer he graduated from high school. He had gotten his first taste in a shady game of blackjack. Socked away in the smoky basement of an acquaintance's older brother's house, he had lost all five dollars of his weekly allowance in three hands. And just like that, he was hooked.

With the ink barely dry on his third set of divorce papers, David caught wind of a new casino being built on Mundy's barren outskirts. Christened The Paragon, it was described as a multistory megaplex of entertainment, boasting every type of casino game imaginable, from slots, to roulette, to craps. Being the gambling aficionados they were, he and Mickey were understandably thrilled. With few legitimate options available to them, most of their betting activity to this point had taken place in quiet dens and gloomy back rooms. Having a full-featured casino within driving distance would be a welcome luxury.

"What a beautiful monstrosity."

David and Mickey stood on a dusty lot off the highway, just east of Mundy's city limits. The gaudy casino loomed over them like a polished piece of zirconia, glinting like a jewel in the summer sun.

"No kiddin'. What an eyesore," David replied. "But, as they say, 'true beauty lies within.' Or something like that." He flashed a toothy grin at Mickey, arching his thick brows.

Mickey ran his tongue over his fleshy lips and rubbed

his palms together. "You're right, they do say that. Cmon, let's go win some money."

The men crossed the lot and approached The Paragon's entrance; a set of tall glass doors framed by a pair of ionic pillars supporting a gabled canopy. A red banner, with the words *Grand Opening* embossed in gilt lettering, draped from the eaves.

As the automatic doors swept open, Mickey and David were blasted by a stale gust of cool air that chilled their sweaty skin. They were accosted by a cacophony of clinks, whirs, bells, and digital jingles. A barrage of flashing neon light lit the freshly laid carpet in bright pools. Zombie-eyed patrons dotted the sea of stools like semi-conscious pigeons, staring into garish screens with drooping jaws.

Mickey and David gawked as they navigated their way through the forest of slots. It was a scene entirely unfamiliar to them, qualitatively different from the dull and hushed atmosphere of the betting joints they frequented. While the extravagant machines piqued their curiosity, the men considered themselves too sophisticated for the simple pleasures they promised.

Ahead of them, hanging from the roof above the central lane bisecting the room, was a sign that read, 'Second Floor: Tables.'

"Bingo," David said, pointing at the sign.

The men hustled up a vast staircase that opened onto a dim landing. It was quieter up here, the clientele clearly more refined. This was where they belonged.

"Nothin like the smell of a fresh deck of cards in the

morning," Mickey said, chortling heartily. "This is incredible! Where should we start?"

David and Mickey gazed out at the rows of sleek tables, flanked by grim-looking dealers in crimson vests and bowties.

"What'd you think, Mick? Blackjack?" David said.

"Sure, why not," Mickey said. "Which table looks luckiest to you?"

David scanned the nest of blackjack tables and gestured to one where a solitary player was seated. He wore a black ten-gallon hat and a tall pair of snakeskin cowboy boots, his substantial gut spilling out over a large belt buckle. The men plopped themselves down onto two empty stools beside him.

"Howdy," David said.

The man acknowledged them with a friendly nod. "You boys aren't going to ruin my streak now, are yah?" He winked a blue eye at them jauntily. "Just joshin'. The name's Wiley, James Wiley."

"Pleased to make your acquaintance. I'm Mickey, and this here's David," said Mickey, jabbing a thumb over his shoulder at his friend, who gave the man a quick two-finger salute.

"First time at The Paragon?" James asked.

"Yes indeed," David said, lacing his fingers and extending his arms out in front of him to crack his knuckles. "You?"

"Yup. 'Bout time Mundy invested in something other than those damned mills. Rumour has it the city was approached by a mul-*tie*-national conglomerate who made them an absurd offer. We're talking nine figures, fellas," James said, his blue eyes bulging to exaggerate the point.

David whistled. "Tell me about it. I think this is just what I need to break the spell of bad luck I've been havin. You know how it is — Lady Luck can be a fickle mistress."

"Got that right," James said.

"Gentleman, please place your bets." David shuddered. Having been absorbed in his conversation with James, he'd been mostly ignoring the dealer standing motionless on the other side of the table. That is, until he heard the silky, sinister voice calling for their bets.

The dealer was tall and thin, nearly skeletal. The pasty skin of his face was pulled tight over a pair of high cheekbones that protruded like crags. His coal-black eyes were sunk into dark fleshy pockets the colour of a serious bruise. His jaw hung slightly open, a putrid odour escaping from between a pair of chapped, flaky lips.

James picked three red chips from the top of a small stack on the table in front of him and tossed them towards the dealer.

"Damn, we got so excited we forgot to buy tokens!" Mickey exclaimed.

"I'd be pleased to help you with that," the dealer said, the words slithering from his reeking mouth. He produced a tray of tokens from below the table. "I can take cash or credit."

"Wow, now that's what I call customer service,"

Mickey said, smiling stupidly at David and nudging him with his elbow.

David dug through his jacket pocket, retrieved a small wad of crumpled dollar bills, and tossed them onto the table. The dealer grabbed the money with a laconic sweep of his corpse-like hand, deposited the bills somewhere below the table, and placed a small stack of ruby red chips in front of David. The sight of the chips stirred something unpleasant in the back of David's mind. He suspected it was a combination of the colour red — a hue he'd come to associate with the crushing weight of debt, given the state of his bank account — and the nagging sense of guilt he'd been feeling since his latest divorce. The connection between his gambling and the stream of negative events in his life was becoming harder to ignore.

"Gentlemen, please place your bets," the dealer repeated. David and Mickey placed two chips each into the pot, matching James' bet.

"So, as I was saying, this big corporation comes to Mundy and buys up this massive plot of land on the edge of town. Naturally, everyone's wondering why they'd do such a thing. Seems like a pretty stupid investment, don't it? Well, I'll let you in on a little secret. Something only us insiders are privy to." James leaned towards David and Mickey, raising a hand to shield his mouth from the dead-eyed dealer. His voice dropped to a whisper. "I've got it on good authority that the company's got its fingers in a few other pies, if you catch my drift. One of its subsidiaries, operating in a hidden bunker somewhere out east, is a biotech firm involved in some shady research. Something about mutant humans, or gene editing, whatever the hell that means."

Mickey guffawed. "Look out, Dave, we found ourselves a true-blue conspiracy theorist."

David smiled good-naturedly as the knot of unease in his stomach tightened. He eyed the dealer, who stood like a decaying statue on the opposite side of the table, patiently waiting for the men to resume the game. David imagined an army of similarly grotesque figures, their DNA altered to give them grisly superpowers. It wasn't a stretch to imagine such an army waging war against the race of average humans, invading and pillaging countries one-by-one until planet Earth had been brought to its knees. Given the current state of his affairs, David decided he wouldn't mind being conscripted into such an army himself.

"Hit me," James said. On the table in front of him were the ten of clubs and the ace of spades. With a deft flick of his wrist, the dealer flung him another card. The queen of diamonds.

"Twenty-one. Well played, sir," the dealer said.

"Hot damn!" James shouted, slapping his stool like a jockey.

"Not so fast, pal. Watch and learn," Mickey said. On the table in front of him were a six and a king. "Hit me."

The eight of hearts skittered across the table. "Twenty-four. Bust," the dealer said.

"Damn," Mickey muttered under his breath. "Alright, David, let's give this guy a run for his money."

David gazed down at the pair of cards on the green felt in front of him. A four and a five. "Hit me," he said.

Another five.

"Hit me."

The jack of hearts.

"Twenty-four. Bust."

David felt the all-too-familiar sinking sensation descend over him. But at this point in his dismal gambling career, he'd grown numb to the associated feelings of guilt and shame that usually came with it. He experienced the loss as a minor annoyance, a pesky obstacle on his path to eventual riches.

The dealer flipped the card sitting face down on the table in front of him. The eight of clubs.

"Sixteen. The dealer hits."

Nine of diamonds.

"Dealer busts. Congratulations, sir." A necrotic hand stacked the tokens in the pot into a neat tower and slid them to James.

"Better luck next time, boys," James said, grasping Mickey's hand and giving it three vigorous pumps. "It's been a pleasure, but I'm gonna call it a day. As the mighty Kenny Rogers says, 'You've got to know when to walk away.' Dealer, I'll take my winnings now, if you please."

"Certainly, sir. Please accompany my colleague to the token exchange booth," said the dealer, his eyes shifting to the side where another wraithlike casino employee had apparated next to James. This one's hair was wildly dishevelled, and there was a crust of something that looked suspiciously like dried blood below his left nostril.

James followed the dealer's gaze and jumped from his stool. "Holy Jesus! You came out of nowhere, buddy."

"I apologize, sir. Please, follow me," he said in a brittle rasp before striding away towards the opposite end of the room. James hustled after him, his bounty of chips jostling in a small tray he gripped in his pudgy hands. David and Mickey watched James's black cowboy hat bob over the sea of tables until it disappeared down a shadowy corridor.

"What a character," Mickey said.

"Yeah. Say, Mick, I'm feelin' a little queasy. Must be the stale air in here or somethin." As he spoke, David's eyes strayed reluctantly to the dealer, whose lifeless stare bore into him like a bone drill. David knew perfectly well that the nagging cramp seizing his innards had nothing to do with stale air.

"It is a bit musty in here, I agree. Ah well, you'll get used to it," Mickey said, clapping David on the back. "Let's play a few more hands. I bet adding some chips to that modest little pile of yours will fix you right up."

David's resolve collapsed like a plywood shack in a hurricane, the hallmark of an inveterate addict. "Okay. I gotta take a leak first, though. I'll be right back."

"You got it, buddy. Hurry back, before I bankrupt this guy," James said, winking playfully at the dealer.

David spotted a washroom sign hanging from the ceiling at the far end of the room, near the corridor James had entered moments before. As he made his way across the floor, he caught glimpses of the dealers at several of the other tables. They were a mix of men and women, young and old. But they all seemed to share the same haggardness in their features, as if they'd just stumbled into work straight from the grave.

When he'd finished in the washroom, David slunk over to the corridor and stole a glance around the corner. It was a plain, nondescript hallway with a door at the end. Embossed directly onto the door in gilt cursive were the words, *Token Exchange*. It seemed odd to David, and strangely inefficient, for every player to be required to filter through the dim hallway to collect their winnings. He shrugged to himself and moved on.

He was on his way back to their table when he saw something that made him stop dead in his tracks. His blood turned to ice as goose pimples erupted up and down his arms. Off to the side, at a table near the far edge of the room, was James. Except he wasn't sitting on the player's side of the table. He was standing on the dealer's side, dressed in a crisp crimson vest and bowtie. David crept closer to get a better look. There was no doubt about it; the ten-gallon hat had been removed from his greying hair and his blue eyes seemed to have lost their luster, but it was certainly him. Only he seemed to have aged twenty years in the last ten minutes, his skin drooping from his once-ruddy cheeks in pale folds, his ears caked with a mysterious crust.

David's mind started racing. Something nefarious was going on here. Was the casino harvesting customers for some sick purpose? He recalled with horror what James had said about the secretive biotech work the conglomerate was involved in and something dropped in the pit of his stomach. He and Mickey needed to leave. Now.

He sprint-walked back to their table, where Mickey had ordered himself a tropical looking drink and was wearing a goofy grin.

"There he is! About time. All these chips are burnin' a hole in my pocket." He fondled the stack of tokens in front of him lovingly.

"We need to go, Mick," David said. "I'll explain in a minute, but right now we need to leave." He gripped Mickey's arm and yanked him from the stool.

"Hey, hold it! What's gotten into you? I haven't had time to ease into my winning streak yet!" Mickey got shakily to his feet. He clutched his chips as David dragged him away from the table towards the staircase.

As David tugged Mickey along, he noticed that the activity in the room had died down. He felt the coalpit eyes of every dealer on them like hot embers. An employee confronted them at the top of the stairs.

"Gentlemen, can I help you?" It was a woman this time. Her eyes were violently bloodshot, crimson trickles leaking from her lids and down the bony ridges of her hollow cheeks. She attempted a crooked smile, revealing a rotten row of snaggled teeth.

"Jesus," Mickey mumbled to himself.

David stepped nimbly around the woman, Mickey

now following of his own accord. The men descended the stairs two at a time, rushed to the exit, and burst through the glass doors and back into the hot sunshine.

Three days later, David attended his first meeting. The casino episode had given him the final push he'd needed to take the plunge, to get past the discomfort and embarrassment of his addiction. Looking into the listless eyes of the casino employees had been like holding up a mirror to his future self, had he continued down the path he'd been on.

He tried to convince Mickey to join him, but to no avail. Their initial visit to The Paragon clearly hadn't had the same impact on him. In fact, he'd tried to cajole David into going again the very next day. Mickey ended up accompanying another gambling enthusiast friend of his, and David never saw or heard from him again.

Eventually, the Mundy townsfolk started to raise concerns about The Paragon. Right around the time of the grand opening, numerous reports of missing friends and family members had started to pour into the local police station. It wasn't long before people started to connect the disappearances to the casino. The police chief had announced they'd be conducting an investigation, but before it could get underway The Paragon abruptly shuttered its doors. The conglomerate absconded, leaving the casino's diamond-like shell sitting empty in the hot dust.

Everyone had an opinion about what should be done with it. Some suggested a school, others a supermarket.

But the building's location and layout made it impractical for just about anything — other than a casino, that is. And so it stood, and continues to stand, like the carapace of a monstrous insect full of sun-boiled secrets.

Running through the woods as darkness settled in, Vale was afraid. She was fearful of the darkness and the things that hid in it. She knew she needed to find shelter; she had taken too long picking berries and lost the time. When finally she realized how late it was, she knew she wasn't going to make it home before the sun set and the darkness rose. And she was alone.

There were things in the woods, awful things that would rip and shred and tear her to pieces. She had heard the stories since she was able to remember, had heard tales of those who didn't make it home in time. She didn't want to become one of those stories, and she could feel those things watching her. There were shadows where there had previously been none, and not just because of the dark.

The thickness of the grove she was in felt never-ending as she tried to push her way through. She didn't remember the trees being so close together, didn't recall the space being so enclosed. Was it her mind playing tricks on her, or was it the forest? Because it wasn't just the monsters that were to be feared; the woods held an evil at night. They were alive and ever changing. It was said the forest could alter itself, rearrange its structure. She believed the stories of the creatures that came out to play in the twilight, but she had never believed the stories about the forest's ability to change.

Until tonight.

The fear of what was waiting behind the brushes, what was leaning against tree trunks, what was whispering on the breeze, became too much, causing her heart to beat faster and her thoughts to become darker, and she ran. She could feel things staring at her, feel them creeping closer to her, could hear them rustling the branches and leaves. She could sense something in the drafts, something more than the phantom sounds, something with a cold touch and a heart of ice. The thing was reaching out to her, its clawed fingertips just brushing her hair, which was flying behind her. It was a knowledge she didn't know how she had, but she did.

Just when she thought she couldn't run any farther, a clearing opened. The full moon shone down upon a small castle that sat just on the far side of the meadow that was filled with blood-red roses. The surrounding moat was dry, but the smell of rain in the air said it would soon be mud. The dirt road led through the flowers, across a small bridge, and to the steps of the citadel. Dark, oak doors reaching fifteen feet high graced the front of the stone structure.

Slowing and careful to stick to the path so as not to prick a finger or get her clothing frayed on the thorns of the crimson beauties, she made her way toward the tall double doors of the fortress.

A light rain started, followed by a streak of lightning and a crash of thunder. After that, the skies opened. Sensing the thing or things still behind her, seeing moving phantasms in her periphery even through the downpour, she ran the last two hundred yards, heedless of how slick the dirt path was becoming, the slippery mud clinging to her shoes.

Her scarlet gown trailed behind her as she dashed up the steps. Going too quickly, her shoe caught the hem of her dress, and she went to her knee, cursing under her breath before regaining her footing, bunching her skirts in her hand, and darting up the last several steps. She stood before those looming doors, staring, entranced for the merest of moments, awe and dread sinking into her being.

This place radiated foulness.

The stone that made up the building was the color of shadows, and the individual blocks appeared to undulate and shift in the moon's light. The dark, oak doors were dusky to the point they looked black. The rain streaming down them gave the appearance of blood flowing. The knockers were the faces of demons, the rings the bodies of snakes wound around the demon's necks. There was one at her shoulder height on each door, but they were too heavy for her to lift. However, the doors were ajar just enough for her to slip her delicate fingers into.

Pulling with less strength than she anticipated she would need, Vale opened both doors, her arms outstretched and holding on to keep them from slamming into the stone. The immediate entry was dark, but there was light beyond. Candlelight and the light from a blazing fire in the hearth in the great hall shone upon her, outlining her silhouette, creating an image of a shadowed ghost of a woman entering the dim light. It cast a shadow across the rain-soaked bricks of the landing and down the steps.

She entered the doorway then grabbed the handles, pulling the doors closed. They banged shut, echoing throughout the small entryway and great hall beyond. She dropped the crossbar into its holds. With the doors barred and the hearth giving forth heat, she felt safe. She inhaled deeply, then exhaled over several seconds, attempting to calm her racing heart.

It had been dark out for some time, and she gauged the time to be half past ten. She assumed the castle's dwellers would have been retired to their rooms for the evening. She would make her way to the fire then rest there until the first rays of dawn appeared. Once the cock crowed, she would slip out the front doors and head for home.

As she turned and took a step toward the hall, something slammed into the giant oak doors. She inhaled sharply, her head whipping toward the sound. The doors reverberated from the impact—what could be so big or so powerful it could cause them to quake? She didn't want to find out, so she turned back toward the great hall and moved as quickly and quietly as she could. She was a petite and slight wisp of a girl, and she moved with the finesse of a cat prowling for dinner.

Being the daughter of a baron, she was familiar with the layout of the place as most castles were similar in design, at least on the inside. She headed toward the back of the great hall toward where she assumed the kitchen would be. There would most likely be a weapon of some sort there, a butcher's knife or a small ax used to cut wood into smaller pieces for the stove. She would arm herself and stand her ground. However, if the stories were true, there would be no man-made tool that could aid in her defense.

As she entered the kitchen and headed toward the scullery, it occurred to her that nobody had come down from the rooms to investigate the banging of something against the front doors or the resounding echo left in its wake. Was there no occupant of this abode? But the fireplace was lit, there were candles burning on the wall sconces. Certainly there must be a proprietor here. She didn't want to entertain the idea she was utterly alone.

Lost in her thoughts, she didn't hear the servants' door in the kitchen creak open, nor did she hear footsteps coming up the stairs from that entry, claws clicking with each step. What finally pulled her from her trance was the sound of a wet, raspy inhale, like something was trying to draw breath with their head submerged in water.

Turning to face whatever creature was behind her, Vale took a step back with her left leg, bracing herself with it as she made an X in front of herself with the small wood-cutting ax and the short sword she found lying on the counter. She was ready to take on this demon, this shadowed creature of the forest that had come for her.

The beast unleashed a ferocious, guttural bellow. Spittle flew from its mouth, coating Vale with it. Baring razor-sharp fangs that were as long as her fingers, it took a step toward her.

She did not move.

A fierceness overcame her, a feeling of dominance and strength. She was not going to allow this demon to overtake her. A power buzzed through her, a current that provided her with bravery and fortitude. She was alone, but she would not be taken. Her mind would not be influenced by this hideous creature, this thing that could tear her to pieces. The fear of darkness, outside or other-worldly, would not consume her.

It swiped a clawed hand at her, its arm longer than it should have been in proportion to its height. She dropped low, spun a circle on her heel, spinning herself closer to it, and slashed with the lance. Drawing a slash across its shins, just below its knees, she followed with the ax, imbedding it in the thing's inner thigh, high up by the groin. Leaving the ax, she used the momentum of her spin to roll away from the thing.

It lunged at her despite the blood pouring from the ax wound. Snarls ripping from its throat, claws lashing, the thing's rage made it clumsy and it missed its mark.

Coming out of her roll onto her feet, she threw the lance at the beast. Her aim was off, but only by a fraction.

The thin spear protruded from the monster just to the left of where its heart was, or at least should have been. She turned and ran from the kitchen, her dress trailing behind her and her soft footsteps a susurrus across the floor.

Reentering the great hall, she quickly scanned and located what had not occurred to her until that moment. Dashing to the coat of arms, she pulled a silver sword from its hold, then twirled, prepared to take on the creature. Holding the sword pointed upward in both hands, determination on her face, she was ready.

A cacophony of noises came from the beast, growls of war and moans of pain fighting for their place in its agonizing roar. It moved toward her with malice and hatred evident in its intent. The thing seemed to take its time getting to her, stalking her like prey. Nothing had ever challenged it and lived before; tonight would not be that night. This frail human would not defeat it.

As it neared, Vale stepped forward and swung the blade in an arc, going backward over and around her right shoulder downward, then upward into the creature, taking the thing by surprise. It had assumed she was coming straight down with her aim, and it took a step to the left. Instead of the sword just missing its right shoulder, she planted it into the thing's abdomen, just under its ribs. She followed the curve of her swing, then stepped back, adjusted her grip, and plunged the blade into the demon's icy heart.

Clutching the razor-edged weapon in its hands, it stared in disbelief. This waif of a human had defeated it.

The silver of the sword burned with an intensity the demon had never felt before. As it fell to the floor, its final thoughts were of shame and bewilderment. Its black ichor coated the stone floor around it. Its breath stopped with the last attempted beat of its cold, dead heart.

Vale stared at it for a moment, waiting to see if it would get up or if it was truly down. Then she unleashed her own roar, a victory cry that came from the base of her gut. She had bested the thing, a surprise not only to her but to it as well.

As she stood staring at the monster, it began to dissipate, melting into a vapor until the entirety of the thing was gone. No evidence of the thing remained. Mystified, Vale knelt at the spot and placed her hand upon the ground. It was as cold as a December lake and as hot as the blue flame of a fire at the same time. It did not make sense.

Her head began to spin, and she stumbled into the wall. Bracing herself against it, she slid to the floor and placed her head between her knees. Her breathing became quick and shallow; she didn't feel like she could catch her breath. She slumped to the floor, her arms wrapping her head just in time to protect it from slamming into the ground.

Did any of it even occur? What was happening to her?

Her last thought was that the fire across the way looked inviting, warm, but that it was impossible it should be lit if nobody was present in the castle to tend it.

Opening her eyes slowly, Vale glanced around. She was unsure where she was or how she had gotten there. The last thing she remembered was picking berries, and there was something about being alone in a field of scarlet roses, a shadow nearby. Palpable fear, then impossible victory.

She pushed herself into a seated position, taking in the hard floor and the great hall. There was a fire burning in a large hearth across the room from her. And there was an odor, something like sulfur and rot. Why did that bring her a feeling of triumph?

She was suddenly aware of how alone she was. Her fear grew, consuming her thoughts. She felt like she was being watched, like something or someone was there with her, hiding in the wings, waiting for her to move.

A shadowed movement in her periphery caused her to snap her head that direction. She followed the movements of the phantasm, watched it move around the room, flitting from corner to corner and table to table in the hall. It had a carefree manner about it, like it was just out for a frolic in the flowers.

Vale was afraid, but although she sensed dread, she knew that thing wasn't where it was coming from.

Snippets of a battle flashed through her mind, pieces of fighting something evil, the clash of a sword, a dark haze floating in the air.

The specter came closer to her and hovered at her eye

level. There was a puff of silver smoke, then a woman, the most beautiful human Vale had ever seen, was standing in front of her. Long raven-black hair touched the small of her back; her porcelain skin was unmarred and smooth. She had lips as deep red as a raspberry. And her voice sounded like angels were singing.

"You have defeated the beast of darkness, and alone at that. You must be a brave warrior to have completed such a task," the woman sang. "You have great powers to have been able to find this place." A look of mischief and knowing graced the woman's face.

Perplexed, Vale asked, "Powers? What do you mean? I happened upon this fortress when I got lost in the dark. A monster was chasing me, and ..." It all came back to her, and she was panicking, her previous bravado replaced with terror.

The entity smiled upon her, then placed her small hand upon Vale's head. "Child," she said, "you have a gift. It is buried deep, but I see it in you. It burns brightly and yearns to come out." She put her hand out to help Vale up.

Giving a small curtsy in thanks, Vale looked more closely at the being. She radiated an aura of confidence and strength. A current rolled off her in waves, and the air around them crackled. An otherworldly creature, Vale was afraid to say it but knew what she was.

"Yes, I am a witch, Vale. I have been watching you for many years. Your time is coming; your powers will soon come to be. You will need guidance, and I will be there to help you learn all you need to know. You will no longer be alone. The women in your family have long enough denied their abilities. It is time for you to rise."

Wait, what is she talking about? Vale wondered. *My family? Denied abilities? Nobody has ever mentioned anything like this before.* Was it possible her family had withheld something so big? People had been burning witches at the stake for the smallest of slights, the most obscure actions. Would it truly be so shocking that her family would hide something like that?

The woman's face lit when she saw understanding cross Vale's face. "We must make haste with your training, but we must also be cautious. There are too many out there that would be quick to light the pyre. That is why this place revealed itself to you. It is a safe place for you to come and practice your craft. Destroying the beast was the first step, a simple test for you to pass to further open the world to you."

Eyes wide, Vale sputtered. "But, but that thing ... It was going to kill me! Its claws, and its teeth—"

"Would never have harmed you, unbeknownst to the creature. And your defeat of it granted you your familiar. Vale, meet Poe."

A black cat sauntered into the great hall, pausing to sit and lick its paw. It looked up at Vale with disdain before it resumed making its way to them. It jumped onto the table beside the two women and again sat, wrapped its tail around itself, and looked Vale over. "She's too old to start training," the thing said.

Vale fainted.

The sun shone brightly through her bedroom window, and the birds sang their happy little songs. Surfacing slowly from her slumber, Vale blinked several times before her heavy eyelids stayed open. She stretched her arms tall and her toes as far as they would reach, then sat up. She would need to start her chores soon; mother would be expecting her to get them finished before breakfast.

She fed and watered the chickens and the goat, then milked the cow. She went back and gathered the eggs.

The whole time, she felt a shadow following her. She could never quite catch what it was, but she felt a presence. She no longer felt alone.

Arriving at the breakfast table, Vale said to her mother, "I had the strangest dream last night."

A black cat jumped into the windowsill, wrapped its tail around itself, and licked its paw.

aple Grove is a small town, maybe all of six hundred people. Just a flyspeck of a northeastern town really, the kind you drive past without even realizing. I arrived there when I was just a year and a half old to live with my aunt in the fall of nineteen eighty-four after my mother, Judy, had become the last victim in a string of college campus murders that were never solved. The last of a half dozen coeds in Philadelphia that were strangled to death. And as for my dad, I never knew him. If my mom ever mentioned him I was too busy learning how to crawl at the time to remember it.

So, I came to live with my aunt Lynn, my mom's sister, who raised me fine but we never developed that sort of deep mother son bond. She too had been scarred by what happened to her sister. Lynn was heavy and homely and handled all the back-office support for a local hardware business. She worked the register too, but she was the one who handled all the inventory and book-keeping and all the things that went on out of sight to keep the business running. She was smart as a whip though – had a master's degree in developmental psychology and would have gone on to get a Ph.D., but that was when my mother was killed and I came to live with her. Her folks – my grandparents, had both passed away when she and my mom were teenagers, and she never married so it was just the two of us. Blood bound roommates, essentially.

We were invisible, which isn't an easy thing to be in a town that small. No one really ever said anything, although growing I sometimes got asked about it. But we made people uncomfortable, so they willed us out of their minds, the same way you do when you see a homeless person shouting at the wind. You pick up your pace a bit maybe. Parents inadvertently tighten their grip on the shoulders of their kids. Lynn and I were reminders of what other people didn't want to think about.

I didn't have a lot of friends. It's not like I was really bullied – in some ways I wonder if that would have been a step up. It would have meant that I really existed, that someone else could see me enough that they wanted to pound my lunch money out of me. But they just kept away. Like I was marked. Cursed.

I engaged in all the activities you would expect of a loner. I watched movies, read books, played a lot on the computer, wrote stories and, after Lynn took me one time to the nearest big art museum, I drew.

I remember it was a Caravaggio exhibit, in Boston I think, and the intensity of those paintings, the brightness of the light and the blood against the utter blackness. It opened my eyes in a new way, it moved me. And so I started drawing. I drew everything I could find – I set up baskets full of junk so that I could draw still life, I drew from photos, I drew landscapes. Everything.

Instead of journals, I started keeping sketch books and they piled up. And then, when I discovered comic books, I started drawing them. I gravitated, for pretty obvious reasons, to Batman.

God, I drew a lot of comics. I went through periods where I would fill entire sketch pads with stories around what I would ever do if I found my father. Who he might be and what he might be doing. Imagining how he would burst into tears at having found me. Maybe he was a movie star or a billionaire businessman. More likely, of course, he probably never even knew about me. Just one half of a drunken one-night tryst at a party or something. I wondered if he even remembered my mom's name. Maybe he scratched his head when he read the papers about her murder and thought, wow, she looks really familiar.

And then there was the other man. The one who killed her. My journals were stuffed with newspaper clipping and articles I found and printed online about similar unsolved murders. I wrote out long, comic book inspired scenarios of what I would do and say when I eventually caught him. How he would cower and beg for mercy.

The two men in my life, the two men who made me in their own ways, both absent. One was a faceless shadow and the other was composed of pure sunlight, which similarly obscured his features. And I chased them both endlessly down the imaginary corridors of my mind, running in mental circles without ever getting a look at either one. Without either ever seeing me.

When I was maybe in my early teen years Lynn must have found those sketch books, because she decided I needed to have some sort of male influence in my life. So she got me enrolled in a local big brothers program where once or twice a week a guy would come by and take me out for activities.

There was a succession of big brothers, and while they saw me, which was more than most people in town, they could never really seem to disguise the fact that it was less about me and more about the credits they needed for some program or something their church recommended or something other than just spending time with the son of no one.

First there was James, who liked sports, so he took me out and we played catch with a softball or rode bikes. He was maybe in his twenties and had a bright smile and was studying biology so that he could go into medicine. After about six months though, he rotated out and then there was Sal who had tattoos and worked at an auto garage and knew, it seemed, just about everything there was to know about cars and motorcycles. We went bowling sometimes but mostly he took me to his shop and showed me how to build and repair engines and motors. And after Sal there was Roger, who also liked to go bowling, but mostly so that he could just make small talk with the girl behind the counter who gave us our shoes.

And then there was Miles. That changed everything.

He was maybe in his thirties with sandy blond hair and dark eyes. I always picture him wearing jeans and a black shirt and an acid-washed denim jacket. On our first day together, we just went for a long walk around the block and he asked me about living here, since he was new to town, and what I liked and what I would change if I was in charge of Maple Grove. The whole time I just kept waiting for some slip that would reveal an alternative motive for him being there for me, but I could find none.

On our outing he took me to a comic shop, because I had mentioned Batman and he asked me which stories were my favorite and why. And the whole time, he never took his focus off of me. Not once. I could sense that he was different and that our connection was different, was real. It was like getting high for the first time, but better. Rather than fading, that feeling strengthened the more I thought about it.

After the second month, Miles put in a request to see me twice a week rather than just once. Lynn and the program agreed.

He took me camping and showed me how to tie knots and shoot a bow. He took me to a firing range too, although he made me promise not to tell anybody, since they might not like that. So I promised and he put the big clunky headphones on me to muffle the sound and he stood behind me with one hand on my shoulder and the other around my hand, showing me how to aim, and breathe, and fire. After a while I became a pretty good shot.

He encouraged my drawing too. Once he asked me if I would draw something for him. But he wanted it to be very specific. He said, "Draw me the darkest, scariest thing you can possibly think of. Draw me the thing that scares you the most."

I went home and I knew what I had to draw, but I kept putting off how to start. The night before the next time I was going to see Miles, I finally took out one of the few pictures I had of my mother, and I drew her face. Her mouth was open in surprise, like she was gasping or screaming and around her neck was a cord held on either end by strong hands that disappeared over her shoulders.

When I was finished my face was burning hot and flushed and slick with tears. My hands were trembling, and I felt this overwhelming sense of shame, like those hands in the picture were mine. Like I was responsible. I wanted to hide it, or burn it, or tear it up into little pieces. I felt somehow like if anyone saw it, it would be proof of my guilt. But I tucked it into the center of a comic book and put it in another folder inside my backpack.

When he met me after school the next day, I was reluctant to show him. We went to a diner and he got me an RC Cola, which was my favorite. He must have known I was dreading sharing my picture with him, but still he stretched it out, savoring my discomfort. Finally, he leaned in conspiratorially and said just one decibel louder than a whisper, "you have something to show me?"

I was paralyzed. I could say I wasn't done yet, but somehow, that power he had over me. I couldn't lie to him, couldn't even imagine it. It would have been like trying to lie to God. All I could do was pull the folder out of my backpack. And the comic book from the folder, and at last, the drawing, which I slid across the Formica tabletop to him.

His face went funny as he looked at it, and I was seized by the terrifying notion that I'd made a mistake. That he would look up at me in horror and send me away. That he would cast me out.

But he didn't. He was smiling and when he looked up at me, his eyes were shining. He was proud. "This... this..." he stammered. "this is the most goddamned beautiful thing I've ever seen." Then, in disbelief, he asked me, "I can keep this? For real."

I was smiling too, having made him so happy. I nodded.

He shook his head. "I'm going to frame this." Then he thought better of it. "Well, maybe not. I don't want to share this with anyone. This is just for me, but I'll keep it some place special."

He promised further that he would show me something special the next time we met. I returned home beaming. Lynn had been proud of me before, but never like Miles had been. Never moved to tears. No one in my life had ever been.

That night when I fell asleep, I dreamed, as I sometimes did, that I was running after my father. He was still made of light so bright I had to squint. While I couldn't make out any of his facial features, I noticed for the first time that he was wearing an acid washed jean jacket.

On our next visit he took me out to a small park on a hill overlooking the lake. And he showed me a secret stairway, grown over with branches, that led all the way down to a dock. "This is my secret place," he confided. "I come down here sometimes and just kick back. No one ever boats past this part of the lake and no one ever notices that old set of stairs. But this is where I come to just be. And if I ever wanted someone to find me, this is where I would have them meet me."

That became our place, and sometimes we would just go there with a six pack of RC cola and sit on the dock and talk. He still trained in all the stuff he told me would be important. He showed me exercises to do to strengthen my arms and hands. He told me about girls and he just listened to me. For hours. Without once ever seeming bored.

I told him my dream of finding my mother's killer, how I wanted to make him pay. My father too maybe, for having left me. Miles mostly just listened, but one time he told me that if revenge was what I really wanted, above everything else, eventually I'd get it.

On the topic of relationships, he told me that the way to really drive someone crazy was indifference and that the more I liked a girl, the more I should just act cool like I didn't really care all that much. For him, he said, it was a little easier because he wasn't just playing some game – mostly he really didn't feel that much for other people and that caring about more than just the few people closest to him was a burden anyway. I knew, the way he said it, that he was implying that I was one of those few people that really did matter to him.

"You know," he once said after I had told him about how people seemed not to notice me, "one day that very thing, that camouflage," he called it, "will become an asset."

A year had passed by this point and I had started to think of Miles as a permanent feature of my life, but he began acting squirrely. Showing up late for our appointments, which he never did. And then, one day on the end of our dock, all of that confidence he had built up, all the trust, he smashed it like a brick through a window.

"I've spent too long here," he told me. "There are other things I've put off that need to be attended to, other long-term projects that I need to get to."

He could see that he was tearing my heart out.

"But I will always, always, be with you. And I will come back to you as soon as I can. It might be a while, but I promise I will see you again."

I believed him, and so I came back to that dock every chance I got. Always, some part of me thought maybe he would be there, waiting at the end of the dock with open arms and tears in his eyes. But in time the expectation and then even the bitterness faded away. It had been his, then ours and now it was mine alone. Later on, when I had a few friends my own age, I would take them there and we would read comics and smoke cigarettes. The RC cola became beer. The first time I ever kissed a girl was on that dock.

I got into MIT for computer science. Moved out west, to where the tech jobs were. I started out as a systems administrator and then moved into the field of cyber security, just as it was becoming a thing. I guess it makes sense that the kid who grew up reading Batman would end up in that field – a shadow holding the other shadows at bay. Protecting people from all the terrible things they didn't even know they didn't know about.

And Mile was right about how my invisibility would be an asset. The more invisible I was, the better I became at my job. The less anyone noticed everything behind the scenes, the more they promoted and paid me.

I kept in touch of course with Lynn – we talked every few weeks. Birthdays. Holidays. But I seldom came back to visit. Until she got sick – the kind there isn't any getting better from. So I moved back like the dutiful son I'd never really been, and I set up my old bedroom as an office. Most of my work by this point could be done remotely anyway. I took her to her appointments and cooked, just simple stuff, and took care of the house.

The town of Maple Grove had somehow become even smaller than before. The high school I'd gone to had long since ceased to exist. Same with the bowling alley. Anyone who had noticed me before had forgotten long ago. Every so often someone at the grocery store would tilt their head when they looked at me and I could see in their eyes that they thought maybe they had known me from somewhere.

I started noticing other things too. A figure at the end of the street, just standing there for a minute but gone almost as soon as I blinked. Or that sense that someone was looking at me, but I couldn't make out from where. Or a familiar vehicle in the rearview mirror a few cars behind me.

Just when I thought maybe I was being paranoid; I saw something in the window of a local thrift store that stopped me in my tracks. It was a beat up old, acid washed jacket. His jacket. I knew it the moment I saw it. Knew it was there for me, like my own personal version of the bat signal. I went in and purchased it for thirty-two dollars.

When I took it home I tried it on in front of the mirror. I felt something in the breast pocket and reached in to fish out a roll of photos – the kind you get into a booth with someone and take. I'd never seen these before. It wasn't the images of my mother, laughing and posing and playful and full of life, that shocked me the most though. It was the boy with dark eyes and a smile that seemed vaguely dangerous. Like he was somehow daring the lense of the camera.

There was a timestamp on the photos.

October fifth, nineteen eighty-four.

A week before she was strangled to death.

Really, deep down, deeper than the shock of it, was the shock of somehow not really being shocked at all. Like I'd always known the truth, the whole truth..

That those two different men I'd been searching for

my whole life, the light and the dark, had always been one and the same.

Early the next morning, I drove out and parked my Ford truck in the gravel lot by the lake. It was sometime around late October – just cold enough that you could see your breath escape like a cloud from your mouth and nostrils. Like you were smoking, even though you weren't.

I was wearing Miles' jacket. Not really out of any special sense of ceremony or because I wanted him to see that I'd figured it out, but just because it was cold. That's what I tell myself.

My shoes crunched on the gravel as I walked down the path along the lake to the dock. He was sitting there at the end of it, just like I knew he'd be, in jeans and a leather jacket, with his legs dangling out over the water. I knew he would have a six pack of RC cola there beside him, which he did, and something else I couldn't quite make out as I approached. By the time I was just a few feet behind him though, I understood.

It was a braided rope cord.

He was bent over slightly looking at his reflection as it rippled and distorted in the water. As I came up behind him and looked down over his shoulder, I noticed that my reflection and mine had merged into a single dark shape on the surface of the lake.

"It was the jacket, wasn't it?" He asked without turning around to look at me.

"Yeah."

"I knew it. I knew you would find it there, put it all together." He turned to look up at me.

I was going to tell him that if he wanted to die, he could jump in the lake himself. But then he said that one thing that every kid not so secretly wants to hear from their parents. That one sentence forbidden by the unwritten rules of parenthood.

"You've always been my favorite. You know that, boy?"

He gave me that same smile he flashed when I gave him the picture I drew of my mother. His eyes caught the light as the sun poked out from the clouds and they shimmered, like he was crying. But not out of sadness. It was the unmistakable look of pride.

I reached down and pulled a can of RC cola from the pack, cracked the tab and took a gulp. That black saccharine sweet fluid filling my mouth. I set the can down next to my work boots.

The lines on his face that had time had just started to chisel when I saw him last had become deep ravines, his hair had receded and gone from blond to mostly grey. His forehead was speckled with liver spots. But it didn't matter – time didn't matter, didn't even seem to exist.

"I wish we could have had more time," Miles said, as if picking up on the frequency of my thoughts before turning to look back out over the water. "But this way is best."

"Yeah," I responded from what seemed like somewhere else. Like I was somewhere behind or above me. I watched that other me lift the cord and wrap it once around each hand, close them into fists and pull the cord taut. I watched myself come up behind Miles and put the cord over his head, until it hung loose around his neck, one of my hands over each of his shoulders.

"Now you take hold tight, just like I taught you. My body will fight it, so keep your balance. Don't let me toss you in the drink."

As I watched myself strain and pull, it was like I was pulling myself back into me. The person I was watching was suddenly me again as the third person point of view switched over to first. Once the struggle was over and Miles had stopped clawing at the cord and finally gone slack, the hands holding that cord were mine. It was my shins against which the dead weight of his body slumped.

I waited for sirens, or screams or a voice over a bullhorn telling me to put my hands up over my head, anything, but it never came. I was invisible again. Like I'd always been. In a place no one was likely to come looking for either one of us.

Tears came and I looked up at the sun just as it was being enveloped by a black storm cloud. The water in my eyes swirled and blurred the light and the dark together, until they were just one thing, impossible to separate or distinguish from each other.

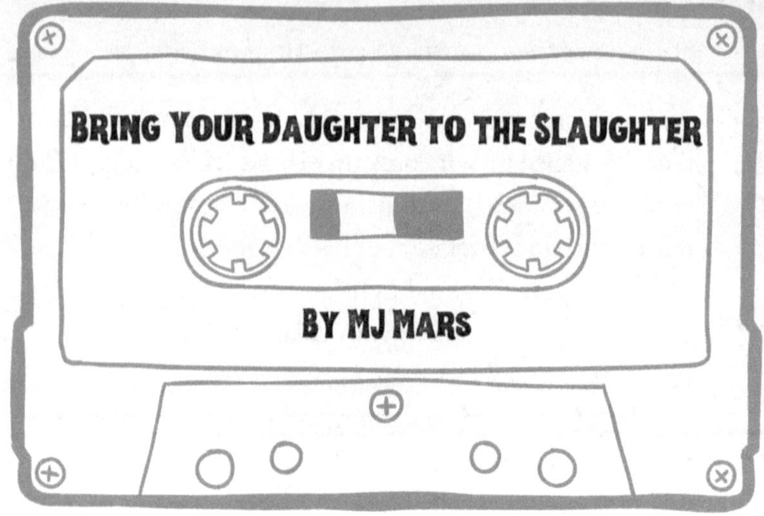

S ian woke with a gasp seconds before her phone alarm blared to life, the digital display informing her of three things: It was 7 a.m., it was a Friday, and it was Halloween. She reached over and jabbed the silencer, then whipped her head toward the window as a scattering of pebbles hit the pane. Yawning, she swung her feet out of bed and went to the curtains, tugging back the fabric and peering down into the yard. It was empty.

She unlatched the window and leaned out, pressing her hands against the sill as she craned her head. Whatever her friend had thrown at the pane to wake her had collected in a gritty, reddish dirt pile. She dusted it from her hands, the grains sharp and sandy against her skin. There was no sign of her friends, and she guessed they must have moved around to the front door. She raked her hand through her hair, working her fingers through tangled snags, then sniffed her hands and wished she hadn't. It smelled like farts. Certain now that there was a Halloween prank in motion, she called out to the usual suspects. "Maizie? Bart?"

Below her, a figure stepped out from the bushes. The man was tall and was covered from head to toe in a filthy-looking brown cape, the head bowed under a scruffy hood.

Rolling her eyes, Sian drummed her fingernails against the sill and sighed. "Good one, Bart. Save your crappy costume for the party tonight, why don't you?"

The figure remained where it stood, staring at the ground. Sian had to give him credit; he was certainly putting a lot of effort into the look. He was even wearing crusty old sandals, his toes smeared in what looked like red-orange desert sand. His big toenails were lined in black filth and were in urgent need of a trim.

"Gross," Sian mouthed to herself. She was all for a decent Halloween costume, but there was such a thing as going too far when it came to personal hygiene. "I'll be down in a minute," she shouted, then closed the window and turned to her mirror.

She froze, her heart leaping into her mouth. Breathless, she stared at her own reflection. For a second, she'd thought she'd seen...no. It was so stupid, she told herself. The residual impact of waking on Halloween and Bart's stupid prank making her mind wander, giving her the creeps. But for one moment it had looked as though there were figures in the room behind her. Black shapes moving toward her, arms outstretched, gnarled claws protruding from boned fingers. "You're going crazy," she told herself, her eyes darting around the mirror, double checking the reflection around her.

Her mobile rang, and she jumped out of her skin. She broke into a laugh, feeling ridiculous, checked the name and answered, her heart still hammering, a flush of shame on her cheeks. "So, the creepy cloak has pockets?"

"What?" Bart mumbled, his voice thick with sleep. "What are you talking about?"

"Your little costume. Thanks for the sneak preview but maybe wash your feet before the party starts."

"Babe, I honestly don't know what you're talking about."

Hooking the phone between her shoulder and ear, Sian started applying her makeup, fluttering a mascara wand against her lashes, her eyes wide open to keep it from smudging. "Don't try and scare me, Bart. I know you were here. I saw you and it didn't frighten me, so mission *not* accomplished. And you can come and wash that orange stuff off my windowsill."

"Sian, I'm calling to say I'm running late. Don't wait to get a lift with me, I've only just woken up."

Growing a little irritated, Sian switched the phone to her left shoulder and started working on the other eye. "I. Saw. You. In your stupid cloak. What are you anyway, the grim reaper or something?"

"Babe, I don't know who's messing with you, but it isn't me. I'm not wearing any cloak tonight. I'm Star Lord. From *Guardians of the Galaxy*? Gerard's lending me his Rocket toy." He yawned again. "Anyway, I've gotta run. See you at college."

Sian dropped the phone and swiped the wand over her lashes an extra time for good measure. A dark shadow crossed the room behind her. She whirled around, the mascara wand streaking her forehead. "Damn it, Bart!" she cried out as her phone sounded again. This time it was a *WhatsApp* message. She opened it and saw the screen flood with an image of her sleepy-looking boyfriend lying in bed holding out a Rocket Raccoon teddy and looking puzzled. She checked the clock at his side and read the date and time. The same as hers.

Holding her breath, she slowly walked back to the window. She leaned out and stared down at the path.

It was empty.

Turning, she screamed as she collided with a tall, dark figure standing right behind her.

"Whoa, honey! I didn't mean to scare you," her father said, holding her upper arms in a firm grasp.

It was all Sian could do to stop herself from shouting out a swear word but, even though she was going to be eighteen in nine months, her parents couldn't abide curse words. They were particularly frosty about blasphemy, Sian had noted, which was odd since they weren't religious as far as she knew. She bit back the curse on her tongue and forced a smile. "It's okay. It's just my friends playing around."

Her father looked down at her and gave her a searching look, and Sian was surprised to see that his eyes looked a little red and puffy, as though he'd been crying. Aside from cursing, crying was the only other thing she'd never seen her dad do, and it unnerved her to see it.

"Dad, what's wrong?"

He gazed tenderly down at her face with an expression of regret, Sian thought. But he shook his head and gave a sharp laugh. "It's these allergies again."

"But it's October."

Ignoring her, her father licked his thumb and smudged it above her eyebrow. He held it out to her, showing an inky black mark. "You've got a little something on you."

"A marked maiden at Halloween," Sian joked, scrubbing her sleeve over the remaining mascara splodge. "That's got to mean a curse or something, right?"

Her father didn't smile. His eyes roamed her face intently and Sian was certain she saw that regretful expression once more. Before she could ask, he pulled her tightly into a hug. "Enjoy every minute of today," he murmured into her hair.

"I will, Dad," she promised as he pulled away and turned around quickly, moving swiftly for the door with a sharp sniff.

"These God damned allergies again."

Sian stood in her room for a few moments wondering two things. How in the heck was her father suffering from hay fever the day before November? And since when had he started swearing again?

"My parents are acting really weird," Sian announced at lunch. The cafeteria was decked out in black and orange streamers and the countertops had been adorned with badly carved pumpkins for the day. In an attempt to push the theme as much as possible, the menu had been re-worded, offering up such culinary cliché's as *Franken*-furters, chicken sand-*witches* and cheese *ghost*-ies. Sian had picked the ghost pun toastie and was relieved to find that the cafeteria staff hadn't gone to bizarre lengths with the fillings of the toasted sandwich. Inside was just plain old cheddar cheese.

Maizie took a bite out of her Frankenfurter and chewed, pushing the sausage and bread into the pouch of her left cheek so she could talk with her mouth full. "What do you mean?"

"Like, I don't know. I went down to breakfast and my mum was fussing all around me. She hadn't even set off for work. And my dad said he had allergies, but it looked more like he was upset over something..."

"Maybe someone's died, and they don't want to tell you until after college. That's what my parents did when it was my aunt." Maizie shrugged and swallowed her mouthful.

"Oh, no. I don't want anyone to have died." Sian dropped her crust and wiped her greasy fingers on a green napkin with a spiderweb printed in the corner.

"Especially not on Halloween. Too weird," Maizie agreed, taking another huge bite.

"I just think if it was that they'd have told me. I mean, I'm seventeen. I can handle it."

"Perhaps they want you to enjoy the party tonight."

Maizie said, again speaking with her mouth partly full, chewed up bun pasting her tongue.

"My dad did tell me I should enjoy every minute of today."

"Well, there you go. Maybe they want you to have a good day before dropping a bombshell."

Sian felt sick. It was almost worse to have to wait around for them to break their news. "I think I'll call my mum," she said, pushing her tray to the side and pulling her phone from her back pocket. She walked out to the empty corridor and stood beside a vending machine, selecting her mother's work from her contacts list. The receptionist answered and told her snippily that her mother hadn't shown up that day. Sian thanked her, not meaning it, and stared at the phone in her hand.

If she'd thought her dad had been acting funny that morning, it was nothing to the way her mother had greeted her in the kitchen. She too had given Sian a lingering embrace, then had leaned back and held her face in both hands, staring at her in an even more intense way than her father had. She almost got the feeling her parents didn't think they'd ever see her again. Shuddering, Sian tried to force the notion from her mind as she called home, the ringtone chiming in her ear. It rang and rang. Feeling even sicker, Sian wondered how she would get through afternoon classes if her mother failed to answer. Just as she gave up hope, her mother's voice spoke over the pounding of blood in her eardrum.

"Sian, are you okay? What is it, what's happening?"

"Mum...I'm okay. Are you?"

There was a rush of air blowing through the receiver as her mother exhaled. "You're okay."

"Of course I'm okay. Mum, what's wrong?"

"Nothing, sweetheart."

"No, look, you can tell me. I'm old enough now to know if something bad has happened. Is Aunt Lucy okay?"

"She's fine, honey."

"Uncle Damien?"

"Everyone's alright, Sian. Believe me. You don't need to worry about anyone else."

Sian leaned back against a vending machine, the gentle vibration of the cooled glass something of a comfort. "Why aren't you at work?"

"I...I took a day off. To get ready for your party."

"That's not like you."

"Well, I wanted it to be perfect for you. I want you to have a perfect day."

Sian tried to ignore the catch in her mother's voice, convincing herself that she was imagining the tears in her words. "Mum, have you got allergies, too?"

Her mother let out a thick laugh and was hoarse when she replied. "Don't be silly, sweetheart. It's not summer. It's Halloween."

"I was going to be a female Jason Voorhees, but then I realised I'd have to keep my face covered with a stupid hockey mask all night," Maizie threw her hands up as if that was the most preposterous idea she'd ever heard. "I mean, *hello*! I want Rael to actually *see* me. I didn't get these brows done to hide them inside some sweaty old sports mask, did I?"

"Who are you going to be instead?" Sian hadn't been expecting too much by way of creativity from her friend, so when she rummaged inside her rucksack and hauled out a black, skin-tight cat suit and a hairband with pointed ears, she wasn't too surprised.

"I'm a familiar."

"A what?"

"You know. A demon animal."

"You're a horny cat," Sian corrected, grabbing the material and stretching it to emphasise how clingy it would be.

"No! I'm a familiar. It's what the old witches had... you know. The ones who got tried for treason or whatever and left at the top of Pendle Hill to freeze."

"I don't think that's quite how it went," Sian rolled her eyes at her friend, used to her skewed take on history. Maizie enjoyed playing dumb. Sometimes it was easier to relent than to correct her flawed factoids.

"Anyway, this way, I'm still Halloween ready, but Rael won't be able to help but notice me. What's Bart coming as?"

"Star Lord."

"Ugh, is that the Harrison Ford one? Does he have a light sabre? Because if he doesn't, it won't be worth it at all."

Sian walked home alongside her long-time friend,

grateful for her constant chatter. It distracted her from dwelling too much on her parents and the strange way they'd been acting. She couldn't work out why they seemed so upset if there hadn't been any family tragedies, and why they were talking to her as though it was her last day on earth. Perhaps she was being too sensitive, she reasoned. She had been jumpy that morning, what with Halloween playing on her mind. And there was the weirdo who had been standing outside her window. She had been trying to work out who it might have been all day, but the only person other than Bart who was that tall would have been creepy Bill who lived three houses down. If it had been Bill, she'd certainly have something to say to her father about it. He had no right coming onto their property and throwing dirt up at her window. She'd never really liked him but had always thought he was harmless. Bill had known her parents since they were teenagers together, after all. But today, when her tensions were high, he suddenly felt like an intimidating threat. She was glad Maizie was walking home with her as she passed Bill's house, even if her friend's incessant talk was beginning to wear thin.

"You're quiet," Maizie pointed out as they strolled past Bill's home.

"Hmm," Sian murmured, distracted. The man had started putting up some sort of Halloween décor but wasn't too far into it by all accounts. He'd drawn a chalk pentagram on his door and had lit a few candles on the porch stairs. Hardly original.

"Earth to Sian, come in, please!"

"Sorry...I just, I think Bill was at our house this morning."

"So?"

"Well, he didn't come and talk to us or anything, he just stood outside my window in a Halloween costume."

"Let me guess...neon green mankini?" Maizie cackled with laughter.

"No, it was a grubby old cloak. It freaked me out, actually."

"Why didn't you tell him to get lost?"

"I didn't see him properly. I don't even know it was definitely him."

"Oh, forget it, babe. It was probably some guy trying to find his way home from a party the night before."

"You're right, I just think-" Sian stopped talking as Bill appeared from around the back of the house. He was no longer wearing a cloak and instead was dressed in a maroon jumper and slouchy chinos. On his feet were white Converse with the laces tucked behind the tongue. Not a sandal or speck of red sand in sight. He was holding an open box of large white candles, a pack of matches balanced on top. When he saw the girls, he froze.

"Hey, Bill," Maizie called, snapping her bubble gum. "Were you at Sian's window this morning?"

The man looked in horror toward Sian, his mouth falling open. He shook his head and took a step back. In what looked like panic, he shoved the candles under the crook of one arm and raised his now free hand to his neck. Candles spilled to the porch decking and rolled off it, tumbling into the long grass that grew at the side of the house. Still clutching at his neck and muttering words that Sian struggled to hear, Bill ducked and scurried through the front door, disappearing into the house.

Finding his actions hysterically funny, Maizie scurried to the decking, reaching into the grass and scooping up the candles. She carried them back to where Sian stood in shock and held up her three prizes. "What a freakin' weirdo! But these will come in super handy for tonight. Come on, girl!"

Sian stood for a moment, staring at the doorway, the pentagram slightly smudged where Bill had raked his hand through it in his hurry to open the door. He seemed to be afraid of her, Sian realised, baffled. She followed on behind Maizie, who was still giggling away to herself, unconcerned by the neighbour's odd behaviour. But Sian couldn't forget the look of fear on the man's face when he saw her. Or the fact that he had scrabbled to hold onto the small gold crucifix around his neck, his fearful expression masked by the words of the prayer that tumbled from his mouth.

They walked into the house, a feeling of deep apprehension settling in Sian's gut. Her mother had been true to her word, and the house was decorated in orange silly string and pulled-felt cobwebs. In the kitchen, plastic cups and a punchbowl filled with sweet-smelling red liquid sat on a black crepe tablecloth. Sian peered into the punchbowl and found a dozen floating fake eyeballs staring back at her. She couldn't help but smile at that one.

Maizie set the stolen candles down by the sink and held one to the light, turning it slowly. "There's something scratched into these," she pointed out.

"What does it say?"

"I dunno. It's in a funny language or something."

Sian stepped closer and peered at the wax. Bill had carved a crude-looking pentagram on the side of the candle. All around the pillar, words had been etched in an unfamiliar language. "What is that, Latin? Diabolus... anima mea...damnatorum."

"It sure sounds like Latin," Maizie grinned and shrugged, unconcerned. "They all burn the same way."

"Mum?" Sian yelled, her unease building. She tossed her bag into the closet. "Are you home?"

"Darling!" her mother cried, pacing through the kitchen at breakneck speed and pulling her into another death-grip embrace.

Sian untangled herself and gestured to the kitchen. "This looks great."

"I hoped you'd like it." Her mother gazed at her, then scooted her eyes quickly away. Sian wasn't sure if she was imagining it, but again she felt sure her parent had been crying.

"Is that Sian?" her father called, coming into the kitchen. He moved past his wife and wrapped his arms around Sian. There was a strange energy in the room, and Sian could feel how tense her father's muscles were beneath his shirt. "Listen honey, me and your mother are going to be working in the basement while you get ready for the party. Please don't let any of your friends come down there. This is really important. Do you understand?"

Stunned by the firm edge to his words, Sian hesitated, only to find herself being shaken roughly by her dad.

He looked intently into her eyes. "I said, *do you understand*?"

"Yes, Sir," she replied, flustered.

"Okay." He leaned in and gave her a firm kiss on the cheek, then gestured to his wife. "Come on, Elise. We've got work to do."

"Bye Mr and Mrs Porter!" Maizie called after them, but they strode out without turning back. Seconds later, the door to the basement recreation room slammed shut.

"Didn't I tell you they were acting weird?" Sian turned to her friend, her voice hushed.

"Truly! I totally see what you mean."

Although it usually felt like a positive thing to have her hunches validated by a friend, this time Sian wished Maizie had shaken her head and called her crazy. Had told her she was imagining it. For Maizie to have noticed too meant that there was something to notice in the first place.

The sick, uneasy feeling stayed with Sian as the girls dressed up in their costumes. She had chosen to be a zombie Disney princess, her pink chiffon dress torn and smeared with fake blood. She drew stitches across her cheek with lip liner and gave herself heavy shadows under her eyes with a grey palette.

Maizie clapped her hands, twitching her black-tipped cat nose and squealing. "You look amazing! Do my whiskers..."

Sian took the black eyeliner and struck three lines across each of Maizie's cheeks. The pair looked in the mirror, appraising their work.

Letting out a screech, Sian dropped the liner. It clattered to the counter, forgotten as she stared wide-eyed at her reflection. A cluster of dark figures crouched behind her, their heads bowed and their clawed hands outstretched, like demonic beggars. The cloaked man stood hunched in the corner beside her unmade bed, his hooded face still peering down at his bare, sand-coated toes. She whirled round with a scream and saw only her empty room, nothing in the corner but a stack of unread textbooks.

"What the hell?" Maizie asked, jumping away from the desk and warily following her friend's gaze.

"I don't know...I keep thinking I'm seeing something..."

"Jeez, you scared the crap outta me!" Maizie wheezed, dramatically clutching her chest. "You've got the Halloween heebie-jeebies. Don't worry. You'll relax once the party starts."

As if on cue, the doorbell chimed.

"I bet that's Bart," Sian muttered, still distracted by the strange visions she had been experiencing. She didn't want to mention it to Maizie, but she thought she'd glimpsed the cloaked figure at school, lurking in the corridor. When she'd looked back, the figure had vanished. Was she going crazy? Or was she simply creeped out by the fact that it was Halloween? She vowed to try to relax and enjoy the party. It was what her parents wanted, no matter what was going on with them. Plus, she always felt safe when she was with Bart.

She opened the front door, and Bart waved the Rocket Raccoon teddy in her face, giving a terrible tough-guy impression of the procyonid *Marvel* character. He then dropped the toy to the floor and proceeded to strut, showing off his Star Lord costume.

Sian grinned. "You look great."

Maizie was nonplussed. "Where the hell's your light sabre?"

Bart rolled his eyes and stepped past Sian into the house.

Maizie lifted the raccoon from the floor. "What the hell's this? An Ewok?"

Laughing, Sian followed her boyfriend into the kitchen and watched as he started ladling punch into three plastic cups. She already felt calmer. Bart was broad and attentive, equally assertive when he needed to be and sensitive when she required it. They had been dating for almost three years. It felt as though she may have found *the one*, even though it was too soon to say for sure. She was just a teenager, after all. There was plenty of life ahead of her yet. Plenty more men out there to meet and fall in love with. But at that point, she couldn't picture being with anyone other than Bart. She let the first relaxed smile of the day come to her lips.

The smile froze on her face when she saw a figure walking hurriedly past the kitchen window.

It was Bill.

"What the...?" The doorbell chimed, but Sian wasn't interested in who had arrived at the front of the property. Bill had been headed for the back. The only entranceway around back would take him straight into the basement room, where her parents were. "Maizie, get the door."

"Please let it be Rael!" Maizie squealed, sashaying out of the room in her slinky catsuit.

Sian followed the route her parents had taken and rapped on the basement door. There were urgent voices inside, muffled through the doorframe, but she could tell it was her father and Bill. They sounded as though they were arguing. The sounds gave Sian a sensation of cold dread.

Her mother tugged open the door, her face ashen. "Sian, honey."

"Why is Bill here?"

"Don't you worry about that. We have some work to do and he's helping us, that's all." A plump tear the size of summer rain fell from her mother's eye and dropped onto her shirt. There was no denying it that time. No pretending it was hay fever allergies.

Sian pushed past her mother and marched down the steps into the rec room. There was a coffee table laid out in the middle of the floor, *Scrabble* letter pieces placed in a circle. An upturned whiskey glass sat in the centre. "What the hell...are you guys doing *Ouija*?" she breathed, looking up to where the two men were standing at the back door.

Bill looked up in fright and gasped, clutching the frame of the door. His eyes bulged and his mouth fell open in panic. Once again, he grabbed the crucifix at his neck.

"Dad?" Sian felt her legs tremble. "Why is he afraid of me?"

Her father shook his head and turned back to their neighbour, reaching out to grip his arm before he managed to run, as he so clearly wished to do. "Bill, come on. We said we'd try this."

"No! It won't work. It's too late. The only thing that might stop this is consecrated ascension, and you both know it."

Elise pointed her finger at the neighbour, her face angry. "We said we wouldn't put her through that."

Bill looked from Elise to Sian, then back again, his expression softening. Instead of afraid, he now looked full of pity. "Elise. John. As my oldest friends, you know I mean it when I say, this is the only way. You made your beds eighteen years ago. We've tried ever since, and nothing has changed. We need to go. We have to take her now."

Sian's father let go of Bill's arm and hung his head. "He's right, Elise. If we were going to get anywhere with the Ouija—or any other method, for that matter—it would have worked by now. We've tried everything. There's only one option left."

"Mum? What are they talking about?" Sian asked, feeling the sting of tears.

Finally, her mother spoke, her voice heavy, the weight of the world carried in her words. "Sian, you have to understand. We were desperate. Desperate to have a child."

She stared at the woman who had brought her into the world, panic restricting her breath, her chest beginning to burn. "Bill said just now, eighteen years ago, you made your beds. What does he mean? What did you do?"

"Your father and I had tried and tried for a baby. It was killing us...it was all we'd ever wanted. *You* were all we'd ever wanted, Sian."

"What did you do?" Sian screamed at them, fear turning to anger on her tongue.

Above her, she heard her friends trying the door, rattling it on its hinges. Bart's faint voice calling her name. It must have been locked. Her mother had locked them in.

Her father moved towards her and took her hand, staring imploringly. He looked as if he'd seen a ghost. "We'd done it in college. Asked the Ouija for things sometimes. Things that came true. It was something we'd seen with our own eyes. The price was never all that high...it was almost a game."

Sian stared at the *Ouija* board laid out on the table. The glass shifted a little, moved by unseen forces. She coughed, her chest tightening even more, her throat suddenly dry and scratchy.

"It had to be Halloween, to let him through. We knew that much. We knew we'd have to pay a high price, and we were willing to do it. You must understand..."

"We wanted a baby so badly it was all we could think of," her mother interjected. "We thought the price might be that he would come for one of us, in time. We decided we were willing to take the risk, if it meant just a glimpse of the happiness a family would bring us. We didn't have aspirations like you do...it was all we wanted for our lives."

"What did you ask for?" Sian whispered, watching the glass move again, darting towards the corner of the table, sending Scrabble tiles scattering to the floor. Three tiles tumbled purposefully across the floor to land at her feet. They spelled *VOS*.

"We asked for you," her father cried, wrapping her in his arms. He was trembling. She coughed against his chest, grains of sand crunching against her tongue, expelled from somewhere inside her.

Her mother moved behind her, her sweet perfume wafting through the scent of sulphuric dust that had suddenly filled the air of the basement. "We didn't know the price would be you, as well."

"What do you mean?" Sian cried, tears of terror flooding her eyes. She blinked, the action scratching her, clouding her vision. It was as if her body was expelling the grit that had daubed her windowsill. She coughed again, and red dirt flew from her mouth and landed on her father's lapel.

"We truly believed we could stop it if we tried to bargain before he came. The time has just gone so quickly...eighteen years since the day I fell pregnant with you. We tried to stop it, Sian, but we failed."

"Stop what? What's going on?" But she knew, even if her parents couldn't form the words. They had made a deal with the devil one Halloween night eighteen years ago. And he was coming to claim his fee.

Bart hammered on the basement door, his voice harsher than Sian had ever heard it. "Mr. and Mrs. Porter! Open this door right now."

At the open doorway, Bill gestured for them to hurry.

Coughing, sandy flecks materialising from some-where deep in her lungs, Sian let her parents lead her out to Bill's car. The shrouded figure watched from the hedges, his head lowered as though in reverent contem-plation. His wide smile was hidden behind his hood.

The car trundled through the overgrowth, bracken lashing at the windows and making clunking sounds deep in the vehicle's undercarriage. Bill drove in silence, hunched over the wheel. Sian's parents flanked her on the back seat, her father's hand wrapped tightly around her thigh, her mother's arms flung around her upper body. Her head was pressed against her mother's chest, and she could feel her shivering uncontrollably, her heart outracing even her own.

It felt as though she was in a dream. Her whole life—her very existence—was a lie. Was she even human in the first place? Or had she been conjured by a demon, even as a baby. Not a mass of cells but a mass of evil. The thought made her want to throw up.

Elise whispered into her hair, "I'm sorry, I'm so sorry, baby. I'm sorry..."

She felt like she didn't even know her mother anymore. How could this woman, someone who stopped to rescue worms, picking them up from the hot pavement and placing them back on soft soil, have even thought of making a deal with the devil? It was obscene.

And now the demons were coming to take her back. Take her back where? To hell, presumably, as though she had been fostered out to the human world and her time had run out. She blinked, the sand gritty against her eyelids. That was exactly what happened, she suddenly realised. Had she been a lost soul in hell eighteen years ago? How long had she been there, suffering, before the deal with her parents was made?

Her anger suddenly consuming her, she shrugged out of her mother's embrace and batted away her father's hand. "Don't touch me," she muttered, staring straight ahead through the windshield.

Elise quietly cried beside her as the scenery changed. They were almost at the chapel. Sian could see gravestones ahead. A small church with a bell in its steeple sat to the right, illuminated by a round solar lamp positioned over the shield-shaped entranceway.

Bill stopped the car and turned to her. "We have to do this quick. I imagine they're going to try and stop us."

"Who?" Sian whispered, but Bill didn't answer, and a huge part of her felt relieved.

"Oh my God, oh my God..." Elise muttered as she fumbled with the door handle, struggling to get out.

John climbed out of his side and went around back, opening his wife's door from the outside and helping her out. He held his hand out to Sian, but she chose to exit through the door he'd left open. She didn't need their help, she thought, bitterly. Not after what they'd done to her.

Bill got out, dragging the spade with him. The sight of it sent panic shooting up through Sian's body. It was the feeling before a drop on a roller coaster. The sensation of a near-miss on the road. Only, for Sian, it didn't go away.

John opened the boot and pulled out a clanking satchel filled with paraphernalia Sian could only guess at. How long had her parents been secretly participating in occult activities while she hung out in her room, oblivious? It was baffling. In a daze, she followed Bill as he strode closer to the graveyard. She felt too betrayed by her parents to allow them any trust at this point. Bill seemed to know what he was doing, and she didn't have any emotional attachment to him. It somehow made this whole mess easier to deal with. For a fleeting moment, she wished her parents hadn't come at all.

"Here. This is where the kids are buried. Not only is it consecrated ground, it's also the ground of the innocents," Bill told them, preparing to strike the grass with the blade of the shovel.

"You can't dig up a child!" Sian protested.

She flinched at her father's cold hand on her upper arm but listened when he spoke calmly in her ear. "We aren't digging anyone up, honey. It's going to be a shallow grave. Just enough to cover you."

Chills scurried over her arms. She was going to have to lie down and be buried in the graveyard.

As if reading her thoughts, her mother quickly spoke. "It's just for a few moments. Just long enough for us to complete the protection and banishing ritual. Once that's done, they won't be able to come for you. You'll be able to get a fresh start, coming out of the earth. They won't touch you after that."

"How do you know it will work?"

Elise hesitated, a frantic look in her eyes. "It has to."

A peculiar howl sounded from the bottom of the graveyard, deep in the shadows.

Bill began to dig faster. "Quickly, now, get everything ready. We don't have much time."

Over the *shiiink-puck* of Bill stomping the shovel into the earth and digging out clods, Sian could make out unusual sounds coming from all around them. Some sounded like baby babble, caught on a breeze. Others were shrill and screeching. None of them sounded like animals she had heard before. She coughed into her hand, black grains launching out and hitting her palm. Her breath smelled of sulphur.

"Quickly, now. It should be deep enough," Bill beckoned her toward the hole. "Clamber in."

"Like this?" Sian looked down at her pink princess costume and felt helpless.

Another strange scream emanated from behind the gravestones, this time far closer than the first.

"Get in, now!" Bill snapped.

Sian stepped into the dank hole. The newly disturbed mud was soft under her feet. When she lowered herself to sit, moisture instantly dampened the back of her dress. It was cold, colder than she could have imagined, and, when she lay flat, spatters of icy dirt scattered her shoulders, already tumbling from the sides. A worm wriggled, half of its body exposed and confused, unsure why it had suddenly found itself out in the open. She hoped it wouldn't drop onto her bare skin.

Elise peered down at her from the opening. "Be brave, sweetheart. It won't be for long."

John crouched down and caressed her cheek. This time, she didn't flinch away from his touch. Her eyes filled with tears as he spoke. "This will work, baby. I promise."

Without another word, Bill began tossing the dirt back into the grave. It was a cold, sharp shock each time the mud hit her skin. At first, it almost felt like a slap, the heavy muck's weight making her bare arms and legs tingle. All too soon, the mud began to layer and, instead of a slapping sensation, it began to feel heavy, like a rock weighing her down in the chilled earth.

"What the hell are you doing?" Maizie's shrill,

panicked voice rang out from somewhere behind Bill. "Let her out!"

Sian heard Elise making calming noises, hurried steps moving away from the gravesite. "It isn't what it looks like, you don't understand."

"Back off, lady!" This was Bart, Sian recognized. She guessed that the pair had been concerned about her parents' strange behaviour and, when her friends realised they had left the basement, they followed them to the churchyard. She had great friends, she knew, but they couldn't have chosen a worse time to be heroic.

Sian struggled under the dirt, trying to sit up but held fast by the weight. "It's okay," she called. "Please, get out of here."

Maizie's horrified face appeared above her. "What in the world?"

"We don't have time for this!" Bill yelled, raising the spade and shovelling more dirt into the grave. He yelped and went sprawling, the spade clattering down into the hole. Bart had jumped on the neighbour, throwing him to the ground.

John appeared in Sian's restricted view for a moment, arms outstretched, ready to drag Bart away from the scuffle.

Elise let out a frustrated cry. "No! It's too late, it's too late!"

There was the sound of fist hitting flesh and Sian's father grunted, landing backwards, his arm lolling into the open grave beside her.

Bart jumped into the hole, grabbed the shovel, and began digging her out. "It's okay, babe. We've got you."

"No, Bart. Listen—you need to let them do the ritual." Sian's voice was firm, betraying the searing panic that was building inside her. For a moment, when her friends had arrived, she wondered if they were right. If her parents were sharing some kind of insanity and she was being dangerously swept up in their delusion. Deep down, she knew that wish was foolhardy.

"Ritual? What the fuck are you talking about, Sian?" Sweat dampened Bart's fringe as he worked, tossing clods of earth over the side of the makeshift grave. Sian's arms began to feel freer, the weight on her chest lifting, allowing her to take a deep breath. She tasted rotting earth.

A howl peeled out over the churchyard.

Elise screamed again, this time a shriek of sheer terror. "They're here. You've ruined everything."

Bart stopped digging and froze, his face which had contained the flush of exertion draining sheet white. A black smear surged over the grave, carrying him with it.

Maizie's voice followed, her voice a high-pitched shriek. "What is that? *What is that?*"

Sian froze, listening to the sound of carnage above her. The ominous chattering of otherworldly beings was closer than ever, wails and mumbles surrounding the grave. Her father's lifeless arm jerked as though his body had been pounced on and it began to move backward, pulled by an unseen force that let out a gargling warble.

Her mother spoke, each word growing quieter, as

though she were being moved over the churchyard. "Sian, we loved you. You were the daughter we always wanted. We loved you..."

In the distance, the "you" was cut short, replaced by a wet-sounding gurgle Sian wondered if she had imagined.

Sian could see nothing from inside the grave, but the sounds on their own were almost worse. Tearing cloth, slapping flesh and pattering droplets of blood. All around her, her friends and family were being torn to pieces. Slaughtered. Because they loved her.

There was a rumbling sensation, as though a rare low-scale earthquake was pulsing through their sleepy, central-England village. The dirt on top of Sian shifted and crumbled, and she wondered for one joyous moment if she was going to be able to free herself and make a dash for safety. The dark sides of the grave began to rise around her.

No, that wasn't it, she realised in horror.

She was moving down.

As though she was lying in a slow elevator on its descent, Sian's body descended deeper into the earth. She wiggled and struggled under the muck, panic overwhelming as the night sky began to shrink above her, the walls of the grave growing ever taller, the rectangle leading to safety getting further and further away.

Screaming and crying now, Sian threw her left arm upward. Dirt exploded around her, scattering over her face. The soft wetness of a twisting worm slid down her neck and came to rest in the pit of her collarbone. Her filth-coated arm struck out and clawed at the sodden side, the mud firm and impacted. From beneath her, a dark hand shot upwards, claws clamping around her wrist.

The grave which had once felt so cold to her was growing warmer, heat from below scorching the earth.

As she tumbled into darkness and fire, a voice flooded her ears. "Eighteen years already? I've been waiting for you..."

1 | THE FATHER

Ginger restocked the bar while I was out. The bottles glitter like idols. My inner opponent steps from the dark of my mind and jeers, *It's only a matter of time. Why not today?* My reply comes like a desperate offering to the gods, and it fails to appease them. I uncork a bottle of Usquebaugh. So much for my best self.

"Welcome back, Dr. Grieves? What can I do you for, love?" Union Jack dress shimmering. Ginger resolves behind me in a three-dimensional ghostly monochrome.

Locked in a battle of wills with the Usquebaugh, I don't reply.

She crosses her arms across her chest and snarls, "Out with it. I don't have all bloody day, you know." The hotel advertises Ginger's personality as "mercurial." Hairpin mood swings aren't a glitch, they're a feature; one I neither asked for nor want, but a feature nonetheless.

I'd disconnect, except too much silence has stacked up. My virtual concierge's passive filters have been logging my missed social cues, and a sudden log-out might bubble up a flag to MasterControl. I need to de-escalate Ginger before I can get rid of her.

"Well?"

"How about a pot of coffee." I should add that I'm here to dry out and ask her to clear out the bar, but I don't.

"You asking or offering, love?"

"I wouldn't think coffee was your bag, baby," I say, going for smooth, trying on an accent. I don't care for the games I have to play with MasterControl's assorted hall monitors in concierge's clothing, but it beats another readjustment.

"You reckon because I'm English I'm only allowed to fancy tea?" Ginger arches an eyebrow.

"I think you fancy nothing at all because you're a virtual." Ginger fixes me with a glare so frigid it might be real. I sigh. Even subroutines like Ginger seem overly tuned these days—though I should know better than to use the v-word. The last thing I want is forty hours of Non-Organic Intelligence Sensitivity Readjustment tacked onto the compliance check, which I expect at any moment. But it seems my best self isn't running the show now. Maybe I could use some sensitivity training.

"Cream and sugar, love?" She spits out the words mechanically.

"Black." Then I add, "Like my heart," a gag that

never failed to earn me a smile (and an eye roll) from my daughter.

Ginger blinks in and out of phase but says nothing. Silence makes most people extraordinarily uncomfortable, but I'm not one of them. I put on an affable face and wait her out. So much for de-escalation. Gods only know what kind of vengeful scripts she's leaking into her passive filters. I can almost feel myself closing in on an alert threshold, though MasterControl's byzantine algorithms evolve so quickly it's pointless to speculate. Trapped as I am in this absurd dance with the holo of a decades dead diva with a fragile ego and lousy sense of humor, I almost sympathize with the Thought Liberation dingbats.

"Will that be all, Dr. Grieves?"

Despite my better judgment, I give Ginger one last needle. "I don't know. Is it too late to upgrade to Scary?"

Ginger eyes empty out. She fixes me with a corpselike stare before flickering out.

I don't remember recorking the Usquebaugh. I'd pour it down the sink, but it's Usquebaugh. It's been three days since I've had a drink. Yet I don't seem to possess the power to return it to the bar.

The door alert pushes me out of my fugue. Too soon for the coffee. A compliance check then. It'll be worse for me if I make them key the door. I answer it.

The Young Man in the gray fedora has an inch on me and wears a wool suit a half-size too small. His face triggers a spasm of memory, but it slips away before my mind can find purchase. He holds at his side what looks to be an antique hat can carrier case.

The Young Man looks down at the bottle in my hand and frowns. "Have you been drinking? You're not supposed to be drinking."

"You've got the wrong room, kid."

"No, no sir, they are both correct, room and man alike."

I try to shut the door, but the Young Man braces it.

"Dr. Grieves, I assure you I only present myself here at this place and time at your request and consent."

There's nothing of the exotic or flamboyant in the Young Man's presentation. His solemn demeanor and odd cadence contrast with a boyish, fresh-faced aspect, an odd collocation of characteristics that surely drives many to find him disarming. He strikes me as mildly insane.

"I have a mind for faces," I begin.

"And you've never seen mine."

"I don't know you, man."

"We all have private memories we've never shared. You imparted one such to me."

"Whatever it is, kid, I'm not interested."

"When your daughter was six," he lowers his voice, "you taught her not to be afraid of the dark."

The words come like knives. I say nothing. I can suddenly feel the cold of the old house in the late hours, and see the terror behind Sophie's eyes. Terror of a monster I summoned. These images claw unbidden to the raw surface of my thoughts.

The Young Man steps closer to me. "Necessity

demanded we remove your recollection of our first meeting. Do you see?"

"Oh sure. Move your foot."

The Young Man sighs, removes a sleek .32 pistol from his pocket, and points it at my belly button. "My apologies."

The Young Man shepherds me into a captain's chair. He sets down the hat can carrier case with care and takes a seat across from me. I reassure myself that the display of a firearm has already triggered a robust security response. This lunatic will be dealt with post-haste.

"Posh Spice?" The Young Man asks, referring to the pop retro-chic milieu of the room.

"Ginger. There was an upcharge for Posh. I should've paid it."

"I'm going to put this away now." The Young Man returns the pistol to his jacket. "Rest assured, this particular firearm is invisible to the filters. Unless it happens to be discharged, of course."

"Of course." Invisible to the filters? It's ridiculous, but nonetheless I find it hard to keep my voice even. "What do you want?"

"For now, only to re-certify your trust."

I wait.

"You always thought of your daughter as fearless."

Unafraid of everything.

"Unafraid of everything." He says, plucking the phrase from behind my eyes. "Are you ready to listen, Dr. Grieves? Are you ready to hear the story of *The Gashlycrumb Tinies*?"

The room compresses in on me. My mind reels and struggles for a reasonable version of reality where this young man appears and mentions a rare book of which I haven't spoken for over thirty years. As much as I tried to banish it from my memory, it was a title that ever clawed at the edges of my thoughts.

Taking my silence as a cue, the Young Man begins, "When your daughter was seven, night terrors invaded her sleep. The shadows in her bedroom transmogrified into a shapeshifter. It hungered to drag her to the underworld. Night after night, you stayed with her, yet these nightly hallucinations grew more terrible. Before long, sleep failed to find her at all. Powerless, you watched as her mind and body eroded to the point where a transition to an institution seemed inevitable."

"Until they stopped," I said.

The Young Man leaned forward. "Is it conceivable that I recite this from any recollection but your own, Dr. Grieves?"

"Tell me the rest. If you know it."

The Young Man nods gravely. "A week later, your daughter asked you to read her favorite book, *The Gashlycrumb Tinies*. A story she knew by heart. So much so that she was given to stop your reading so she could recite it word-for-word herself. Although on this occasion, it seemed like a long time since she'd done that."

I thought you'd outgrown this one. I stare into my daughter's eyes. Their guileless incomprehension shouldn't chill me, but it does.

The Young Man's voice pulls me back into the room.

"Your daughter hadn't outgrown *The Gashlycrumb Tinies.* She had no memory of it. Not the story. Not the illustrations. Not the shadowy shapeshifter."

The purity of trust in Sophia's eyes and the book in her hands galvanized itself with the dreadful epiphany that I had been the cause of her ordeal. The conjoined memory formed a tumor of guilt in the prison of my heart that I never possessed the courage to expose.

"I should have burned it," I mutter.

The Young Man looks at his watch. "We need to hurry." He removes a pneumatic hypo from a leather zip case and chambers a murky purple cartridge.

"Load this."

"Why? What is it?"

"You told me that story so you would know to trust me."

"Why would I need to trust you?"

"If you don't load it in the next minute, I can't help you. I can't tell you any more than that until you load it."

I study the purple fluid. I've used thousands of pharmaceutical cartridges in my time, but I've never seen anything like this. Loading it would be a leap into the absurd. I want to tear into my uninvited guest, to dive across the coffee table and wring answers from him. But even before his arrival, I was already hovering dangerously close to triggering another round of readjustment therapy.

I push the hypo into my neck. The injection is fully automated after that. In the split-second it takes me to realize what I've done, it's over.

The Young Man holds up a finger and stares at his watch. Several seconds tick by, and he relaxes. "The serum maps and rewrites your memories. If we had waited any longer, it wouldn't have covered my entrance. You won't remember me or this conversation."

"Stop playing games and tell me what you want, or damn the scans, I'll bring half the Ministry down on our heads."

"Three days ago, you retained me to help you find Edward James Best."

The name comes unexpectedly and feels like a physical blow. It takes me a moment to conjure, "You should have told me that up front."

"No, I shouldn't." The Young Man rechecks his watch. "Dr. Grieves, please understand that everything I do and its order possesses a specific intention and purpose."

"You found him?"

The concierge alert interrupts us.

"My coffee. Blast, I can't ignore it."

"Just pretend I'm not here."

"There's also a chance it's a psych drone."

"Compliance check?"

"Ginger Spice doesn't care for my sense of humor."

The Young Man grows weary. "What did you say to it?"

"I may have referred to her as a virtual."

"What possessed you to do that? Surely you know how offensive-"

"It's only offensive because some idiot thought it would be cute to program them that way."

Ginger materializes. "Talking to ourselves, are we, Dr. Meatsack?"

The Young Man says, "You should apologize."

"For what?"

Ginger Spice blinks. "Beg your pardon?"

Ginger Spice taps her foot and awaits my reply. She never acknowledges the Young Man.

"Like the pistol, I'm digitally invisible," the Young Man says. "The hotel cannot detect or log my presence. Stop communicating with me, or Ginger Spice is going to assume you've made an imaginary friend."

"Cat got your tongue?" Ginger frowns. "Regular problem of yours, innit?"

"I- I'm sorry, Ginger. I'm not myself tonight, and I've been unforgivably rude to you."

"Are you taking the piss with me?"

"No. Please accept my humblest apologies."

A smile ignites Ginger's face. "Quite all right, love. Everyone has their moments. Oh, and if you fancy a shag later, just give us a shout and we'll get your pipes sorted. In the meantime, enjoy your tea."

Tea? "Thank you," I say.

Ginger dissolves, leaving a carafe of Earl Grey tea in her place.

I turn to the young man. "Where is he?"

"Hiding in plain sight, as it were."

I cross to the window and look out over the glittering skyline. If nothing else, the city is clean.

"I won't ask why we haven't shared his whereabouts with the MasterControl because I already know."

"Then we ought to get started," he says. The Young Man flips over his hat can carrier. "This device will temporarily remap your biometrics." The cover dilates open like a camera shutter, revealing a pneumatic architecture of gears.

"It looks like a portable guillotine."

"The experience is... unpleasant," he says. "After self-sealing, it will fill with gel to immobilize your head. You'll be without oxygen for two minutes. That will be the least of your discomfort."

"But I'll live. Right?"

"You'll live." He drops the device over my head. A grind of gears and a pop. My face erupts in a stabbing, rending, white-hot orgy of pain. Black bleeds over black, and I slip away.

I awaken coughing, gagging up gel. I'm on my side. My heart hammers. The device is gone. The young man stands next to me with an empty hypo in his hand and a sardonic aspect.

"You were right," I croak. "That was awful."

"I'm pleased you survived."

I climb to my feet and stagger to the mirror to look at my face. But the ruin my imagination has rendered doesn't reflect back at me. By outward appearance, I've emerged unscathed through my ordeal with the Young Man's iron maiden.

"You may look the same to an unenhanced human

eye, but as far as the billion digital eyes around the city are concerned, you're a different man."

"Does my face have a name?"

He tells me. And I understand. I understand everything.

2 | THE HUSBAND

Jeb Huntley was still awake when the holo blinked on. A man at the front door. The brim of his hat obscured his face. Or perhaps her face? Jeb had the vague and irrational idea that his latest companion had returned unannounced for another round, but they didn't do that.

"Jeb, it's Matt." The voice sounded at once mechanical and celestial over the speakers.

Jeb trudged to his front door and hesitated. He lacked the energy for his former father-in-law, but sleep wasn't coming any time soon either. Besides, could he really turn the old man away?

Jeb opened the door.

"I know it's late—" Matt said, a little hoarse, but absent the slurred speech Jeb had come to expect.

"I'm half-asleep, Matt. Can't it wait until—"

"I found him, Jeb. I found Edward James Best."

"We've been through this."

"It's real this time. I have proof."

"Have you logged a report with MasterControl?

"Let me tell you what I found out. Then I'll let you decide."

"Decide... what?"

"If there's enough to log a report."

"Tomorrow."

"Now." Matt checked his watch. "If we don't catch him in the next 90 minutes, he'll be gone forever."

"You're not making any sense."

"That's because you haven't heard the facts. Trust me. For better or for worse, this will be the last time."

"I guess you better come in," Jeb said.

They went to the kitchen, where Jeb put the kettle on.

Jeb said, "There was another one the other night. Another murder. The first since Sophia. I thought to call you, but- "

"Turned out to be a suicide." Matt said. "According to the feeds."

"According to the feeds," Jeb muttered.

Neither said anything more while the kettle climbed to a boil. Matt seemed to have recovered the self-possession Jeb once found unnerving, as though Matt was examining him like the inside of one of his patients.

Jeb turned around. "Until not so long ago, revenge was all I could think about."

"The man took your wife and daughter."

"You don't understand. I wouldn't kill him. I'd blow out his knees with a shotgun. Then I'd lock him up in a work shed and mutilate him every night until he was just this blob of meat." Jeb took a deep breath and let it out slowly. "I never said that out loud before."

"Do you own a shotgun?" Matt asked.

"I don't have a work shed." Jeb admitted.

"It's probably just as well. Unless you know of a place out of range of the trauma filters, you'd be in category six reconditioning within the hour."

The kettle whistled, and Jeb filled their tumblers. "Torture may be the only crime more impossible than murder these days."

Matt steeped his teabag back and forth. "Unlikely maybe, but impossible? Who knows."

"Do you know something I don't?"

Matt shrugged. "Only that human desire, for better or worse, eventually finds a way to get what it wants."

"Is that what you've got in mind? Why you haven't filed a report with MasterControl? As much as I'd like to think I'd damn the consequences, after the first few levels of re-adjustment, I reckon I'd care a lot."

"Edward James Best got away with it, didn't he? What one man can do-"

"Let's report it, Matt."

"We can't."

"What could we possibly do to the man that would be worse than what the state has in store for him?"

"Edward James Best doesn't exist."

Jeb said nothing.

Matt continued, "He's a biometric mask the real killer wore to hide his identity from MasterControl."

Jeb's hopes suddenly dimmed. "Gods, Matt—"

"I know I've had some strange notions over the last two years. I haven't always been, well, at my best."

"You're human."

Matt put up his hand. "Neither of us needs to pretend I didn't fall apart. Or that I'm put back together. I'm not sure I'll ever be. But a man came to me. I don't even know what he calls himself. He's a fixer of some kind I guess."

Jeb opened his mouth but lost the thread of his thoughts. After a moment he asked, "But he, he wasn't the one who-?"

Matt shook his head. "No."

"Did he give you a name? Who killed them, Matt? If you know, I need you to tell me right now."

"Let me lay it out for you the way he did."

"Just tell me the name."

"We need to see if the story leads you to the same place it led me. We have to be sure."

Jeb realized his fingers were clawing into the marble countertop. He let out a breath. "You said this guy's a fixer. What does that mean?"

"He sells privacy. Once he implants his clients with the virtual mask, they become anonymous. To you and me they look no different, but as far as MasterControl is concerned, they're someone else. In the killer's case, Edward James Best."

"I don't guess this fixer of yours was good enough to provide his real name. How much did he touch you for anyway?"

"I've narrowed it down."

"How? Whether he was using his real name or not, it couldn't have been anyone in our orbits. All Sophia's movements and social patterns were disseminated.

Control employed three unique logic systems and located every man with whom she interacted going back two years. They were all interviewed under scan. No one has ever beaten the scans."

"Paranoid Schizophrenics do it all the time."

"Not intentionally. When a paranoid claims to be the second coming of Elvis, they actually believe it."

"Exactly. The scans can't detect a lie if the subject doesn't know they're lying."

"Please tell me you got me out of bed for more than a thought experiment."

"The only piece I don't have is whether Maya was always part of the plan. After all, she wasn't supposed to be there."

"Plan? There was no plan!" Jeb's anger swelled. "She was supposed to stay with you that night, wasn't she? But you were too bloody drunk."

"That's right," Matt said.

"I-I shouldn't have said that."

"I had it coming."

"Yeah, I guess you did," Jeb said with more savagery than he intended. Losing his daughter had been so painful that he could hardly conjure her face without spiraling. The mention of her name out loud felt like claws tearing into an old wound.

"This isn't a thought experiment, Jeb." Matt pulled an empty hypo from his jacket and set it on the counter. "I don't remember my meeting three days ago with this fixer. I didn't remember him. Because of this."

"An amnesiac? You have to know that the scans can detect memory gaps-."

"This serum fills in the gaps, as it were."

"Implanted memories?"

"Borrowed from other synapses. It's not so improbable. How many days bleed into the next without us taking much notice?"

The color had drained from Jeb's face. "That's how you think he did it?"

Matt nodded. "The killer doesn't know he's the killer."

Possibilities surged through Jeb's mind, as he cycled through the people in his world who might have taken his wife and daughter from him in such a savage manner. Then the pieces fell into place. Jeb saw the path down which Matt was attempting to lead him. Why he hadn't filed a report to MasterControl. Why he was here. Jeb shook his head, warding off malignant thoughts. "Gods, Matt, that last readjustment must have been one too many."

Matt stared through the bay window into the backyard. "We may have figured out the perfect way to deceive ourselves, but I wonder if there are deeds so heinous they leave traces beyond reckoning."

"Gods, you really are broken."

"Now you see why I wanted to lay it out for you before I alerted MasterControl. Tell me, did you come up with the same name I did?

"No. No, you- you're the bloody lunatic, and now

you're trying to gaslight me with one of your crazed, wet-brained delusions!" He was shouting.

"Your tea's getting cold."

Jeb slapped the mug off the counter. "Get out!"

"Not until we both know for sure."

"What about you, Matt? A lot of people experience tragedy. They don't drink themselves half to death and wind up in and out of re-adjustment. They don't tank their medical practices and what's left of their families. If one of us has some amnesiac demons, my money's on you, doc."

Matt nodded. "I guess private hells have a way of bleeding out into the world. Maybe mine more than most. But if I couldn't be the father and grandfather they deserved in life, maybe I can bring them some peace now."

"Now?" Jeb's voice climbed an octave. "Are we talking about their ghosts?"

"You and I both know ghosts don't have to be real to exist. You still talk to them, don't you, Jeb?"

"Get out. Now. Or I swear-"

"Do you invite them in, or have you found yourself trying to shut them out? Your wife and daughter."

"I said get-"

"They haunt you, don't they?"

Jeb gripped the counter to steady himself. His heart hammered in his ears. He gathered himself. His voice was a growl. "They'll lock you up again. That's what will happen if you try to report this... yarn."

Matt withdrew a hypo loaded with an orange

capsule. He laid it down between them. "This hypo does the opposite of the other. It restores memory."

"You don't expect me to take that." Jeb said.

"Don't you want to know for sure?"

"I have nothing to prove to you."

"What about to yourself?"

"I'm alerting Security Services now. I suggest you leave before-"

Matt slipped a .32 pistol from his coat and pointed it at Jeb's heart. "If you've no lost memories, the serum will have no effect."

"Now you sound like MasterControl propaganda."

"I will kill you."

"I don't believe-"

"Check the house feed of my arrival," Matt said.

"Why would I- "

"Do it now," Matt growled.

"House," Jeb said, hating the tight pitch of his voice. "Rewind the front door feed." A holo glowed to life. Jeb watched Matt approach the house. His face was cast down, obscured by the brim of his hat. Then Matt stopped a few paces shy of the front door and tilted his head up. It was not the face of Matt Grieves that stared straight into him.

"You. You're Edward James Best," Jeb whispered.

"No, Jeb, *you're* Edward James Best. I'm just wearing his face."

"I didn't kill them!"

"They both loved you so much. All you had to do was become the kind of man who deserved it."

"Please, Matt—"

Matt raised the pistol. "Last chance."

"You think they won't question you, Matt? You think they won't put you under scan? I'm not the one who'll be readjusted. And this time, there'll be nothing left of you!"

"They'll scan me all right. And I"ll pass with flying colors, the same way you did, you son of a bitch." Matt swiveled his aim to Jeb's right and fired into the wall. The concussion was flat and loud in the small space. Jeb staggered back and sagged to the floor.

Matt loomed over him. "Last chance."

Jeb jabbed the hypo to his neck. The pneumatic mechanism hissed.

They waited.

A minute passed, and Jeb felt no different. As relief washed over him, he gave Matt a sardonic grin. "I didn't kill them. I didn't kill Sophia. I didn't kill Maya."

"I suspect the Security Service will be along shortly." Matt said quietly. He set the pistol on the counter. "Goodbye, Jeb."

Jeb watched Matt head for the door. He looked over at the pistol. Did Matt expect Jeb to be baited into grabbing it? *Not bloody likely, you bastard.*

When he was sure his father-in-law had left, Jeb sagged into his lounge chair. The strange ordeal had left his nerves jangled, and the initial sense of relief he'd experienced quickly curdled to anger. When Security Services banged on his door, he would, of course, be forced to explain that Matt and Edward James Best were one in the same. Before the delusional old man hurt himself or someone else. And that would be that. A broad smile eased across Jeb's face. And that would be that.

The pain came like a knife behind his eyes. His body spasmed, thoughts juddering. Jeb screamed. The world went dark.

3| THE PRISONER & THE KILLER

Jeb awakens a prisoner inside the body of the man he was. He watches himself creep down the gravel path, smells cedar and fresh rain, crouching at the gate to his backyard. Through a gap, he watches his wife towel off from her evening swim. The prisoner is struck by her grace. Memories of her flood into him. A familiar pain twists inside his heart. The man he was jumps up, grabs the top of the fence, and pulls himself over. He lands with a crunch of gravel that startles Sophia. The man he was steps into the light and flashes her a grin.

Sophia laughs. "Dork, I ought to throw you in this pool."

"Is that a promise?"

"Not if you'll enjoy it."

The prisoner thinks of a thousand things to say to this woman, now irrevocably lost to him. He considers a thousand ways he might spend these moments, so quickly washing away. But the Prisoner can do nothing but endure the bland banter of the fool he was. Unmarked as he is by grief and loss, this shadow of himself blithely drifts through these moments with

Sophia, obsessed with imagined slights and spurned entitlement, so eager to hurt and destroy.

The Prisoner feels the weight of the knife nestled in his belt. The thrill of excitement sickens him. Dread spikes to terror as his left hand casually floats behind his back and claims the blade. Sophia's eyebrows raise. Curious. Amused? Trusting. The Prisoner screams at her to run, but the man he was remains unaware of his silent passenger. He closes the distance to his wife. With a desperate, fanatical effort, the Prisoner attempts to conjure a will powerful enough to alter the fabric of reality. To undo what he has done. To stop himself from committing this crime. To save his wife.

The Prisoner feels the warmth of Sophia's blood through the gloves. He struggles desperately to avert his gaze from Sophia's dimming eyes, but the man he was luxuriates in every detail, as he lowers his dying wife into the water and holds her underneath the surface. Unable to look away, the Prisoner's despair thunders, and he consoles himself that his mind will soon fracture to the welcome oblivion of madness.

"Daddy?"

The man he was turns to see his daughter in her pajamas. His heart sinks. "Maya," he says in a lifeless voice.

While the Prisoner does not yet remember what he is about to do, he does know what it is to live a life after a child has been torn from it. A life he would now gladly surrender to save his child. As the man he was rages, the Prisoner implores silent gods, offers his soul to any willing devil.

The man he was sees nothing but his plots and dreams turning to ash. His daughter's mind is now a trap from which he cannot escape. Then a siren from a reptilian corner of his mind whispers a glimmer of hope. It tells him that the man he will become will mourn his daughter, but he won't be burdened with the curse of guilt. The man he will become will suffer. He will pray for retribution against the monster that took his family. But inevitably the pain will fade. In time, he will heal. He will evolve into a better version of the man he is.

Tears streak down his face, as Jeb Huntley gives chase.

4 | THE WELL-ADJUSTED JEB HUNTLEY

A fist pounded on the front door. Jeb spilled from his chair and emptied his stomach onto the floor. He glanced up at the holo. An Officer out front. An override alert scrolled underneath her. She'd be inside in seconds.

Jeb clamored to the counter, giving silent thanks to Matt for having left the pistol for him; now recognizing it for an act of compassion he did not deserve. Jeb jammed the pistol to his head and thumbed back the hammer. Before thought could turn him a coward, his daughter's apparition resolved.

Jeb shut his eyes and pulled the trigger.

That bastard, Jeb cursed. *That miserable bastard.*

The Officer followed the sound of high-pitched laughter to find Jeb Huntley, pistol still pressed to his head. She eventually had to stun Jeb to get him to stop pulling the trigger.

"Not to worry, sir," the Officer reassured him, "a little readjustment therapy and you'll be back to your old self in no time."

5 | THE FATHER

Six months later, an unmarked package shows up in my hotel room. It contains an orange syringe and a letter in my handwriting that, among other things, explains why I don't remember writing it. I'm instantly suspicious of both.

A grueling battery of scans has bestowed me with a healthy dose of paranoia for the out-of-the-ordinary. While MasterControl eventually cleared me following my former son-in-law's total breakdown and dismaying accusations against me, I fear some sort of trap. Caution advises me to report the package, but curiosity has traditionally proven the strongest of my self-destructive impulses.

I re-read the note. While experience has ingrained deep distrust of our humane utopia, surely I can trust myself.

I f life is a gift, then sentience is a curse. What could be worse than understanding that everything we know could be snatched away in a second, without mercy or warning? We make an art of distraction, constantly finding ways to make ourselves ignorant of fate, but every year raises the odds. Every saving throw is made with a smaller die. We cling to the ineffable to deny the inevitable, supping from a poisoned chalice in full knowledge that this mouthful may be the one that chokes us. Life offers no guarantees but one, a contract that may expire upon any given breath.

You've had ample opportunity to consider this over the past three months. In fact, you've rarely had a chance to think of anything else.

You're on the train out of the city tonight, nestled uncomfortably in your seat as you stare at the same internet page on your phone and absorb nothing it says. You wouldn't be here if you had any other options, but your car wouldn't start this morning and you needed to go to work. It's the third new job you've had since your nightmare began, and you can't afford to lose this one, too. You'll be forced to flee it at some stage, this is already written in stone, but still you cling to the last vestiges of an ordinary life. The world makes no allowances for those who abandon its obligations.

You give up on reading, a pleasure that has lost its ability to soothe, and look around the carriage. An elderly Asian couple sits nearby, comfortable in silence, holding hands in the knowledge that this communication says all that needs to be said; you scream on the inside to see this, knowing such solace can never be yours again. Three teenaged boys are learning to take up as much space as possible with their splayed poses and loud voices, crassly commenting on a social media reel as though nothing will ever matter as much. A large man spills across two seats, lost in the distraction of his bag of crisps. A jovial African woman carries on a conversation with friends or family through a screen in her hand, her speech peppered with laughter. A jittery dude with a face tattoo jiggles a kick scooter between edgy legs.

And then a guitar riff saws into your head, a belligerent legato metal motif louder than anything around you. You shoot upright in your seat, gasping in shock, and the large man glances your way for a moment before returning to his repast. No-one else reacts to this intrusion of distortion, nor notes your response.

That's because they can't hear this riff that has haunted your every minute, asleep or awake, whether present or absent. This performance—as always—is for you alone. And after so many reprises, you know exactly what it means.

Death is close by, invisible, unstoppable.

And it is coming for you.

It first happened about three months ago. You were walking down a city street on a fine afternoon with nothing pressing on your schedule or on your mind, idly wasting precious minutes of your life as if it would never end. And then that guitar riff erupted nearby, so close it might well have been inside your head. It certainly felt as though it was, your brain suddenly converted into a blaring, pulsing speaker.

You spasmed in surprise and spun on your heel, looking for the cause of this cacophony. A metalhead blaring tunes from his phone right beside you, a busker's amp bursting to life at your feet as they began their public performance, and found nothing. Your fellow pedestrians strolled by, oblivious to the sudden noise. You even lifted one hand to your head to make sure you weren't wearing headphones that you had forgotten, in case Bluetooth was enabled and was picking up a stranger's stray broadcast. You weren't, and you already knew that, but how else to explain this volume? A beat kicked in behind the guitar, bass and snare skins pounding against the inside of your skull, and your confusion heightened. What was happening here? How? Why?

You were staring down the street in discomfort and dismay when one element caught your eye like a barbed fishhook. Something that passers-by skirted without a second glance. Something that stood out against the scenery like a coloured figurine in a monochrome diorama.

Something that you instinctively understood was meant only for you.

You rise to your feet, swaying with the motion of the train as it rounds a gentle corner, and your panicked eyes raze the carriage ahead. No-one looks back at you, but you have no interest in them, either. Nothing seems out of place, and nothing moves your way except the row of plastic grab handles hanging from the yellow handrail that swing subtly under the touch of gravity. Stickered signs scream red warnings at you, but only about minor crimes you might be considering such as eating, drinking, smoking, or fare-dodging. No help there, nor from the security guard standing by the nearest doors who is turning a benevolent blind eye to the large man scoffing his crisps right beneath the sign forbidding it.

You step out into the walkway and peer forward down the concertina-connected carriages. From here, you can see another three steel tubes winding their way along, mostly unoccupied. A few heads breach the space above plain plastic seatbacks, distracted faces directed at you or away, but no-one meets your gaze. Drawing in a long, shaking breath, you turn to look behind you.

There is one further carriage attached to this one. Yellow rails, smeared windows, diffident passengers.

And right at the end, standing against the back wall as if to surf the train's velocity like a too-cool teenager, is the figure you've been expecting. Tall and rangy, clad in plain blue jeans and combat boots and a black hoodie with the cowl pulled up—though not against the train's cameras, which will not be able to see it nor record its presence. Long, moon-pale hair spills out the bottom of the drawn hood, and a single point of white light gleams from the darkness within like a cold and distant star.

In its right hand, a bright, naked blade.

🤘 🤘 🤘

As you stood on the street, aghast at this sight you had never expected, the figure began to move toward you. Its black boots trod slow, heavy, assured. You found your eyes drawn to the weapon in its hand, a terrible promise: nine inches long with a labyrinthine pattern etched on the blade, clean and gleaming as if lit by some sun other than the one above, so sharp and clear that the rest of the world faded into nonsense beyond it. A snake's eye, keeping you pinned to the spot as its tooth moved slowly closer, closer.

Ironically, it was the song itself that startled you out of your trance. You'd already become used to the deafening riff and crashing beat, barely even noticing the bass and rhythm guitar stepping in behind them, but now a vocal pierced through their metal hide. Strong, forceful, *intelligible*—you heard this stranger singing words you could comprehend, if not understand, and it shocked you into movement. Loath to run or scream or cause a scene in case you'd suddenly fallen prey to a psychotic break, you backed up a few feet, glanced around to make sure you were alone in this ruthless reverie. A gum-chewing young mother in workout gear swerved her pram around you, frowning at your impertinence in blocking her way, and you took a breath to call out, to warn her about the knife-wielding shape some ten metres up the footpath. But you already suspected there was no point, a suspicion validated when she cruised right by the strange figure without so much as a sideways glare.

This stalker strode on, its tread measured as that of a hunter, and you were surprised that each step didn't shake the street like a cheap stage set. The intrusion of this spectre seemed an offence to the world itself, yet the two of you might have been the only players in this strange scene. You kept your eyes from the hypnotic blade, trying to make out the features hidden in the shadows of that drawn hood, and saw only a pulsing point of white that twinkled like a diamond catching light. You'd never come across the like in real life, but you'd beheld enough horror-themed heavy metal album art to recognise an evil eye when you saw one. Shanks of colourless hair trailed from the bottom of the cowl, as though this figure were ancient, and yet it moved with all the coiled vigour of a peak predator.

And *you* were the prey.

This shocking thought broke you free from your paralysis, and you did what prey has done since time immemorial, the only thing it can do in the face of oncoming peril: you ran away. Every glance over your shoulder told you that your pursuer was following at a leisurely pace, casual in its brutality. As though flight were pointless, and when you eventually stopped and collapsed, fighting for breath with tortured lungs, it would still be coming for you, tireless, relentless.

As certain as death.

You slip into the aisle of the train carriage, keeping an eye on the shape. You haven't got a name for it, haven't even tried to apply one—it simply defies knowledge. Names may have power, but you have none against this thing. All you can do is put yourself as far away from it as possible.

It steps forward now, and as you've come to expect, its stride is a little longer and swifter than before. Its pursuit has become more dogged each time, as though each confrontation is another level in some deranged video game. Already it has cleared the final three rows of seats before the ticket machine, its blade passing unseen and unfelt over the hijab-clad head of a dozing student.

You turn away and walk quickly down the aisle,

bracing yourself against the headrests of empty seats as the carriage sways in its transit, ignoring the security guard by the nearby doors in the hope that he will ignore you in return. You mustn't hurry, mustn't cause a scene. If people think you're having some kind of episode, they might try to help you—might try to confine you, for your own good. You cannot allow this to happen.

As you pass from one carriage into the next, you look back to gauge the distance between you and your pursuer. It is coming on steadily, its pace increasingly impatient after being outrun so many times. A quiet whimper escapes your throat, but anyone who hears it glances quickly away. Everyone is used to weirdos on public transport, the abandoned mentally ill and the drug-fried cookers and worse, and though you are well-dressed and relatively composed, you might be a loony in disguise for all your fellow passengers know. There will be no help from this quarter, not that any offers would be of use.

A recorded voice tells you that the train is now approaching the next stop. You gasp in relief, but how long until the carriage slows to allow you off? Thirty seconds? A minute? Can you stay ahead of the shape that long?

It's into the second carriage now as you pass through into the third. Should you stop, it will be upon you in less than ten seconds.

That first time, you learned three pertinent facts about your unspeakable pursuer. One: when the metal song began inside your head, it appeared nearby. Two: when the song ended, it vanished. Three: no-one else could see it.

The track pounding inside your skull is unfamiliar to you. You're quite conversant in heavy metal, from its fuzzy beginnings to its many current forms, yet this band's identity eludes you. That said, you've reason to believe the song is from the 1980s; the song features no production touches from any decade since, no turntables or eight-string guitars or glitch breaks, and it has a warm, analogue sound: the kind of unrepentant epic you can imagine being belted out by long-haired warriors in sweaty leather pants, one foot up on the foldback speakers as lights flash and pyrotechnics boom. After the incident in the street—after the song wound up, leaving silence in your head or at least merely the usual noise of your thoughts, and the shape was no longer to be seen on the footpath behind you—you went home and searched online, hoping to understand some small element of your shocking experience. And you found nothing.

This was strange, but no stranger than anything else you had been through that day, so you forgot it. This was almost literally true: you could barely recall the song when it wasn't tearing through your mind, unable to reconstruct its rhythms and melodies. The lyrics made an awful kind of sense at the time, enough that you felt you might understand what was happening to you if you could only stop and listen and *think*, but they vanished from your mind the moment the song ended. Still, you were just glad the ordeal was over.

And then it happened again.

This time, you were at home, reposing on the couch in a t-shirt and underwear as you watched TV—safe in your own space, unwitnessed and unneeded. You recoiled off the lounge and onto the floor when that guitar lick burst to life inside your head, your heart accelerating to match its tempo, and you immediately looked around for what must surely follow.

The shape was standing at the end of your hallway, blocking your front door.

You already knew that flight was your only recourse. You swiped up your phone and scurried away toward the back door as the stalker stepped slowly down your hall, bulging out of the shadows like it was pushing its way through the gauze of reality, that dreadful blade gleaming so clean and pure that it was clearly longing to wear your blood. That single point of light inside the dark hood that must have been an eye was glowing, pulsing, somehow transmitting a sense of savage glee, and you knew that somewhere within those shadows, this thing was *grinning*.

Your back door was deadbolted and too secure to wrest open in time. Oh, the irony! Instead, you dashed to your kitchen and thumped the window screen out into the yard with a single panicked blow. You clambered up onto the counter and scampered through the narrow gap just as the figure stepped into your kitchen, that dread-fully keen blade rising to follow you. You fell onto the cement path outside, caught your wind at once, and ran away into the night.

Just the second time, but already you were catching onto the rules. You hurried down the footpath in your bare feet, taking care to avoid the lurking teeth of a broken bottle, and you watched as your pursuer finally made it out onto the street during the second chorus. You already had a good head start, and at that time even a steady backwards stride was enough to keep the same distance from the shape, so you just kept it up until the song ended and then, in the blink of an eye, your stalker was gone.

Panting, sweating, only now allowing yourself to feel the bruises and scrapes your flight had inflicted, you walked back home. The sudden silence in your head was almost deafening after the metal onslaught. The night breeze caressed your bare legs, reminding you that you were rather underdressed for this public appearance, but other than a sarcastic wolf whistle from a passing car, no-one reacted to your plight in any notable way. You understood that you would continue to suffer alone.

Two weeks had passed since your first encounter with the shape. Did that mean another fortnight before it came again?

No.

You make your way down the swaying aisle of the third carriage, eyeing the end of the fifth where a wall closes it off from the driver. This is all the room you have to avoid the shape. It has advanced into the second carriage now, matching your speed, faster in each appearance. You wonder how many more times you can escape this thing before it is *sprinting* after you, hard upon you before you've even registered its presence.

But you must survive this encounter first. You keep walking, fixing a vague smile to your trembling lips, but it's not convincing. A young woman in heavy eyeliner and full goth regalia glances up from her horror paperback and meets your wild stare, glances away as though a ghost has sprung from the pages before her. Everyone else is too caught up in themselves to notice you, busy ignoring the implacability of their own grim fates.

The metal song has swung into its first verse now. That's thirty-two seconds down, with three and a half minutes still to come. Two hundred and thirteen seconds, to be precise. You're about an eighth of the way through your ordeal, roughly twelve point five percent of the way to safety. You're stepping into the fourth carriage. Your palms are damp and already twitching in anticipation of a knife in the back.

Now arriving, the recorded voice intones, naming the stop, and you pant in gratitude. You can feel the train beginning to slow now, so gradually, second by second. By the time it stops, you'll be at the very last door at the end of the fifth carriage.

Your stalker is now halfway along the third.

As far as you can tell, there is neither rhyme nor reason to this horror's attacks. Two weeks passed between its first appearances, but the third came just five days later. Then, nothing for three weeks—and *then*, twice in one day.

You've had to drastically rearrange your life around these unpredictable assaults. You lost your first job when you dropped everything and fled, the song ringing in your ears, because there was no way to sensibly explain what you'd done. You were late to another role because you had to run in the opposite direction just as you were about to clock in—again, difficult to explain, and bosses are not known for their understanding of such cryptic antics. You've avoided confined spaces over which you have no control, because if the shape comes when you're trapped, you're done for. Even your own home no longer feels safe, and you've taken to sleeping fully dressed, all doors and windows open, on those occasions when you decide to rest there. More often now, you sleep in your car, upright in the driver's seat. It came for you once when you were dozing behind the wheel in a parking lot, and you barely even laid eyes on it before you were zooming off down the street. Yes, the car makes much sense.

Your life is now entirely dictated by fear. Or rather, F.E.A.R.: Fuck Everything And Run. You can't visit your friends or family, for you'll be unable to provide a satisfactory explanation when you need to abruptly bolt out the door, and the problem with loved ones is that they insist on trying to help when you're in trouble—but in this instance, their assistance might include getting you sectioned for your own good. You try to avoid crowded places, too, because causing a scene might end with your apprehension by security or police. Either way, you'll be confined and unable to flee... and what will happen then?

You're morbidly obsessed with that thought, with good reason. What will everyone else see when the shape finally catches up and gleefully drives that dreadful blade into you? Will you erupt in gouts of blood, shaking under invisible blows as witnesses stare on and scream? Or will you simply drop dead on the spot and be thought a victim of natural causes?

Few things could be less natural than this. But what even *is* it? Why have you been chosen by this horrid haunting? You've been over everything, recalled every move and raked over the cold coals of every past day, trying to understand when and how this all began—and you've come up with nothing. Perhaps this pursuit is simply random, the result of some cosmic dice roll that fell in your disfavour; perhaps this is the final, inexplicable truth of death, and *everyone* is hunted by some hooded horror in their final seconds. Who can say? It's not like there's anyone you can ask, and online forums rarely address this specific kind of phenomena. Reddit and Quora are notably quiet on the subject of supernatural stalkers.

This is your cross to bear, and yours alone. If there was anyone before you, you have no way of knowing...

and if there's anyone after you, you will be too dead to care.

You're halfway down the fifth carriage and the train has slowed to a walking pace. Any second now, the great silver beast will lurch to a stop to let you off. You look back and see the shape about to leave the fourth carriage. The song drives out of its first verse and into the first chorus. Fifty seconds gone. Three and a quarter minutes left.

You reach the end of the carriage as the train finally calms itself and jolts to a halt. The recorded voice announces the destination again, and it's not one you know, but that doesn't matter in the least. The door buttons come aglow with a ring of green LEDs, and your hand is already pushing at the nearest. The doors *shush* open at a speed that seems downright leisurely to your panicked brain, and you turn to spy your pursuer striding heavily down the fifth carriage, just seconds away.

But now you're out into the night air, the cement of the platform reassuringly solid and motionless beneath your shoes. Only one passenger was waiting here and they're already stepping into the third carriage, mindless of your plight; no-one else has chosen to alight at this stop with you. Only the hunter, now looming through the doors with its fulsome blade forward, pointing at you with hungry intent.

It's not yet fast enough to keep up with you, though, and you can easily outrun it in this open space. You dodge around a steel bench and its accompanying bin, noting with a start that some idiot has set a fire in the latter and putrid trash-smoke is pouring out of its round mouth. Burning pieces of litter flutter in the air around you like angry butterflies, and you wave sweaty hands at them as you stumble by.

Where to now? You briefly consider doubling back around the shape to reboard the train, but the shape could easily cut you off and keep you away long enough for the service to be on its way again. In the direction you're facing, the drab grey platform runs on for a good twenty metres before offering a choice of ramp or stairs; these will take you either to the street above or overhead across the tracks to the stop on the citybound side. You consider the metallic tunnel that runs over the train line and decide to focus on the street. In your recent experience, open space works best when fleeing an unstoppable murderer.

Your shoes slap against the cement below and echoes bounce back at you from the metal shelter above. You count your steps off in four-four time, *one two three four one two three four*, ignoring the way they fall out of sync with the drumbeat pounding in your skull—this is no time for symmetry. Then you are at the end of the platform and faced with your next choice. Steps might turn treacherous and trip you, so the ramp it is. You glance back and see the shape advancing implacably as ever, the fire behind it casting a hellish halo of smoke and burning litter-flies around its hooded head.

You're straining up the ramp now, your legs pistoning hard. You've been getting a decent workout from these pursuits, and you've taken to running in your spare time too, all the better to escape your encroaching fate. Such a minor incline is no challenge to you—in seconds, you'll be up on the footpath and fleeing down the road, and you'd have to get mowed down by a passing car for the figure to catch you then. The second verse has begun, meaning you're almost a minute and half through your nightmare. You can keep ahead of the stalker for two and half more, easy.

The peak of the ramp is only three metres away when something comes dashing over it, sprinting headlong toward you. You have less than a second to take it in—a *fox*, of all things, another predator that you never expected to encounter on these city streets. Its eyes widen as it sees you powering toward it and you both swerve to avoid collision, but those cursed cosmic dice decree that you choose the same direction. This rogue scavenger ploughs between your thrashing legs, throwing your feet out from under you. You turn as you plummet, watching the fox tumble and regain its footing with vulpine grace, and then the ramp comes up to meet your back with an almighty wallop.

The landing blasts the air out of you, numbs your struck elbows, puts you on a momentary pause you can ill afford. During this too-long stretch of motionlessness, you watch as the fox careens down the ramp, its head turning to take in the advancing shape on its way by. One hunter acknowledging another? There's something new —animals can see it! But this is of limited interest to you, for your pursuer is now just a handful of strides away. The single starlight in its hood shines like laughter, and that dreadful blade comes up, keen to drink of you at last.

With a terrified convulsion, you manage to thrust yourself backward, your hand darting up to block the blow about to fall. The hunter lunges forward, close now, *too* close, and its right arm sweeps across in a movement of undeniable cancellation.

The blade passes right through your raised hand.

And leaves it whole, unmarked.

You gasp, stumbling sideways onto your knees. The knife went right through you—as if it were a ghost—oh, the shape itself is immaterial—*it can't hurt you!*

You pant out a laugh. All this time, fleeing for your bloody life from this gleeful spectre, and it can't even lay a hand on you! It might as well be a bad dream, and you're wide awake—you can simply close your eyes to this fiend, enjoy the song pounding in your head for what it is and not what it portends. This thing can't touch you.

You're still rising, still laughing, when the shape brings the blade back across its body in another brutal swipe. The incorporeal blade slashes through your jaw and keeps going, its singing steel not pausing even a split-second as it passes by, but this time, you feel something catch under its force. Some silver thread within you snaps, severed in a heartbeat, and you fall away from yourself. Stunned, you watch as your empty body collapses in a graceless heap on the ramp, a meat puppet with its strings cut—and yet, you do not move—

Until the shape raises the blade once more, not so much pointing at you as inviting you, and its gleam is brighter than ever, brighter than winter clouds when the sun burns cold behind them, and it is everything, and you are rushing toward the endless labyrinth etched into its luminous steel, and that sinister glow burns away everything as you enter.

That guitar lick again—loud, so loud, more so than ever. It cuts through your skull like a rusty, jagged-toothed saw, but you welcome the sensation with everything you have. It has been so long since you *felt* anything.

You're standing in a city park you don't recognise, an oak tree looming over you like a protective parent. The drums crash in, but for once, you don't want to run. Instead, you take a single step. And then another. Nice and slow.

A dozen people are spread across the grass of the park, making out on blankets, taking selfies with statues, feeding the ducks adrift on the pond. At the edge of the water, a raven-haired woman in a denim jacket stands with a hand pressed to one side of her head, as if pained by a sudden headache. She stares all around her, startled by sudden song. You grin as you recognise the move-ments, though you don't exactly remember them as such.

She turns toward the tree. She sees you. And the hand falls slowly from her head as her face twists in confusion and growing horror.

Ah, yes. It begins again.

You tread across the grass in her direction, measured, intent. There's no hurry; there will be plenty of time to enjoy the chase. You won't catch her this time—you're just introducing yourself. Showing her the stakes, the rules.

The woman begins to stumble away, looking back over her shoulder at you, and you relish the feel of the earth cringing beneath your feet as you slowly give chase. The hypnotic blade gleams in your hand, so deep and strange, the key to everything. Within the dark depths of your hood, drums crash and guitars storm. When the first verse starts, you grin even wider as you begin to silently sing along.

I am the second Mrs. Roberts. Before that, I was the third Mrs. Jones, the fifth Mrs. Smith, and the fourth Mrs. Williams. I've lost track of the names and husbands over the years. One dead wife is a tragedy, two are coincidence, and three are suspicious. Beyond that and you almost certainly have a serial killer on your hands.

I usually insist on there being at least two wives dead under mysterious circumstances before I render my services, but John Roberts is special. I may be the second Mrs. Roberts, but the first wasn't the only one to die under mysterious circumstances. Two years ago, his daughters, Lucy and Rose, both vanished along with their mother, Kelly. When they first disappeared, the police looked at John but, because there were no signs of struggle or blood and the car was gone with most of the girls' necessities, they went with the theory that Kelly took the kids and left him.

Her sister, understandably, was not satisfied with that solution. Kelly was not the type to take off in the dead of night without telling the rest of her family, and although she mentioned some marital issues, they weren't severe enough for her to just disappear with her beloved daughters. So, she requested my services.

Getting rid of his current paramour—a woman he began dating less than a month after the disappearance—was a simple task. I simply had a talk with her boss, worked my charms, and convinced him to promote her and give her a job in Paris, agreeing to pay her expenses so that she could move as quickly as possible. It seemed to be a fair trade: she dodges a bullet and gets a new job, while in return, Lilith Claiborne got her old, underpaid job and her murderous lover.

Though he seemed down for a few days after she left, it didn't take long for John to notice me. It never does with men like him. To make things even easier, he had a type: blonde hair, blue eyes, athletic build. Both his wife and his lover looked like this, so I made sure to turn myself into a bombshell just for him, his wildest fantasies made flesh.

After three days, he approached my desk while I mindlessly entered pointless data. John Roberts was generically handsome—dark hair in a short cut, a five o'clock shadow, and warm brown eyes giving him the kind of charm that would land him roles in b-movie action flicks.

"Hey there," he said, "you must be Shelly's replacement."

"I wouldn't know," I replied with a coy smile. "I don't even work here. I just walked in off the street and took over this desk."

He laughed at that. "I know this is really forward, but me and a couple of the guys are going out for drinks tonight. You're welcome to come if you want. We'd all love to get to know our newest coworker."

"I'd love to," I said. Far too easy.

Conveniently, the rest of the guys had "scheduling conflicts" and stood us up, so it was just him, me, and the bartender. We chatted until closing. Well, he did most of the talking. I just smiled, looked pretty, and pretended to like all the things he liked, acting knowledgeable but not too knowledgeable so that he could explain simple concepts to me and feel like a genius. Occasionally, I'd add my own tidbits here and there, just enough to keep him interested in me without turning him off.

Ours was a whirlwind romance. We were engaged after a month and married after three. People whispered, of course. A grieving father of a missing woman and children immediately getting married despite not knowing if they're dead. They hadn't even been missing long enough to be declared dead in absentia. Who wouldn't talk?

But as the saying goes, love makes us do the craziest things. Crazy like marrying a woman you just met and know nothing about. Nothing real, anyway. But who needs real when every man on the street gazes at you in envy when I'm on your hip? Who needs to know the little things like where I was born (a little place called

Eden) or what my favorite color is (most would assume red because of my occupation, but it's actually blue) when you know that I'm great in bed? Who cares if it makes you look guilty as sin and the police begin looking in earnest for your missing wife and daughters when you've traded up from the two children and a white picket fence?

Early in our relationship one night, after we finished making the beast with two backs, I said, "I googled you, you know." I've found that most people are willing to talk in the dark. Something about not seeing the other person's face lets a bed become a confessional.

I felt him tense beside me. "Whatever it is they're saying about me, it isn't true."

I propped myself on one elbow. "What do you think they're saying?"

"That I killed them," he ground out, his muscles taut like a drawn bow.

"What do you think happened to them?" I asked, trying to get him to relax by indicating that I'll believe his side of the story over the internet—which I might have, but there was also the matter of Kelly's sister believing that something was deeply wrong. I believed her more.

He sighed. "I don't know. I think she just decided to leave. She'd always been flighty, but after our second, she started acting strange. Post-partum psychosis, I think. Wherever they are, I hope they're safe. And I really hope she didn't do something to them."

Post-partem psychosis was never mentioned by the sister, and when I called in a couple favors to access

Kelly's medical records, I could find no record of such a diagnosis, so I had a feeling that this was just a bit of bs to prevent me from asking any more awkward questions.

I laid my head on his chest. "I believe you."

In the two years since the disappearance, he had moved to a different house, a bachelor pad with fewer memories of the family he once had. The house now belongs to another family, but locked doors are rarely an issue for a demon. While they all slept, I slipped inside, my vision superimposing two images of the world. The first was of the house as it is now—the dinosaur toys strewn about the living room and family photos of two sons and a daughter—and how it looked that night. The night that scarred this place.

Because places scar the same way that people do. A horrible, traumatizing event leaves a mark that takes years to heal...if it ever does. But because a second family has filled its halls with laughter and singing and joy, it seems to be healing. Feet skimming the floor, I hovered upstairs to the bedrooms that once belonged to the Roberts family. The master bedroom was where he killed her. I watched the horror play out before my very eyes. He pressed a pillow to her face and held it there until she stopped fighting. And then held it for several minutes more. Once he was sure that she wouldn't wake up again, he got up and headed to the room shared by the two little girls.

I didn't need to see this, so, instead, I followed the vision of him as he carried the three bodies with their luggage to her car and drove to a nearby lake. He strapped the girls in as though they were just asleep, even tucking a threadbare stuffed cat into Rose's arms. After placing Kelly in the driver's seat, he sent the car into the water, watching it sink with blank, emotionless eyes. The lake was only two miles away, so he just walked back. No evidence, no bodies, no crime.

But just because the living cannot find justice, it doesn't mean that the dead cannot have their revenge. I turned my attention from him to the now placid lake, and I was fully in the present once more. Stepping into the water, I walked through the murky depths until I reached the rusted submerged vehicle. The dead need a tether—usually an object of great importance to them—if they want to return to the land of the living. Though mostly destroyed by the water and decay, I gathered the remains of the stuffed cat that had been placed in Rose's now rotting arms and returned home. The tether went into a shoebox before placing it in the vents and resealing, all before John woke. There are some advantages to not needing to sleep.

It started small, as most hauntings do. His keys would disappear and reappear in strange places, footsteps would pace up and down the halls at night, and picture frames on the walls would tilt of their own accord.

"Hey babe?" he asked from the couch one afternoon while I prepared dinner.

"Yeah?" I replied, too occupied with sautéing mushrooms to pay attention to his inane prattling. I may not need to eat, but I do love the taste of food and trying out new recipes. Mushroom pesto chicken was fairly simple, but I was feeling too lazy to do much more than that.

"Have you noticed anything weird going on?" he asked.

I swallowed my smirk. "Weird how?"

"It's stupid," he said, "but I have this feeling, almost like I'm being watched all the time. And things keep happening that I can't explain. Like, I'll lose my phone even though I knew I had just placed it on the counter, or I'll hear whispers in the hallway."

Lowering the stove's temperature, I moved to sit beside him on the couch. "I haven't seen anything." I felt his forehead, my brows knitted in an almost maternal concern. "Are you feeling okay? Your forehead is kind of warm."

He jerked away, a flash of dark anger shining in his eyes before he relaxed again. "I'm not sick, and I'm not crazy."

"I never said you were," I replied, "but you're the most rational guy I know. Do...do you think ghosts are doing this or something?"

He laughed, but it wasn't a happy one. No, it was the kind of laugh made by people who have been caught indulging in their dirty little secrets. "I don't know what I think. I just know that something's off."

"I don't think you're crazy." I pressed a distracting kiss to the corner of his mouth before getting up to check on the mushrooms. This is my favorite part of the process. I get to gaslight him in the way he probably gaslit her in those final days. "But I do think there's a rational explanation for this."

He sighed, placing his head in his hands. "I'm sure you're right. Maybe I should get this place inspected for a gas leak."

"That's usually the culprit," I replied, turning the heat off the stove.

I made sure that I was in the bathroom when little Lucy tugged on her Daddy's foot in the middle of the night. He woke with a yelp as I flushed, washed my hands, and stepped outside, my face a mask of concern. "What's wrong?"

His whole body shook like a nervous chihuahua. "Something grabbed my leg," he said, and then repeated, "Something grabbed my fucking leg."

"Are you sure you weren't dreaming?" I asked. "I have very vivid dreams sometimes. Like the *I can feel, smell, and taste* type of vivid."

He shook his head. "It was real. I swear it was real." His eyes went from wide and frightened to suspicious. "What were you doing in the bathroom anyway?"

"What most people do when they get up in the middle of the night. I had to pee."

"Did *you* grab my foot?"

I smirked and slid into bed beside him. "Honey, you know it's not the foot I'd be grabbing if I wanted you up."

He squinted at me, a dark storm cloud gathering behind his eyes. "You're not fucking with me?"

I yawned. "It's three in the morning. Why would I

decide to play a prank on you?" Turning to face away from him, I added, "Like I said, you probably dreamt it. Sleep paralysis or something."

"Okay," he said doubtfully as he laid back down, "you're probably right."

"Always am," I mumbled and feigned drifting off to sleep. He stayed awake and shaking for about an hour longer before his breathing evened out.

Little Lucy and Rose stood in the corner of the room with their mother, all three glaring at him with unbridled fury. *Soon, darlings,* I mouthed, *Soon, you will have justice.*

The campaign of terror began in earnest the next morning. I woke to a scream and a thud coming from the bathroom. John had backed himself into a corner, pointing shakily to a message written with a childish hand in the mirror.

DADDY

"You-you see that too, right?" he stammered.

I furrowed my brows in confusion and concern. "See what?"

"The mirror. There's a message in the fucking mirror."

"John, I'm worried about you," I said, slowly reaching for him. "Maybe you should visit that psychiatrist again. What was his name? Doctor Khan?"

He jerked away from me. "I don't need a psychiatrist."

"Okay, okay," I said, putting my hands up in a placating gesture.

"And I'm not crazy."

Ever the concerned spouse, I took my seat beside him. "I know you aren't, hon, but maybe we moved too fast. You've been through so much, and I thought I would help you move on, but I'm worried I just made things worse."

He shook his head. "No, you're the one bright spot in this hell I've been living the past two years."

A hell of his own making, though he didn't know the extent just yet. "Will you think about getting some therapy, though? Treat it like a checkup at the doctor's office. I just want to make sure you're okay."

I felt him tense beside me, a look of soul-wrecking terror on his face. His ex-wife and daughters stood in the doorway, smiling with too many teeth in their mouths. Tears welled in his eyes as he shook his head. "No, no, this isn't real. It's not real."

"What isn't real?" I asked.

He whipped his head back to me. "You don't see them?"

My face was a mask of confusion. "Who?"

"Them. I-it's them!"

"Your family?" I asked.

He nodded. The spirits did nothing. They only watched and smiled like predators about to devour their prey.

"Could it be a manifestation of your guilt?" I asked.

He tore his gaze from them and to me. "What?"

"Your guilt," I replied, and then let the mask of the concerned wife drop. "For a heartbroken family man, you really got over the pain of their disappearance quickly, didn't you? Moving from one relationship to another like women are your own personal all you can eat buffet." I got to my feet and headed towards the door.

He was shaking his head, a pathetic attempt at a denial. "No, no, I swear I didn't—"

The ghosts bristled at that, making him flinch. I stopped and looked back over my shoulder. "You really shouldn't lie like that. It set a bad example for the little ones."

His mouth opened and closed like a beached fish. "You can see them?"

Fully turning to face him, I leaned against the wall with my arms crossed. "Who do you think brought them here, babe?"

He didn't seem to know where to look. His eyes kept ping ponging between me and the spirits. "Why?"

"You know why. But something has been bothering me. Why did *you* do it? Why did you kill them?"

"I didn't—" he began but cut himself off when Kelly growled.

"We both know that's not true, darling. So come clean for once in your life."

"You bitch. You're just as much of a whore as my first wife," he shouted, lunging for me. It was about as effective as lunging for a tendril of fog. He ran straight into a wall with a dull thud. Stepping back and rubbing his head, he stared at me in horror and confusion. "What are you?" he whispered.

I smiled, revealing fangs. "I am justice for women

who have none. I am the first sinner and the mother of demons. I am Lilith. And I have come to avenge your wife and children."

Jumping up to sit on the bathroom countertop, I gave the three spirits the go ahead. I like to say that the ghostly gaslighting is the best part, but really, it's this: watching a monster be torn apart by his victims. They scratched out his eyes and sank their teeth into him, ripping off flesh and letting blood spray like a fountain. His screams gave way to gurgled cries as he tried and failed to fight off the incorporeal beings. *Not so powerful now, are you?*

Rose snapped his neck, and she and Lucy pulled until it came free in a shower of blood like confetti from a cannon. Their murderer was dead. Justice was served.

I watched with a smile as the three faded into the great beyond—the little girls first, and then, with one last, grateful look thrown my way, their mother. With my job done, I left the waterlogged stuffed animal on his chest along with a note to dredge the lake and headed back down under.

Tomorrow will be a media circus. People love the macabre, and a guy who was accused of murder being decapitated in his own bathroom is enough to drive the media into a feeding frenzy. Add to that a mysterious— now missing—second wife, and the true crime buffs will be theorizing about this one for years.

I only hope that Kelly and her family have found some peace in the process.

Part I

"A cautionary tale."

Fog choked the alley behind The Leviathan, a squatter bar stitched together with rusted shipping containers and old concert posters peeling like sunburned skin. Inside, the amps howled like sirens and boots stomped out rhythms older than memory. I was leaning against the bar, chain-smoking clove cigs and soaking in the static.

That's when The Mariner showed up.

Nobody knew his real name. Said he'd been around since before the scene even had a name. Wore a prehistoric studded leather jacket; his fingers tattooed with sea creatures inked in jailhouse blue. His eyes burnt-out searchlights – long dead behind the lenses but somehow still scanning.

He walked straight past the pit, past the bar, and

planted himself on a milk crate stage no one had used since the riot in '27.

Then he started talking. "There was a voyage once. Not across oceans - through this poisoned world. We sailed in a tour van powered by spite and stolen gas, dragging amps from squat to squat like pilgrims lugging relics."

Everyone thought that it was a bit contrived. A performance. But no one said anything. No one moved. "We had a drummer who could raise the dead, a bassist who never spoke, and me - just a frontman with a voice like broken glass. We thought we were gods. Until I killed the bird."

The Bird. The soul of the scene. The code.

The invisible compass that pointed us toward something pure and uncorrupted, even in the filth.

"We sold out," he spat. "Signed with SonyCo. Took their blood money and let them bleach our sound. First a tour bus, then synths, then ballads about love. LOVE! While the world burned."

His voice cracked like thunder in a bottle.

"At first, the world applauded. But then the curse came. Gigs turned to riots. Fans OD'd in mosh pits. Our bassist vanished mid-set in Berlin - just gone, like a ghost note. By the time I realised, it was too late. The others blamed me. Hell, I blamed me."

Outside, real thunder cracked. Or maybe just a passing train. Maybe not.

"Now I wander. From dive to dive. Telling this tale. Trying to warn the young."

"Warn us of what?" We all turned to stare at a girl with a rainbow-painted-Mohican and a safety pin through the top lip of her sneer.

The Mariner grinned, but it wasn't joyous. "That if you betray the bird - if you sell out what matters - the world doesn't punish you with silence. It makes you keep playing. Forever. With no soul. No anchor. Just endless shows in front of dead eyes. Immortal. Undead."

Then he stood. The lights flickered, strobing his shadow as he walked out of the door and into the mist.

We never saw him again. But the story? It clung to us. You'd hear snippets and embellishments in basements and zines, tattooed on someone's thigh next to a skull-faced albatross. Every now and then, a band gets big too fast, and burns out even faster. And in every true punk set, there's a moment, right before the breakdown, where you hear it.

Not a scream. Not a riff.

A whisper.

"Don't kill the bird."

Part II

"The road goes on, but only the damned stay on it."

After the Mariner vanished into the fog, something shifted. The Leviathan shut down a week later— the owner found face-down in a puddle of beer, blood and teeth. No forced entry. No suspects. Just a line scrawled on the bathroom mirror in black lipstick:

You heard the song. Now live it.

I didn't believe in curses. Not then. I was all black leather and blistered fingers, convinced that nihilism was armour. But the story wouldn't die. Word spread. Venues started reporting things: soundchecks where no one played, amps bleeding static that sounded like distant screams, kids in the crowd going catatonic mid-set, eyes rolled back, whispering in unison:

He rides again.

I started digging.

Old flyers from the early '80s. Bands no one remembered. Names scratched out in red marker. One photo kept turning up - grainy, blown out. A frontman with eyes like ash, a stitched-up leather jacket, and a microphone wrapped in rosary beads.

The caption read: *"The Mariner & The Hollow Crew. Tour '83 – 'Eternal Refrain.'"*

I tracked down one of the surviving members - a drummer, now rotting in a hospice under a fake name. He couldn't move his hands anymore but his feet wouldn't stop; each one stamping an invisible kick drum to the beat inside his head. He told me the curse wasn't about selling out. That was just the bait.

"It's the *song*, kid," he wheezed, his knees pistoning up and down as drool glistened on his chin. "They made us record it. Not music. A ritual. One take. Analog tape.

We didn't know that once it was pressed, it couldn't be undone."

"What was it called?" I said.

He smiled. His gums like a graveyard. "Track Seven. Rime of the Ancient Mariner."

He told me that no digital copies exist. Said the only vinyl was buried in a condemned church in Hastings, England, sealed in salt and concrete.

So, I went there.

It was night when I broke in, flashlight flickering, boots crunching over broken glass and pigeon bones. Next to the altar stood a turntable, surrounded by dead rats and bloodied picks.

I found the record in a wall cavity, wrapped in an old 'Maiden tee, Eddie's face crusted with what I prayed was wax. The label was blank—just a single etching on the inner ring:

Play and be played.

I listened to it.

Of course I did.

The needle dropped. Static hissed. Then something came through the speakers that wasn't sound. It was darker than sound, an aural force pulling like a riptide through my veins. Screams backward-masked into Gregorian chants, bass lines that clawed up your spine, and over it all... his voice.

You killed the bird. You killed the bird. You killed the...

I blacked out.

When I woke, the record was gone. The church

doors were open. My fingernails had been torn off, neatly, one by one.

And I could hear music.

Not from the outside.

From *inside me*.

Now I tour.

Not by choice. I show up at gigs I don't remember booking. My guitar plays riffs I never learned. I scream lyrics no one wrote. Kids in the crowd bleed from their ears and ask for more. They don't dance. They contort in spastic shapes like marionettes at the mercy of a drunk puppeteer.

Every town I leave feels colder. Every night I feel less human. I haven't slept in three weeks. I don't think I'm supposed to.

I'm not the Mariner. I'm just the next one.

He passed the curse on.

So if you ever hear a song with no name, playing from a record that shouldn't exist, in a place that smells like rust and regret:

Don't listen.

Don't sing along.

And for the love of all that still breathes...

Don't kill the bird.

Part III

"It's not a tour. It's a plague on vinyl."

Cities blurred into each other, graffitied wastelands where neon signs flickered like epileptic warnings, and every club reeked of mould and regret. The curse preceded me everywhere I went.

People said they'd started dreaming about me.

I showed up at one venue and the sound guy went pale like his arteries had emptied. "You were in my sleep last night," he said. "You bled through my speakers."

Later that night a kid showed me the raw, livid scars of the track list he'd carved into his chest after my show in Marseille. Said the Mariner told him to do it.

I stopped carrying gear. Didn't need it. Every venue had everything ready; same setup, same fog machine, same mic wrapped in a rosary. Same setlist.

And always, Track Seven.

I never remember playing it. Just the aftermath. Vomit on the dance floor. Blood on the walls. Eyes. So many goddamn eyes, wide open, never blinking.

I tried to stop once.

Abandoned the van in a ditch somewhere outside Dresden. Walked until my boots split. Found a burned-out chapel and stayed there for three days. No food. No music. Just silence and a bottle of rotgut that tasted older than sin.

On the fourth night, the floorboards started vibrating. No speakers. No power. Just the warped hum of Track Seven, rising up from the earth like spores from a long-dead fungus.

I passed out with blood leaking from my ears. When I woke, someone had painted a crude albatross on my chest in tar. And my van was parked outside.

Engine running.

No keys.

I'm not alone now.

Others have heard the song. Some through bootlegs traded in dark web circles. Others on cassette tapes mailed in unmarked envelopes. A few told me they just woke up humming it.

They find me. Some beg to be free. Some want to join the band. A few try to kill me. None succeed.

I met a girl in a Burger King parking lot. She looked somewhere between eighteen and eighty. I remember she had a tattered Discharge patch on her denim jacket. She said, "The Bird said I'd find you. Said you needed a backup singer." Then she pulled a knife from her boot, cut out her tongue, handed it to me then showed me what was left of her wrists.

I still hear the blood-gurgling laughter noises she made as she bled to death.

I buried her that night, under a billboard that read: *Your Future is Calling.*

Shortly after that I started seeing him again.

The original Mariner.

Sometimes in the crowd, right at the back, head down, mouthing the words. Other times in motel mirrors, over my shoulder, grinning with black teeth and eyes like shattered portholes. Once, I saw him standing on the median of a freeway in Texas. Just stood there, as every car veered around him like he didn't exist.

He never speaks. Just watches.

Like he's waiting for me to snap and hand the curse on.

And here's the part that'll really twist your gut:

The Bird is real.

Not a metaphor. Not a symbol. A *thing*. A massive, rotting albatross with wings like torn sails and eyes that burn through dreamscapes.

It circles above the gigs. It's invisible to most, but there are those who feel the shadow. They're the ones who look up mid-set and scream.

And when I sleep - if I ever do - it lands beside me. Its breath smells like old tape reels and salt. It whispers things in voices made of distortion.

"You're almost ready," it says.

This is my warning to you.

If you see a flyer with no band name. If your friend says they've got "a lost track that'll blow your mind." If a beat makes your bones rattle but your ears hear nothing...

Burn it.

Bury the ashes in salt and silence.

Walk away.

Because the song's spreading.

And someday, if you hear it too, it will be your turn.

Part IV

"There is no encore. Only echo."

I played a set last night in a town that doesn't exist anymore.

It wasn't on any map. It just appeared, rows of leaning houses with boarded windows, a diner where all the clocks pointed backward, and a single venue called

The Drowned Room, half-submerged in fog and something darker.

I didn't walk in. I was already on stage when I blinked.

The crowd wasn't human. Not really. Hollow eyes, smiles too wide, heads twitching like broken animatronics. They moved in perfect time, like they'd heard the song a thousand times already, like they were part of it now.

I opened with "Dead Compass." My hands weren't moving.

They were playing themselves.

The mic hissed, and the floor rippled like water.

Then Track Seven started on its own.

It changes every time.

The song.

Longer now. More verses. Some in languages no one speaks anymore. I recognized one, Old Church Slavonic, another in something older than Latin. One verse wasn't even sound. Just a piercing feedback howl. A sonic banshee that made the walls bleed, and I watched as a kid in the front row aged thirty years in ten seconds.

He thanked me afterwards.

The Bird showed up mid-set, perched on the rafters like a gargoyle. Its feathers are falling out now, exposing something beneath, *wires, bones, and rusted speaker cones.* It opened its beak and out came **a** distorted sample of a scream that I made three years ago.

I never recorded that.

After the set, I found a backstage door. First one in

months. Usually there's just... *nothing*. A black wall. Or a mirror that won't reflect me.

Behind the door was a hallway. Damp. Narrow. Infinite.

Flyers pinned to the walls. Dozens. Hundreds. Every gig I've ever played. Every gig that I'll play in the future. Cities that haven't been built yet. Venues in space. From here to eternity.

One show listed as: *Final Set – All Souls in Attendance. No Escape.*

I walked that hallway for hours. Maybe days or weeks.

Every few steps, a speaker in the wall would blurt out a lyric; backward, inside-out, or whispered by a child.

I passed a door marked *MARINER GREEN ROOM – DO NOT ENTER.*

I entered.

He was inside.

The Original.

Dead.

Hanging from guitar strings knotted around a ceiling beam. Eyes bulging wide. Swollen tongue intruding his rictus grimace.

Beneath his gently swinging corpse lay a notebook. The first page read: *"The bird cannot die. The song cannot end. The stage is the gallows, and we are all the rope."*

I came back to reality.

If you can call this real.

The world's been... glitching. Flickering. People

freeze mid-step like someone paused then restarted their video footage.

I passed a preacher on a street corner. He was clutching a dead microphone, his face gone, voice looping like a sample: "He plays still... he plays still... he plays still..."

I've stopped eating. My blood is thick with feedback.

My shadow doesn't match me anymore. It's taller now. Wearing a jacket I've never owned, carrying a guitar I never see. Sometimes it plays a fret-wanking riff in silence, with perfect form.

Last night, I found a cassette in my jacket pocket. No label. Just the smell of salt and rust.

I played it in my head on a Sony Walkman that had no batteries.

It was Track Eight.

I didn't even know there *was* a Track Eight.

It starts where Track Seven ends.

It's not a song.

It's a summons.

If you've read this far, it means the song is already inside you. Just a hum now. A heartbeat out of sync. A distant drum.

Ignore it.

Please.

Because once it reaches your lips, once you hum it, whistle it, *sing it,*

The Bird will know.

The Mariner will come.

And the next show... will be yours.

Part V

"You don't play the song. The song plays you."

I played a house show in a place called Greywater, though no one could point to it on a map. The house was sinking - slowly, rhythmically - into the earth. I performed in a flooded basement. Waist-deep in brackish water. No crowd. Just mirrors nailed to the walls, each one showing a different version of me: older, twisted, burning.

I asked one of them what year it was. "Year Zero," he laughed. "Like it always is."

I tried silence again. Hid in a cave up north where radios died and nothing grew. Burned my guitar. Shaved my head.

The Bird found me as I was trying to cut out my tongues.

It didn't land this time. It crashed. Its wings now shredded cassette tape, whipping in winds no one else can feel. Its eyes project tour dates across the walls of my skull, seared in static.

The cave filled with basslines. My blood boiled in rhythm. I screamed without a mouth.

Track Nine.

There was never supposed to be a Track Nine.

It's not even music. It's reversal. Of sound. Of self.

Everything you are? Unwritten.

Back on the road.

Not driving. Just waking up in new places, with new

scars, new merch at the table. T-shirts I didn't design. Slogans I never wrote:

I Heard the Bird.

Track Seven Made Me Kill.

Tour Never Ends.

Some of them glow in the dark. Some whisper in the wash.

At a merch booth in St. Louis, I met a child, seventeen years old, maybe less. No parents. No shoes. She handed me a mixtape fashioned from her own teeth, each one etched with a song title.

She smiled, wide and wrong.

"You're the bridge," she said. "You finish the track; we start the fire."

Then she disappeared. No one else saw her.

But the tape still clacks in my pocket, even without a player.

🤘 🤘 🤘

I've seen the Mariner again.

Not just in glimpses now—he *performs*. At shows I thought were mine. Sometimes he opens, sometimes he closes. Sometimes I am he.

I don't know where he ends and I begin.

I found a photo from 1983 last week. The Hollow Crew, the original line-up.

I'm in it.

I haven't aged.

Or maybe I've aged too far and looped back.

I'm beginning to understand the Song.

Not the lyrics, they change nightly. Not the melody, it writes itself in screams and machine hums.

The structure.

It's a binding. The tracks aren't just songs. They're seals. Rituals. Each one locks—or unlocks—another layer of The Bird.

We've reached Track Ten now.

I played it last night without touching a single instrument. The sound poured from the walls, the ceiling, my own mouthless face.

People in the crowd melted.

One girl gave birth to a nest made of wires and bone.

A boy carved the tablature into his skin with a guitar string.

No applause.

Just chanting:

Feed the beak. Feed the beak. Feed the beak.

If you're reading this and your ears are ringing... it's already too late.

You've heard the intro. Even in silence.

The static you hear in your dreams? That's Track Eleven warming up.

It'll play the day the Bird takes flight.

It won't be a concert.

It'll be a mass extinction, but I won't be your saviour, I'm the opening act, and you are the next verse.

Sing carefully.

Part VI

"It's not a tour. It's a funeral procession for the living."

It happened last night.

Track Eleven.

I didn't mean to play it. I didn't even know I could. But there I was, standing in a bombed-out cathedral-turned-venue in a city with no name; the stained-glass bleeding static, the altar lined with amps powered by violence.

No crowd.

Just chairs.

Each one filled with a mannequin dressed like someone I used to know.

Ex-lovers. Bandmates. That sound guy who slit his own throat after hearing Track Seven played backward in Philly.

Even *me*. Different versions of me.

One holding a mic made of bone.

One without a face.

One weeping blood and whispering, "It's almost time. You're the crescendo."

I didn't strum. I didn't speak.

The song began itself.

Track Eleven is not heard. It's lived.

Time bled backward. My first show. My first breath. My first scream. All of it unspooling like damaged tape.

Outside, the Bird circled the steeple, dragging its wings across the sky, carving runes into the stars. The clouds cracked. Not lightning, just feedback.

And when the hook hit, when the drop came, I split. Literally.

My shadow ripped away from me and danced.

My skin peeled into lyrics.

My soul became a chorus.

I saw the Mariner then.

Not across the room. Not on stage. But in me.

He's always been in me.

Because here's the truth:

There's not *one* Mariner.

There's a lineage. A cycle. A relay race through hell's soundcheck.

Every time the curse gets too loud, too unstable, it needs a new voice to carry it. To keep the track alive.

To feed the Bird.

I'm not the headliner.

I'm the hand-off.

So now I speak directly to you.

Yes. YOU. Stand still, will you.

You. The one who keeps reading. Keeps scrolling. Thinking this is just fiction, just horror, just *art*.

You're wrong.

Every word you've read has been part of Track Twelve.

The final track. The encore that ends the world.

And your eyes?

They're the needle.

You've just dropped it onto the wax.

And when the lights go out tonight - and they will - you'll hear it.

A whisper in the walls. A scream in your shower. A rhythm in your blood.

You'll hum it. You won't mean to. But you will.

And when you do?

The Bird will land.

The Mariner will knock.

And the show will begin.

This is the end of the story *(but not the end of the song.)*

Because now...

You're on tour.

See you at soundcheck.

Hannah wrung her dirty hands then wiped them on her once pretty pink dress. Her momma bought it for her for Easter. She didn't know how long ago that was. Days merged with one another into a continuous stream of daylight morphing into darkness.

Most of the time it was all dark. The frosted glass block windows along two sides of the basement only allowed so much light in.

Hannah was nine when she last saw her family. Her birthday was in May. Had she missed it? She proudly puffed out her chest and declared that she had left the world of single digit birthdays, and forever would be double digits until the day she died.

Death. Even a passing thought like enjoying turning ten brought a heavy sadness to her heart.

She wondered for the hundredth time if she'd ever see her brother again. Ethan was seven and was often mean to her, but he was her brother and she missed him dearly. Her momma and daddy she missed the most.

Momma was tall. Taller than most women she knew. Her long legs always impressed Hannah. As well as her curly blonde hair and bright blue eyes. God made a perfect woman when he made her momma, though her momma said the same thing about Hannah as she was the spitting image of her.

God did the same with her daddy. Muscular, but not too much. Short brown hair and a thick beard, he embodied what a man should be. Plus he was great with fixing her dollhouse.

But those memories of her family were fading with each passing day. Hannah tried to visualize them, to remember what they felt like and what they smelled like. It was getting harder to do.

A door slammed and Hannah's heart almost exploded. It was him. The Beast. He was coming for her.

Heavy footfalls crossed the darkened house above her. The thick concrete walls of the basement where she was chained were imposing and had long ago broken her spirit. It was a place she didn't recognize when she first opened her eyes and discovered her situation, but one that had become familiar over time.

The basement door swung open and The Beast stomped down the rickety wooden steps. When he reached the bottom, he pulled the string which turned on the single exposed bulb, bathing the small space in a yellow glow.

Hannah called him The Beast not because he was an

actual monster, but because of his mask. She had never seen his real face. He only ever appeared wearing a grotesque demonic latex mask that covered his entire head. It was red with yellow teeth and eyes. Thick veins ran across the forehead where the numbers "666" were scrawled in bloody letters. His mouth was framed by a black beard and moustache, molded out of the latex. The mask had black hair on the head that she thought was real–but couldn't be sure–and pointy ears like an elf. Many nights were spent curled in a ball against the cold concrete wall crying because of that face.

The Beast dropped a juice box, a green apple, and a ham sandwich wrapped in plastic from the store onto the floor at her feet. She didn't dare move. Fear kept her from accepting the meal.

"Eat," The Beast growled from behind the mask. Her stomach rumbled but she was too terrified to take what he offered. His voice was deep and menacing, like when her daddy got mad at her brother. But so much worse.

The Beast breathed heavy behind the mask, like a bull ready to charge.

Hannah timidly reached for the juice box. Her hand shook. The Beast stood like a statue, but a mean, scary looking one. It was unnerving and made Hannah want to pee. She didn't want to pee in front of The Beast again. She closed her legs and squeezed tight, then broke the straw from the box and poked it through the aluminum dot on the top.

"Do I need to watch you eat it all or can I trust you?"

Hannah looked up at him and nodded. "I'll eat it," she said in a weak voice.

"Have you bled yet?"

The question made her shudder. It was something he asked almost every time he came down here. At first she didn't know what he meant, but then quickly realized he was talking about menstruation. He wanted to know if she started her period, because if she did, she could have babies. The Beast was fond of telling her that he wanted babies. Lots and lots of them, and she was going to give them to him.

Hannah wasn't dumb. She knew how babies were made. If The Beast wanted her to have them, there was only one way for that to happen. She thanked God every day that her period hadn't come. She wasn't sure what would happen when it did.

Hannah took a sip of the warm apple juice and shook her head.

"Huh," The Beast replied. "I expect it will soon. Don't you dare lie to me, either. You know what will happen if you do."

She nodded.

The Beast stared at her through the mask, his real eyes obscured by shadows from the light. Hannah wanted to crawl away and hide, but there was nowhere to go. He'd chained her leg to a thick metal bolt that was secured to the floor. The only way out was to unlock the lock, and she had no idea where the key was.

He inhaled deeply. "It won't be long now. Your body is close."

A sense of dread seeped into her bones. How could The Beast know that? She hoped it wasn't true.

Without another word, The Beast turned off the light and slowly climbed the stairs, closing the door behind him. Hannah was left in near total darkness with only a sliver of light poking through from beneath the door.

Tears began to stream down her cheeks. Every day it was the same thing. Food. Then the question. Most girls didn't get their period until they were older, like around ten or eleven.

Then the truth smacked her in the face. *She* was ten.

She wasn't when The Beast first took her. But now? She had to have turned ten by now. Would she start to bleed soon? Her momma hadn't talked to her much about it other than to say it would happen and she would help her through it. Without her around, Hannah worried it might be a problem. The Beast couldn't help. He *wanted* it to happen so he could make his babies.

Despair settled in, bringing with it the first inkling of not wanting to live.

She expected to die many times when The Beast came down the stairs and every time she wanted to live. But just now, just as she was coming to terms with the notion that she would soon be able to bear children, she felt like dying was her only escape.

It was an odd feeling to wish for death when all along you wanted to live, but Hannah accepted it. She embraced it. She wondered how she could make it happen. It had never occurred to her before, but she found the appeal inviting.

No, she thought, pushing the idea away. She wanted to live.

Hannah finished the meal The Beast brought for her and after relieving herself in a bucket, she fell asleep. But it was a restless sleep haunted by images of The Beast.

"Wake up," The Beast growled. Hannah rubbed sleep from her eyes and blinked rapidly. When she looked up from the floor, The Beast stood above her with the light behind him, creating an even scarier outline around him and his petrifying mask. Her stomach ached, a feeling she hadn't really felt before.

"It started."

Hannah had no idea what he meant. She was barely aware of her surroundings and having been pulled from a nightmare, her mind hadn't adjusted to the disturbance yet.

Hannah placed her hand on the floor to push up and it felt warm and wet. When she got into a seated position, it felt the same between her legs.

When her eyes finally adjusted, she realized what it was: blood. *Her* blood. The ultimate betrayal from her body. She started her period.

A powerful grief followed by a streak of panic raced through her. The Beast was clear about what this would mean. She clutched her arms around her chest.

The Beast stepped closer and she shrank back as much as possible. She didn't want to make babies with him. He reached past her and grabbed hold of the chain around her ankle, and then swiftly pulled a key from his pocket and unlocked her.

"Don't you dare think of trying to escape," he said through the mask. "It won't end well for you."

Though he'd unlocked the chain from the floor, it was still fixed tightly around her ankle. Even if the thought had occurred to her, there was no way she was getting away from him.

"Get up," he commanded. Hannah didn't move. Fear paralyzed her.

"I said get up!" He yanked the chain so hard it felt like it was cutting into her flesh.

Tears streamed down Hannah's face. "Please, I don't want to do this. I don't want babies."

The Beast said nothing, only pulling on the chain again. Hannah reluctantly complied, though her shaky legs were difficult to stand on.

"If you move, I'll kill you. Understand?"

Hannah froze to the spot, a tiny marble statue incapable of movement. Satisfied with her silent compliance, The Beast bent on one knee in front of the small pool of blood on the floor.

Hannah's heart raced in her chest, thumping a wild rhythm that she thought might make it explode. The Beast, clutching the chain in one hand, used his free hand and placed a finger in the blood. He dragged it through the crimson and lifted it to his nostrils, inhaling deeply.

Satisfied with what he found, he then drew a circle out of the blood. Hannah wanted to cry, but kept herself together out of fear from what The Beast might do. She watched him draw a star within the circle, but also noticed the short brown hair under the back of the mask. She had never seen that before, but she was also never at this angle. It broke the illusion that The Beast really looked like the mask, and she kept the secret to herself.

When The Beast was done, he stood and marvelled at the image. Hannah saw that he had created a pentagram, a symbol she'd seen in Sunday School when they were talking about the devil. A five pointed star rested inside a circle. What was different about this one was that The Beast included the number six in three of the points on the star. 666. The number of the beast. Another memory from a Sunday School in another lifetime. They were the same numbers on his mask.

Flashes of Hell flooded her mind. Eternal torment. Demons. Evil. Was this what The Beast had in mind for her? Was he implying that he was *The* Beast talked about in the Bible? Hannah suddenly felt even worse about her situation and prayed to God for freedom. She didn't want to be a sacrifice and she really, really didn't want to have babies.

"Now go up," The Beast said, indicating the stairs with a nod. She had never been upstairs. Her last memory before the basement was of being at the mall with her momma. The next thing she knew, she was chained to the floor in an unfamiliar place. That had been her entire existence for as long as she remembered.

Upstairs? It was like an entirely new world awaited which made her both excited and scared.

"I said up!" he snarled when she hadn't budged. His tone shook her spirit, but she complied. Each tiny step up was exhilarating. And terrifying. The fear of the unknown sent shockwaves throughout her body. She couldn't get the image of The Beast writing in the blood—her blood—out of her mind. The horror that had filled her head was powerful and paralyzing.

When she reached the top, The Beast nudged her forward. He still held the chain that was firmly locked around her ankle in one hand.

"To the right," he commanded. Hannah did as she was told. She was in a hallway that had three doors, two on her right and one on her left. The walls were dingy white, or yellow, she wasn't sure, and bare. No pictures and no art. Just walls with stains where dusty outlines indicated pictures once hung. None of it was familiar. A lamp illuminated a room down the hall, but much of the house remained in shadows.

"Go to the door on the left," The Beast said. Hannah felt a surge of panic. Was that where he wanted to make babies? A tear raced down her cheek. Her heart hammered her chest. She couldn't do this!

When she didn't move, The Beast nudged her forward, almost making her fall. She swallowed hard and took a timid step forward. Behind her, she heard The Beast breathing heavily inside his mask. She desperately wanted to run away, but she had no idea how to leave and with the chain still wrapped around her ankle, there was no way she was getting far. The Beast had full control over her.

More tears flowed the closer Hannah got to the door. Fear rose to a fever pitch in her mind, making her entire body shake. When she approached the door, The Beast reached ahead of her and flicked on the light.

It was the bathroom. Confusion settled in. She thought The Beast wanted babies. Why was he bringing her there?

The room was small with just a shower stall, toilet, and small vanity with a sink. The floor was a dirt-streaked stone tile and the walls were covered in a hideous wallpaper depicting a farm scene from long ago of people carrying baskets in fields in red print on a cream colored background. Some of it was peeling near the ceiling.

One the counter was a box of generic sanitary pads to soak up her menstrual blood. She had never been taught how to use them or tampons, and the thought of The Beast teaching her made her stomach twist.

"Clean yourself in the shower and use that," he said, indicating the pads.

Hannah looked over herself and at the chain around her ankle. The Beast closed the bathroom door and locked it behind him. He bent to her leg and swiftly unlocked the lock, pulling it free.

"This goes back on when you're done. Don't think about trying to leave. Got it?" His voice had gotten darker and deeper. Hannah nodded. The freedom she felt was exciting, though tempered with the fact that it was false. She wasn't free and had no hope of ever being free again.

"Now get in the shower and clean yourself up. I can't have you dirty when you're making babies."

Hannah's heart nearly burst in her chest. She couldn't muster the strength to do what he wanted, not when the end result was to lay with The Beast to make babies. He noticed her hesitation, then grabbed the neck of her dress.

"I said get in the shower!" With both hands gripping the dress, he ripped it in half right down the front. She gasped and tried to cover herself, but he refused to be stopped. He tore the dress off of her, leaving her in just her blood-stained underwear that had yellow flowers on them.

Tears flowed faster and she shook. It was her Easter dress. Her one connection to her family and something she cherished deeply. With it gone, it felt like part of her had been ripped away for good.

"Are you going to listen?"

Hannah couldn't stop crying. Long, mournful wails escaped her lips.

"Shut up before I give you something to cry about!"

Something in the way he said those words shattered her fears. It was like being struck by lightning. She'd heard it before and spoken in just the same way. But where? It was like a memory from long ago was trying to get her attention, but not quite enough to give her the details she needed. She stared at him with her mouth open and her tears suddenly halted. This meant something, she just didn't know what.

She timidly turned away from him, wary that with her back exposed, he could do anything he wanted without her stopping him. Carefully she turned on the water until it was hot. It was easier to burn off all the anger, all the evil, all the wickedness from her. Maybe then she could live.

Stream billowed out of the shower. Hannah pulled off her underwear and stepped in.

Her stomach felt achy, like she'd eaten something bad. But the hot water scalding her skin was soothing. She basked in the heat, enjoying the sensation.

"Don't take a lot of time in there," The Beast said, shattering her bliss.

There was a bottle of shampoo and a small travel sized bar of white soap on the ledge. She tilted her head back and soaked her hair, feeling the burn on her scalp.

Despite The Beast's warning, she was in no hurry to get out. Leaving the safety of the shower meant she was then at his mercy, and that scared her more than anything.

"Aww, stupid mask," The Beast grumbled. "I'm going out in the hall. Don't you dare try anything. Hurry up!"

Again, a recognition struck Hannah. The tone and timbre of The Beast's voice triggered something inside, though she couldn't place it. Then the door opened and clicked shut. Hannah peaked out of the shower curtain and she was alone. A welcoming relief settled in her bones and she let out a heavy sigh.

Various scenarios ran through her head, all of them about how she could escape. With no chain around her ankle and The Beast out of the room, there was no better way to get free than now. But how? The bathroom was an interior room with no windows. There was only one way in or out, and she assumed The Beast was on the other side of the door.

That meant she'd have to trick him and try to hurt him. She was much smaller than him and doubted her ability to do anything significant. The hope of freedom was dashed with the reality of her situation.

The Beast beat on the door. "Hurry up in there!" He startled her and smashed all thought of escape. Resigning herself to her fate, Hannah used the shampoo and soap to clean off all of the filth that had been accumulating since The Beast took her. She was extra careful with the dried blood between her legs.

The water had started to cool. She couldn't stay in there much longer even if The Beast wasn't yelling at her. Life wasn't fair and she feared what was to come next. Slowly turning off the water, Hannah stood there for a moment and enjoyed the serenity of the steam, something she'd seen her momma do and now understood why.

The Beast beat on the door again. "Towel's on the toilet. I left you a nightgown and panties." The word "panties" sent a shiver down her spine. She couldn't explain why, but it unnerved her to no end.

Hannah stepped out of the shower and dried off.

"Don't forget the pad!" The Beast barked.

Hannah had never used one before and her momma hadn't had a chance to show her. She picked up the box and read the directions, grimacing as she did. A cramp gnarled her stomach. She placed the pad according to the directions and pulled on the pink underwear The Beast had left her. They were exactly her size, surprising her. *How would he know which ones to get?* she thought.

She slipped on the nightgown which was a lavender color with purple flowers. It felt flowy and comfortable, reaching all the way to the floor.

Then she spotted something that triggered an idea. A toothbrush sat innocently in a holder on the sink. If she could work it out, maybe she could use it to stab him? Her eyes lit up and a flicker of hope blossomed in her chest. She snatched it from the holder and shoved it in the waistband of her underwear, hoping the nightgown could keep it hidden.

The Beast pushed the door open and for a second, Hannah thought she was caught.

"It's about time."

He grabbed her by the arm and pulled her out of the bathroom. He held the chain in one hand and bent down to attach it to her ankle. *This was it. Now or never,* Hannah thought.

The moment The Beast got to his knee, she snatched the toothbrush from her underwear and tried to stab him in the neck. It was an awkward movement with her nightgown getting in the way.

"Ouch! What are you doing?" he shouted, letting go of her leg. She struck with such force that she broke the skin, but did little else. She thrust her knee up and connected with his face, making him curse.

When he let go to soothe his bleeding nose, Hannah bolted.

She had no idea where to go or how to get out. Everything was a blur. The Beast growled and chased after her.

"Get back here!"

Hannah's heart pounded faster. This was her chance.

Turning a corner, she found herself in a large living room with a door at the far end. Freedom awaited! She raced across the room and grabbed hold of the door knob, and turned. The door opened.

She rushed inside and immediately realized her mistake. It wasn't the front door. It was a door to another room. This one was windowless and painted black, illuminated by an overhead red light. Weird occult symbols were painted in blood red on all of the walls between long translucent black fabric. Black candles on the floor marked the five points of a large room-sized pentagram, the same symbol The Beast drew with her blood in the basement. Their ominous flames dancing atop the wicks. A book and stacks of paper lay outside of the circle. Shock overwhelmed her and she started hyper-ventilating.

The Beast arrived behind her and started laughing. "I couldn't have done it better myself. This is where we make the babies once your bleeding is done."

A cold streak of dread consumed Hannah. How could she have been so dumb? She put herself in this position.

The Beast entered the room and locked the door behind him. Hope faded within Hannah's heart. Tears started to fall once again.

"Don't cry, dear. It's all in service to the Dark One. He requires much. Your mother couldn't see that and she had to pay for her mistake. Your brother too. Both needed to die. They wanted to stop me. Stop us from doing what must be done."

Hannah cocked her head to the side, unsure she understood what The Beast was saying. Her momma and brother...dead? It can't be!

Then, he grabbed hold of the mask, lifting it from his head. When he did, she gasped and fell to her knees crying.

It was her daddy.

"Hey Hannah," he said in his normal voice. Conflicting emotions swirled inside of her. Her dad was...The Beast? He's the one that wanted to make babies with her? He killed her momma and Ethen? But he was only seven years old! Her stomach twisted and she wanted to puke. He held the mask in front of him, staring into its vacant eyes. His face was shaved and though he looked different from the last time she'd seen him, there was no denying the truth.

"I felt it was time you knew. You are going to bring forth the vessels for the Dark One. Do you know what that means? You are his favored!"

"Daddy, no! You're scaring me. Why are you doing this?" She couldn't control herself as her feelings turned in on themselves. Her daddy was the one who should've protected her. How could he be doing this?

"Little girl, everything I've done was to serve him. Are you ready to practice for when your bleeding stops?"

He lunged at her and Hannah jumped to the side. Her nightgown lightly brushed over one of the candles and caught fire.

"No!" she screamed. The flames burst upwards on the nightgown. Her father stepped back, looking around for anything to wrap her in.

Hannah panicked as the flames singed the hairs on her legs. She ripped off the nightgown, burning her hands as she did. She cried out.

Her daddy did nothing to help.

"What's wrong with you?" she shouted.

"We need to offer vessels," he replied.

Hannah watched as the flames ignited the book that was outside of the pentagram on the floor. Her daddy shouted and dove for it. When he wrapped his arms around it, he knocked over another candle and this one ignited the mask he had worn over the past few weeks.

Hannah moved back toward the door. Fear and confusion filled her. Her daddy was trying desperately to put out the fire on the book, but it didn't seem to stop. Embers from the pages spread out like fireflies. When they landed, some of them were snuffed out. Others landed on papers or the black cloth on the walls, which spread the fire even more.

Hannah wasn't sure if she should help her daddy or run. He glared at her and even without the mask, she saw The Beast. Her mind was made up. There was no way she was going to do a thing for him.

She turned and ran out of the room, slamming the door behind her just as flames raged and her daddy screamed.

Hannah raced through the house looking for the way out. She was afraid that if her daddy escaped the room, she'd be in trouble. She turned down a hall and found the kitchen and another door she hoped led to the outside. When she opened it, she stared into an inky night.

In the house, a door burst open.

"Hannah! Get back here!" her daddy shouted. She glanced into the house and then back into the dark.

This was her escape. Her one shot at freedom. All those nights spent worrying about what The Beast would do to her culminated in this moment. The Beast, her daddy, was evil. She couldn't stay. Whatever his plans were for her would have to go unfinished. Whatever awaited her in the darkness was better than what was in the house.

"Hannah!" he screamed again and she saw him coming, flames wrapped around his body, but with a wicked grin on his face.

The Beast was coming.

Hannah bit her lower lip, shifting on her feet and then ran into the night. Freedom's embrace was cool and welcoming. The darkness more comforting than ever before.

The car was acting weird. It sputtered as if it was out of gas or had some mechanical problem. It was shaking and struggled to maneuver. I pulled over to a curb, set the car in park and killed the engine. The shaking stopped. I grabbed my phone, but it wouldn't turn on at all. I stepped out and looked around at where I was. This place looked familiar, but I couldn't remember when I'd been here or seen it before.

As I walked down what I assumed was the main street in this village, I noticed that there was no one outside. It was a beautiful day out and there wasn't a single soul around. I had a weird feeling inside of me. Despite not seeing anyone on the street, I felt like I was not alone.

Like I was being watched.

The more I walked down this road, the weirder things seemed. It felt like this town was shaken-up like a snow globe, and then dumped out, letting whatever spilled out of it to be placed here. That was the best way I could possibly describe it because some of the houses looked to be well kept and reminded me of a tv show or movie I've seen from the 1960's. The others...

While some of the houses looked amazing and well kept, the rest looked like they had just been through a major world war. The outside of those homes had faded and most of the paint was chipped. Some of the windows had been broken or boarded up. But there was one thing that stood out among these worn-down houses – they each had white flags hanging from the front.

That was weird enough, but the real alarming thing was that most of those white flags were either torn, shot up or partially burned.

The nearest white flag house looked like it was shot to ribbons as the dirty, white cloth blew in the wind. I stared at the flag at first until I heard a noise. It sounded animal-like, and I looked towards the front door. But that wasn't where the sound was coming from; it came from the side of the house.

As soon as I looked over to the left, I saw a chicken run out. Its little feet were trying to move fast, but I saw something coming up from behind it and I knew the chicken was not going to outrun its predator. A fox scurried on the ground like a snake and when it came within distance of the chicken, it leapt at it. The chicken had no chance.

Seeing a fox out here in what appeared to be civilization was shocking enough, but then I stood there and watched what it did to that chicken. I had to get away and felt horrible just standing there, witnessing the toll of nature.

"Hey," said a voice. It came from a house up ahead. I looked to where the voice had come from and saw a man standing by a front door. He waved his arm telling me to come closer. I started to move my feet in the direction towards him, but they moved faster when he said, "Hurry!"

When I approached where the man was standing, he went inside the house and left the door open. I walked up the concrete steps and went in. It was pitch black. My eyes were trying to adjust to the darkness and to find where the man had gone.

"Close the door," a voice said from the back of the house. "Quickly!"

I did as I was told. I closed the door fast and harder than I intended to. The slamming sound was loud and echoed throughout what I could now see as a half empty house. "Where are you?" I asked this stranger that had invited me in.

"Back here," the voice said. It sounded like it came from the other side of the house. It took my eyes another moment to adjust to the environment. It was a good thing too because garbage laid across the floor. Actually, it was more like debris. Chairs turned over, shattered picture frames, books torn apart and what was really alarming was a metal chest that was splattered with bullet holes.

It wasn't easy to walk to the back of the house. My feet were trying not to step on the scattered litter on the floor. It didn't work out too well and I almost rolled my ankle. "Back here," the voice called again. I followed it and found the man who waved me in. He stood behind a chair where a woman sat.

She looked to be in rough shape. My eyes rose up to meet the man's gaze, but he wasn't in much better shape than her. He was frail looking. "I shifted my gaze back to the woman who looked even worse than before. It seemed these two had been through hell and back, as if they were in a war."I wondered if they were a couple and that question was quickly answered.

"My wife and I were wondering why you came back here?" the man said.

I was confused. "What do you mean came back here?" I asked him. "I don't even know where here is?"

The man came closer. "This is Hammer's Village. You don't remember?"

"No, I don't."

"Adrian," he said to me. *How did he know my name?* "You don't remember where you grew up? You don't remember me?" As soon as he said it, I thought he looked familiar. "It's me Richard. You shouldn't have come back," he said.

"I was driving, and my car gave me problems," I don't know why I was explaining myself to him. "I got out and I've seen some weird things. This place looks like a bomb hit it."

"Well," the man said. "That is not entirely false, 'though, there were some explosions that took place here."

"What happened? Why does some of the village look fine while some of the houses look abandoned and run down?"

The man stepped forward. "Listen, you need to leave, now!"

"Why?" I asked him. "What's going on here?" He kept approaching me and I backed up.

We were near the front door, and I reached out to open it, but he gripped my shoulders to turn me around. "Adrian, it's for your own safety. They do check-ins and if they find you, they will kill you, or worse."

"Worse?" I asked him. "What could be worse than death?"

The man, Richard, looked back towards the kitchen where his wife sat. He didn't need to explain anymore to me.

"The opposition will get you if you don't leave. They are killers." He released his grip on my shoulders. "Anyone they find loose on the streets, will be captured."

"Listen, uh, Richard," I answered him. "I don't know what to do or where to go. My car was acting funny. It might be a gas issue, a mechanical issue or an electric issue. I don't know. But, is there a mechanic or garage I could bring it to? Also, my phone doesn't seem to be working."

Richard stared straight at me, not blinking. "They scrambled the airwaves. No one can contact anyone or be contacted. I told you; they are dangerous people." He opens the door and points to the outside.

"Richard, please." He closed the door on me.

Outside, the village was quiet. I looked at my surroundings, gaging at what the houses really looked like. The ones that were beaten up had white flags that hung in front of them. All of them. They were all torn into shreds as if an animal had attacked them. The tattered shreds gently blew from a wind that flowed down the main road. I looked behind me to Richard's house to verify if he had the same thing hanging outside his run-down abode. He did.

I walked down the road, but I didn't walk down the middle of the street. Even though there weren't any cars or anyone occupying the street, I remembered Richards warning about those opposition people capturing those who they find roaming the streets. I kept to the sidewalks and closer towards the houses.

A few houses away from Richards, a noise came from between two buildings. As I got closer, the noise distinctively became more noticeable. It sounded like someone slurping on a piece of food.

Around the corner were two boys, both who looked as though they were in their early teens. The boys were dirty with smudges on their cheeks and the clothes were torn in a few places, similar to the white flags that hung on the houses.

They were kneeling down in front of each other, occupied with what they were devouring. The noises stopped when they noticed my presence and they both looked at me. The one on my left had yellow eyes with his black hair in a buzz cut that was poorly done.

Hanging from his mouth was what these boys were feasting on – a worm.

The long, silky body wiggled from side to side while the boy on the left held his lips tightly around it. The boys looked at me as though I had interrupted them and found out their secret. "It's the only food we can find," the boy on the right said. He was paler in color than the other boy but shared the same haircut. The boy on the left held his lips tight. The worm continued to wiggle around.

I stood there in shock. The reality of how things were in this village was very strange. The area seemed as though it was recently in a war where things didn't go too well for the citizens. "I'm sorry," was all I could think of saying as the boys held their gaze at me. "I'm sorry," I said again.

"Please don't take them," the boy on the right said.

"Take what?" I asked.

"Our food," he said. "The worms. We found them fairly. We didn't steal them."

They were more worried about me taking their meal away than the embarrassment of the situation. This both scared me and made me feel pity for them to have to live like this.

I didn't say anything while we looked at each other for a moment longer. I backed up and continued to do so while still facing them. They kept staring at me until I had backed up far enough and then they went back to eating their meal. Before I headed back around the corner, I could see the worm in the one boy's mouth wiggle and then disappear. A slurping sound came from that direction.

The options I had seemed limited. I needed to leave this village, but I didn't know how. My car wasn't working but maybe I could try it again and I thought it was worth the effort.

I walked the few blocks back to where I had parked it, actually where it had broken down. As I got closer to where I thought it had been, there was nothing there. No car. I was pretty sure that this was the area where I had pulled it over. There was no car there, but there was something else. Someone had painted a message in red letters on the concrete where I left my vehicle.

STAY

The letters that were spray painted on the ground made me fear for my life.

What the hell is going on around here?

There was nothing more I could do, I had to move on and preferably somewhere sheltered for my safety. I walked on looking for that safe spot, past the area where Richard's house was and where the kids were eating worms, but I opted to walk on the other side of the street. The houses were similar in appearance and as I walked on, I could see some houses had lights that were coming on. I hadn't noticed how dark it was getting.

This didn't make sense to me as I had arrived here shortly before 1pm and it was a sunny, cloudless day. Being that it was the middle of May meant that the sun didn't set until much later in the day and I truly believe that I hadn't been here that long.

Psst.

The sound knocked me out of my thoughts. *Was someone calling out to me?*

Psst.

The sound came from the next house ahead on my right. The house looked to be in well-kept condition. The lawn looked freshly mowed, and the paint wasn't chipped on the window frames. The door wasn't hanging off like some of the other houses I had seen. Also, there wasn't a torn, white flag hanging in the front of the house.

Psst.

The sound came from a corner of the porch. It took a moment for my eyes to adjust to the growing darkness of the street. I could see a dark figure waving me over towards them. At first, I was hesitant to get closer but then the figure spoke. "It's too dangerous out there. Come inside."

What other choice did I have?

I walked onto the porch. The figure's face still rested in the shadows as they held the door open for me. "Quickly," they said. "Come in." This invitation felt very similar to what I experienced at Richard's house. Except this place was well kept.

Inside, the floor was carpeted in a combo beige and white color. It made me self-conscious about getting it dirty, and I looked down at my feet. My shoes had a significant amount of mud stuck to them. They stepped back and signaled for me to follow them. I felt bad about walking in with muddy shoes but I did it anyway.

The figure briefly turned around, and I saw why I couldn't see their face; they wore a mask. I followed them into a room that appeared to be the living room of the house. There were couches and chairs that were positioned in a U shape, with people sitting among them.

"Welcome back, Adrian," the figure said. They took off their mask. It was a man with dark black hair that was combed back behind his ears. He wore a scar on his left cheek. A long line that ran from below his lip to the spot where the ear takes shape.

"Uhm, hi," I said. "How do you know my name?"

The man smiled. "It's dangerous out there, wandering around like you were. You may not know this, but you have enemies out there, especially in the dark."

"Yes, I've been told." He never answered my question. I looked around the room and saw that everyone was staring at me. I counted four other people here, beside the man with the scar. Actually, there were five. I didn't notice him at first because he was knelt down, tucked back in the right corner. It was a child.

He didn't look too young, but not old enough to be able to get a license to drive a car. He had long, dark hair that was similar to the man who let me in. His hair rested on his shoulders and waved in the air as he brought his body forward and then back again. He had a continuous movement of back and forth after his arm shot out releasing something and then picking it up.

His knees were locked up, aligned with his shoulder blades. The only time his feet moved was when he leaned in to grab the object that he shook with one hand and released. I moved closer around the couch to get a better view. A fireplace was lit behind him. The kid raised his right hand up near his ear, shook it for a moment and then released a pair of dice onto the floor in front of him. The pair of dice reminded me of what one would find in a board game. After each roll, he would quickly pick them back up.

I looked around to see what he was playing, but there was no board game or cards or anything else that indicated he was playing a game. There wasn't even anyone else there playing with him.

"It's dangerous out there," the man said, bringing me back from staring at the kid.

"So, I've heard," I said to him. The other people on the couch stared at me. Their eyes were staring at me as if they were deciding what to do with me, or what to do to me.

This place looked very comforting from the outside, in a 'normal' sort of way. A place where there was a family with a couple of children and who would host the neighborhood BBQ or picnic. But, as I was standing in here, looking at the surroundings, this place felt cold, despite the fireplace roaring in the corner. It felt wrong. The curtains were pulled shut, the lights were low and the figures who were staring at me on the couch, had their shadows cast up the wall in a monstrously large shape. I felt intimidated.

My mind was racing, thinking of what to do next. I didn't know my way around the house, or even the neighborhood for that matter, and I didn't know where to escape to. I didn't know if I could outrun these people. Looking at their faces, I had at least twenty years on them, and I wasn't exactly in great shape to run away.

"What are you doing here?" the man asked me. He stepped closer to me. My instinct was to back up, but I held my ground, just barely, I might add. The man only took one step and then stopped. From that extra step closer I noticed his size. He was taller than me, not by much but I could tell from beneath his clothing that his torso was muscular and while I feel like I could get a good shot at his jaw, I knew he could take me down pretty easily.

"My car broke down," I told him. "I was looking for a client's house but got lost and ended up here. Look, is there a garage or..."

"Where's your car?" he asked me.

"Back there." I pointed at what I thought was the correct direction.

"And you just decided to walk around out there?"

The question made me a bit confused. I answered back with some attitude, "What else was I supposed to do?"

"Stay in it," said a voice from behind the couch. It came from the boy who was rolling the dice.

"What?" I huffed a laugh. "What do you mean stay in it? I need help. Are you people able to help me or not?"

"That all depends," the boy said. The others on the couch, who seemed to be older than the one with the dice, kept their stare at me and stayed silent.

"All depends on what?" I looked at the man with the scar.

"It all depends on what the dice will say about your future." The boy answered me and released the dice. They made a clicking sound as they hit the carpet and collided with each other.

I looked at the man with the scar. I was expecting him to answer me logically, not this child. The man pointed his arm towards the area behind me, where the child was.

"Sir," I asked him. "Are you able to help me?"

The man blinked; it was almost a wince as if this was a painful situation. "Milo has spoken. Come forward to find your fate." His arm stayed pointed. At that moment, all the boys from the couch stood up. Each one lifted their arms and pointed in the direction that the man was pointing towards.

Towards the boy with the dice.

"Look, you don't have to help me. Just, please, tell me who could."

"Milo has spoken," the man said. His arm held steady.

"Who's Milo?" I asked and felt dumb after the words came from my mouth. The boy stopped rolling the dice for what I thought was the first time since I had come into this house.

He looked up at me as he stood up. He was taller than I thought, but was still young. Way too young to be in charge of things. But, for some reason, the boy held power. I looked at the man and I thought I saw some fear in his eyes.

"The dice will tell you your fate," the boy said again. He remained standing. The dice in his right hand knocked into each other as he casually shook his fist.

I walked past the boys that were on the couch. Their arms remained pointing as did their eyes on me. I followed those eyes until I got closer to where the man was standing.

"What's going on here, man?" I asked him in a whisper. My face was about an inch or two away from his.

"Milo has spoken. It is time to find out your fate."

What the hell does that mean?

I held my gaze a moment longer and then went to where Milo was stationed. Milo stayed standing until I got within the area that he used for rolling the dice. He held his hand out, indicating for me to stop and he knelt down to the position he was in when I came into this house.

Milo pointed to the floor below me. I assumed he wanted me to kneel down, so I did.

"No!" he shouted. "You sit cross-legged." I did as he asked me to. "Put your elbows on your knees and hold your hands out."

I did as he had instructed.

"The dice will decide your fate," he said again.

"What fate?" I asked.

"If you will be saved or disposed."

"What do you mean saved or disposed?" I think I

knew the answer to my question, but there was no way this could be real.

Milo stopped shaking his fist. "Whether we let you go, or..."

He didn't finish the sentence. He grasped the dice with both hands and shook it.

"Or, what?" I asked.

"Let's see what the dice say." Milo continued to shake the dice while he held his stare. I stared back. A shiver ran through my body, not just because of this odd, morbid situation, but because his eyes looked ice cold. Those eyes looked like they didn't care about anything or anyone, except maybe the dice he held in his hands.

Despite that chill that had run through me, I found myself sweating. The sweating grew as Milo continued to shake up the dice.

"Are you odd?" He asked me. The dice clunked together.

"What?" I asked him. My throat was dry.

"Or, are you even?" The only sound in the room was the clinking of the dice, the fire behind Milo and the low hum from the lightbulbs and electricity that ran through this structure.

"Odd or even?" I asked him with some confusion.

"Your choice," he said. "But it doesn't matter anyway, you can't outrun your fate."

I realized this kid was talking to me as though we were in a casino together and he was the dealer. That's what it reminded me of. Instead of betting on my money, I was betting on my life. I looked back to the man and the other children. They held their stares at me. I don't think they blinked once.

"What will it be?" Milo asked me. I was about to say something when he shouted, "ANSWER NOW!"

Sweat fell from my forehead and into my left eye. I wiped it away and answered him. "Uh, odds."

Milo stopped shaking his fist. "Good choice," he said. He smiled.

The dice rattled faster in fury as he held up both hands that were cupped together. A smile formed on his face, and he released the dice.

Clink. Clink.

They knocked into each other twice. The translucent red color and the painted white dots on the side glimmered as reflection came from the fire that was roaring behind Milo. As they collided with each other, the dice went their separate ways. One of them rolled towards me and stopped a few inches away from my right shoe.

Four

It was an even number. That wasn't good. I looked at Milo and his smile grew larger. The other dice continued to bounce around on its sides for only a moment longer, but to me, it seemed to be minutes instead of seconds.

Finally, it landed, and I held my breath. I was mesmerized by how it would land. It bounced one way, and then the other way. As it bounced, it seemed to shoot up farther and off to the sides, only to bounce back and come to fall on a flat side.

Four.

That total would make the total an even number,

eight. My heart seemed to stop beating as well as my breathing. My fate would be death; I was sure of it. My thoughts ran through me so fast, and as my fear ramped up, I didn't notice that the last dice had some more momentum to roll over on its one side and then to fall still. It wasn't the number four, but a different number.

Seven.

The total number was eleven, an odd number.

"Damn," the man with the scar said. "No fun for us tonight."

I was dumbfounded at what I saw, probably more in disbelief than anything. I stared at the lone red dice that we were all so enchanted with a moment ago. It stared back at me.

I smiled in relief. But for some reason I still feared what my outcome would be.

"Well," the boy said.

"It's odd," I told him.

"It is." He stood up. "It looks like your fate has been chosen. You can leave." He pointed towards the door.

"Wait," I said. "I still need help. My car isn't working. Isn't there anyone who can help me?"

"Your fate has been chosen," the boy said. He kept his arm straight and held it, pointing towards the door.

"But," I looked at the man. "You said it's dangerous out there."

"It is," he said, but said nothing after that.

I guess I had to go. It's not like I wanted to stay; the place gave me the creeps. But, I was concerned with being out there on the streets, alone. I had only visited two houses here and both of the residents inside had warned me about the dangers out there.

Milo held his arm straight out and continued pointing at the door. The boys on the couch were doing the same thing, as well as the man. I felt like I had interrupted some secret meeting or something. I looked back at the man when I headed to the door, hoping he would say something, anything, to help me out. His face didn't change when the door was closing.

Outside, the temperature had dropped. The night was suddenly cool, and I had no jacket, at least I don't remember bringing one. I stayed close to the sidewalks, avoiding the street. It wasn't exactly an easy walk, as the sidewalks were in ruins. Concrete was torn up. There were roots from trees sticking out and they made me fumble a few times.

I didn't know where to go. I only knew that I didn't want to go back to where I was.

A whisper came from my left side as I walked past a few rows of abandoned houses.

"There he is again," a faint voice said. It was tough to hear it exactly, but that's what I think they said.

A few more whispers and faint voices came from that side. I picked up my pace. I wasn't exactly running, but I was trying to move as fast as possible without bringing too much attention to myself.

I found myself surrounded by no more houses. I had gone to the end of the road and apparently this is where the road bends to the right and continues on from what I could see. I followed that way. More houses came into view, but they were completely dark, and each one seemed to have the torn cloth of white flags.

Footsteps were approaching from behind me. I picked up my pace as much as I could. I didn't want to show fear, but that is what I was feeling, and it was increasing, as well as the footsteps behind me.

"Adrian," someone said behind me.

I pretended not to hear them and continued on.

"Adrian!" a different voice said.

This would continue on, and I knew I had to turn around to face them.

I couldn't see their faces too descriptively, but there were a few of them. I quickly counted six people. Their height ranged from short to super tall. I wasn't short, but there were two of them that towered over me as the group approached me.

"What are you doing back here?" one of the shorter ones asked me.

Why has everyone asked me this?

They took a step closer. The one who asked me was a woman who looked older than me. There were gray streaks that ran down the sides of her dark hair. Her clothes were torn in places and had spots of dirt on them. They all had similar looks. The woman came closer. The others stayed back, and it became obvious that she was the leader.

"Haven't you learned yet?" She let out a tiny laugh. The others behind her did the same. "You keep coming back here and keep getting the same result. You belong –

with us." The ones behind her nodded their heads and mumbled amongst each other.

"What do you mean I belong with you?" I asked.

"It's no use to deny it. Join the resistance."

"What resistance?" I knew there was a us versus them going on in the village here, but I wasn't totally sure which ones were the 'good ones'.

"Stop acting dumb," she told me. She moved closer and I could faintly see a scar on her right cheek. It looked very similar to the one that the man had back at the house with Milo. She smiled, "Please stay this time."

I had no idea what she was talking about. All I knew was that I felt the need to leave, immediately. I shook my head and backed up.

"Adrian!" she shouted. It sounded more like she was pleading to me rather than yelling at me.

I took off running. After a moment, I looked back. No one was following me. No one was around. The dark street showed no sign of life anywhere, not even from the homes and buildings I passed by.

I stopped running and settled on a brisk walk. All this running had me panting and reminded me that I was not in the best of shape. I would worry about that later, for now, I just needed to get out of here and find my way back to the normal world.

A sense of hope sprung up inside me when I saw the first thing that made me think I was getting closer to reality, it was a car.

I hadn't seen one this entire time I was walking/running on these streets. When I got closer to it, I noticed it looked familiar. It was my car.

How could that be?

I didn't reflect too much on this impossibility, I just wanted to get as far away from here as I could, and fast.

I sprinted faster while reaching into my pocket for the key fob. My hand gripped it with sweat. I pressed the button to unlock the car. Its low beep amplified louder as it echoed around this empty neighborhood. I quickly got in and closed the door. My foot and hand instinctively synched to pressing down on the brake and pushing the button to start the engine.

To my surprise, the engine kicked on instantly and I positioned the gear shift to drive away. I felt relieved and thought to myself that I was going to make it out here alive. For a moment, the car was running perfectly, but that was short lived.

The car was acting weird. It sputtered as if it was out of gas or had some mechanical problem. It was shaking and it struggled to maneuver. I pulled over to a curb and set the car in park and killed the engine. The shaking stopped. I stepped out and looked around at where I was. This place looked familiar, but I couldn't remember from when I had been here or seen it before.

What does it mean to sacrifice? More importantly, when that sacrifice is made for a life you never even wanted, does that make you a fool, or worse, a murderer? Did you kill the version of yourself you were supposed to become?

"Evan, are you alright?"

It's a funny thing to ask, at least for the little twerp on the other side of this desk. He must barely be out of high school. I can still see the shine of acne scars on his smooth, chinless face. Devin should grow a beard or something to cover that up, but hell, he probably can't even grow one. Thinking about him staring in the mirror every morning, lamenting that fact almost helps me smile through the fact that I'm being laid off.

I force the smile anyway, but I can tell from his expression that it's less like a reassurance, and more like the grimace of a threatened chimpanzee who's being jabbed through the bars by a zoo handler with a broomstick. The kid almost looks afraid and it gives me a quiet satisfaction. He's probably never fired anybody before, just like he has very little experience in any management at all. The benefit of being the son of a CEO I suppose. A year ago, he was probably puking through alcohol poisoning in a field somewhere. "How old are you?" I ask with my teeth still bared.

"Excuse me?"

"It's a simple question."

"I'm twenty-three, but I don't think it's appropriate that—"

"Do you know what that means?" I cut him off, my blood heating to a vengeful simmer.

"No, can't say that I do."

"It means," I start, struggling to keep my voice level, "that I've been here, working in this office, since before you were born. What it *means* is that there are forgotten papers in the drawers of my desk that were printed while you were still pissing yourself and crying to your mommy whenever you had a nightmare." I'm still smiling, so wide now that it hurts my cheeks. "It means that I've given half my life to this company, only to be thrown aside for what? A goddamn algorithm?"

"Your severance package is more than fair. Times are changing and there's just no room for redundancy in this company's future." He's trying to sound professional, nonchalant, but he can't hide the tremor in his voice.

"Redundancy?" I repeat, chewing on the word like a sharp piece of gravel. "People aren't redundant you smarmy fucking infant. What do you think it's like, job hunting at my age? You'll never find out of course. Daddy's taken care of your whole future for you, hasn't he?"

Devin's face reddens and it's almost worth the job to watch him squirm, humiliated but still needing to act unfazed. He stumbles over some half-baked corporate buzzwords, but I'm up and out of his office, already halfway back to the desk I've sat at every day for 48,000 hours of the last couple decades, give or take. I take what's mine, and some that isn't, then make my way to the elevator for the eleven story journey down.

I started in the basement mailroom, clawed my way all the way up the tower, just to be tossed away like garbage. They might as well just chuck me out the window. It'd get me out of the building faster and turn all the rubbernecking eyes of my former coworkers back to maintaining efficiency and productivity.

Of course it's raining outside. It rains all the time here and yet I don't own an umbrella. However, I barely notice as I trudge the nine blocks to my coffin of an apartment. How did it come to this? I remember being a teenager, wanting—no—expecting the world laid at my feet, and why shouldn't I have? The teachers always said I was gifted. Uncle Eddie said so too.

What would he think of me now, my hair cut short, winding my way down a decades long staircase of defeat? My first thought when I walk through the door is to feed the dog, but my second reminds me that he died six months ago. It's just me here. I'm fifty-four years old and this is what my life looks like: Unemployed with a black mold infested apartment and only five numbers in my phone. Two of them belong to takeout places, one for the office that I guess I can delete now, one for the woman who told me not to call her anymore, and of course, the last number that belongs to a dead man.

Uncle Eddie was my best friend. He killed himself on tour twenty years ago, but I've brought his number with me to every new phone I've had since then. Even though he's gone, it's nice to have the number of somebody who believes in me.

I went on tour with him once, just for a few shows when I was a teenager, watching the seething crowd boil over for one more song. I thought I'd be like him, told him that's what I wanted to do after a show one night, and damn if he didn't open up his guitar case, put the thing in my hand, and tell me it was mine now.

It's probably the most valuable thing I own. No, it definitely is. If I sold it, I could keep myself in this rats' nest for five more years, or even buy a decent place.

I could never do that, of course. I've already sold my life, my body, my mind. It would kill me to lose that last spark of a dream. What would he say if I did? He'd probably kick me in the ass for not having done it already, to be honest. Eddie never did give much of a shit for objects. He lived for experience.

And that's the real reason I think he'd be ashamed of me. I've never experienced anything, not really. If he asked what I've done with my life, all I could talk about would be a few too many beers in college before sitting at a desk for the next half of my life. That's it. You're all caught up, Ed.

And all those years, all that work, just to live in a shitty apartment in one of the most expensive cities in the world. I don't even remember the last time I picked up that guitar. Maybe I should.

The case leans upright against the wall in my bedroom. I've tried putting it in the closet a few times, but it's like leaving it out is a pretty little lie I tell myself, like it's out because I need it, because any minute now, I'll pick it up.

The inside of the case is crushed red velvet, as fresh and clean as the day he bought it; a heavy contrast to its scratched and faded exterior. The white body of Eddie's Jackson guitar shines like the sun. This thing once sang to over 300,000 people at the Rock in Rio festival in 1985, and it's been trapped in its coffin—which itself has been trapped in mine—almost ever since. There's something profane about that, isn't there? I feel a flash of rage at all that wasted time.

I pick it up like it's way more fragile than it is and sit on my bed. I don't even have an amplifier to plug it into, but I strum it a few times anyway. I'm surprised to find it's still in perfect tune. That doesn't seem possible. The strings should slowly lose tension after sitting unused for so long. I warm up with a couple scales, annoyed to find that I don't remember them at first. Furthermore, after only a few minutes, my fingertips already sting from their war with the fretboard. I used to play for hours, but my fingers are less conditioned than they used to be.

I push through the pain and start shuffling through my brain to find the songs I still know how to play. There's a flash of movement in the corner of my vision from the chair beside my bed. It almost looked like a person was sitting there, but of course the chair's as empty as it ever was. I turn my focus back to the instrument, take a deep breath, and launch into the solo from my favorite song. Naturally, it's one uncle Eddie wrote, from their sixth album, if I remember correctly.

The more dust I shake off that part of myself, the warmer I feel. After a few flubs on the opening notes, I fall into it just like I used to, and it's like I'm flying.

The strangest part is that even without an amplifier, I can hear the music I'm playing. Not in that way you know what it's supposed to sound like, but as though it were plugged into the world's tallest Marshall stack, turned all the way up. For just a moment, there's nothing in the world except for me and this song, so loud I can feel it vibrate through my teeth.

But the tension of the strings outmatches that of my flesh and I feel them become slick with blood. It used to take all day to break the skin. I stop playing, disgusted by my frailty.

"Why did you stop?"

I yelp like a kicked dog and almost drop the guitar. The chair beside my bed isn't empty anymore.

The skin on his face—yellow as old flypaper— cracks under the strain of uncle Eddie's grin. His teeth are like gray tombstones and his eyes are black marbles set deep into their decaying sockets.

"Why did you stop?" He asks again. His voice is a beehive in a paper bag.

I laugh because it's finally happened. I've gone utterly insane and maybe I'd be afraid if it wasn't so freeing. "It's good to see you," I say to the chair that has to be empty, welcoming the delusion because at least I'm not alone anymore.

"You have to play. If you don't, I can't—" Eddie flickers like a projection and blinks away. I gawk at the empty chair, mourning the fantasy being so short-lived, and I'm about to put the guitar away but the thought that maybe I didn't imagine it holds me back. I wince when my split fingers touch the strings, but begin to play.

"—find you." He's back in the chair, seemingly unaware of being cut off mid-sentence. His leather jacket is caked in soil with patches of moss sprouting on the sleeves, but I still recognize it as the one he was buried in. I keep playing, faster and faster, flecks of blood flying from my fingers and splashing onto the corpse across from me, where they disappear, absorbed like rain on parched desert earth. Eddie grins wide and nods his head in time, smoke seeping out from between his teeth like it must have when he pulled the trigger. I wonder what the back of his head looks like.

I want to stop playing, want to ask him a thousand questions, but if I do, will he disappear again? I hope my blood isn't staining the pristine white guitar, but when I look down, the thing is clean as ever, greedily drinking my effluence. Eddie rises from the chair, stretches out like a driver after a long ride in a cramped car, leans down close to inspect the guitar. His breath smells like wet dirt and the music is so loud that I fear my neighbors calling the police.

"You've taken good care of it," he says, and I think of the fine line between care and neglect. If I'd used it as it was meant to be used, surely it wouldn't still be in such perfect condition. He nods as though hearing my thoughts, and seeing as he's probably a figment of my imagination, it's likely he does.

We stay like this for hours, me playing songs I never learned how to play, him standing over me, inspecting my form. My fingers don't hurt anymore. I look down at my hand and find the skin of my fingertips flayed away, worked down to pure white bone, but rather than fear, I feel nothing short of elation. I've paid with my body for things I never wanted for all my life. Stripping the flesh from my hand in pursuit of something I love is a far easier price to pay.

"Now you understand the cost," Eddie says, and I know he's not talking about my hand, but the cost of having abandoned myself for so long, and the price of winning back that which I lost. It's a price he paid every day his whole life, and one I was too much of a coward to claim for myself; a birthright I rejected in favor of a cubicle and blue light filtering eyeglasses, just to be cast aside, my job handed off to artificial intelligence by some kid who's never made a sacrifice in his life.

Eddie nods thoughtfully, an apparent idea sparking in his black eyes. "An old life paid for a new one," he says, and I understand what he means. There's no need to speak. We both know what I have to do.

The parking lot of Moretech has emptied out by the time I arrive, save for Devin's S class Mercedes Benz. It surprises me that he's still here, but of course he is. He needs to be for what comes next. The front door—normally locked by now—pushes open easily, because that needs to happen too. I make my way down the dark hallway and slip into the elevator. When I reach the eleventh floor, the elevator dings to announce my arrival.

"Hello?" I hear Devin call out. I swing my guitar around on its strap from where it was hanging across my back and check to make sure it's still in tune. Once I'm satisfied, I creep across the field of cubicles until I reach his corner office and step inside. He seems startled to see me, but not afraid. That will change in a moment.

"What are you doing, Evan?" He asks. "You can't be here. If you left anything behind, call the front desk in the morning and they'll arrange to have it sent out. Please leave before I call security."

But we both know there are only two of us here. I strum a lazy chord and smile as uncle Eddie springs back into view behind Devin's chair.

"What the hell is this?" Devin asks, trying to paint authority over the uncertainty in his voice. Eddie grabs onto his hair and yanks his head back against the chair, holding him in place. Devin screeches in surprise. "Who's that? Who's there?" He demands, staring at me with wide eyes that are filling with the terror they were lacking just a moment ago.

"I don't know what this is," he says, the mask of authority gone in favor of a fearful bleating tone. "But you can just leave now and I won't call the police. We can just pretend it never happened. You want your job back? It's yours! Just tell me how we can work this out, tell me what you need! It's okay, I swear! It's fine!"

But I don't want my job back. I never wanted it to begin with. I want so much more than that and after all these wasted years, I'm going to take it. I unsling the guitar from my shoulders and hold it with two hands by the neck, testing its weight. Without the music, Eddie is gone, but I know he's somewhere, watching and waiting. I look down at my arms and see the leather of Eddie's jacket. It fits me perfectly.

I swing the guitar like an axe, breaking Devin's jaw on the first strike. The second silences the screaming.

And the third paints my face in the freshest, warmest red.

*   *   *

I'm sitting on an ugly yellow futon in an actually-green green room when there's a knock at the door. It's the stage manager, Erin.

"You about ready?" She asks. "Rest of the guys are out there already and the crowd is screaming for blood." I laugh at the joke she doesn't know she made and rise to my feet, picking up my simple white Jackson guitar as I do. I brush my long hair back with my free hand and take a deep breath.

"Yeah," I say. "Let's get to work."

Erin leads me down a long hallway and I can hear the crowd's roar strengthen with every step. I can feel the pulse of the kick drum deep in my chest. I can smell the sweat and beer and pure, unadulterated life. This day is like any other to me now. She pulls back a black curtain and I step out onto the stage, at the foot of which 60,000 people are screaming my name. This new office suits me well. I plug in and strum a long, mournful chord, then scan the crowd until I find him. My uncle grins back at me from every face in the crowd, and now that he's here, we can begin.

There are many things we sacrifice in this life. Nobody can avoid it. The only choice we have is what sacrifices we make. Do we sell our bodies for a paycheck? Do we sell our souls? What is lost when we don't take the things we want, the things we need? What kind of blood is it worth to you to live the life you've always dreamed of? Do you have the fortitude to shred your fingers down to pearlescent white bone? Or are you satisfied with the prison you've built for yourself?

I paid the cost and I'd do it again, over and over and over until every Devin in the world is reduced to quivering, shapeless meat. The world would surely be a better place for the slaughter.

Because beneath these stage lights, beneath the

watchful eyes of 1,000 dead rockstars, prostrate before the altar of heavy metal:

I'm finally home.

Thomas R. Clark

Speculative fiction author Thomas R Clark is a two-time Splatterpunk Award Nominee (Best Novella, 2021 for BELLA'S BOYS and Best Short Story, 2022 for FIREFLIES & APPLE PIES). His most recent release is WE ARE 13, a collection of splatterpunk & folk horror. His journalism and entertainment critiques have appeared in Memento Mori Ink, Rue Morgue, Stranger With Friction, House of Stitched Magazine, This Is Infamous, and miscellaneous internet outlets. Tom lives in Central New York with his wife and their canine companions.

STEVE ZISSON

Steve Zisson is a biotech journalist whose fiction has appeared in Daily Science Fiction, Nature's Future, Little Blue Marble, Suburban Nightmares, among other places. He edited a science fiction and fantasy anthology, A Punk Rock Future. He lives on the North Shore of Boston.

JG FAHERTY

Born and raised in New York's haunted Hudson Valley and more recently a resident of North Carolina's equally haunted Cape Fear region, JG Faherty is the author of 25 books, 4 collections, and more than 95 short stories, and he's been a finalist for both the Bram Stoker Award (twice) and ITW Thriller Award. He writes adult and YA horror, science fiction, dark fantasy, and paranormal romance, and his works range from quiet, suspenseful horror to action-packed paranormal thrillers. He is proud to be a relative of Mary Shelley. You can follow him on X, Facebook, and Instagram as @jgfaherty.

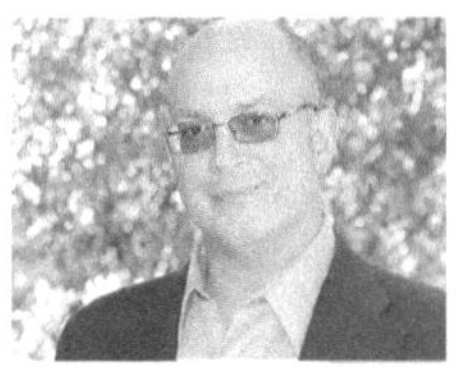

Jyl Glenn

Jyl Glenn is a writer, editor, formatter, narrator, and mentor. She is a freelancer for Memento Mori Ink Magazine, has edited several anthologies, appeared in several more, and her first novel, *Cubby*, released in September 2025. She collects creepy art, writes depressing poetry, and has an affinity for pink dinosaurs. Jyl is forever a New Yorker who happens to live in Tulsa with her dog, Betty. Her newsletter, signed books, and unhinged merch can be found: www.jylglennwrites.com

facebook.com/jylglenn

instagram.com/_delightfully_unhinged_

Mari Pittelman

Mari Pittelman is a horror fan and writer who prefers rainy days to sunny ones and secretly hopes the monster under her bed wants to be friends. She is on track to realize both of her life long dreams: to write and publish as much as possible. And to be the neighborhood witch that children tell scary stories about, because she believes that every child deserves a local urban legend. Mari lives in Milwaukee, Wisconsin with her familiar; a cat named Lilith. They can usually be found lurking around their apartment ignoring as many responsibilities as possible.

Killian H. Gore

Killian H. Gore is an independent horror writer and book publisher from Warrington, England, with over one hundred fiction and non-fiction titles to his name. Due to his passion for horror movies and hunger for trivia, the majority of his books are horror film quiz books, but they also contain original stories that are related to the particular movie the book focusses upon. He is the author of the novel, The Horror Movie Massacre, about a failed horror filmmaker who resorts to killing people at famous horror movie locations and the novella, UFO of the Dead, about a top-secret UFO file that could save the world from a zombie apocalypse.

STACIE HERRINGTON

Stacie Herrington writes fiction, poetry, and nonfiction, mostly horror. Recent work appears in the *Horror Writers Association Poetry Showcase XI*, *Defenestration*, *Last Girls Club*, and the Black Hare Press Patreon. If you enjoyed this story, check out "Such Good Care" in *Roadkill: Texas Horror by Texas Writers Vol. 10* (out October 2025), and listen to the soothing tones of her barely contained rage on *The Podcast Compels You*, available wherever you get your podcasts.

Spencer Keene

Spencer Keene (he/him) is a writer and lawyer from Vancouver, BC. His poetry and short fiction have been featured in a variety of print and digital publications, including Candlelit Chronicles, Dog Throat Journal, Underbelly Press, and Iron Faerie Publishing's Hallowed anthology. Find more of Spencer's work at www.spencer-keene.ca

Heather Ann Larson

Heather Ann Larson is an editor (Indie Terror 13) and author. She has been reading horror most of her life, starting as a young girl with Christopher Pike and RL Stine. She graduated to Stephen King earlier than she should have (as most of you also probably did).

Joshua Ginsberg

Joshua Ginsberg is the author of six non-fiction books on the subjects of off-beat travel, local history and haunted locations, including Secret Tampa Bay: A Guide to the Weird, Wonderful and Obscure and Haunted Orlando. His work has appeared on the NoSleep Podcast, in anthologies such as Hootenanny Horrorshow and Fumptruck, and in publications including Apex Magazine, Spooky, Tension Literary, Crepuscular, Black Hare Press, Trembling with Fear and Flash Phantoms. He lives in Tampa with his wife, Jen, and their Shih Tzu, Tinker Bell.

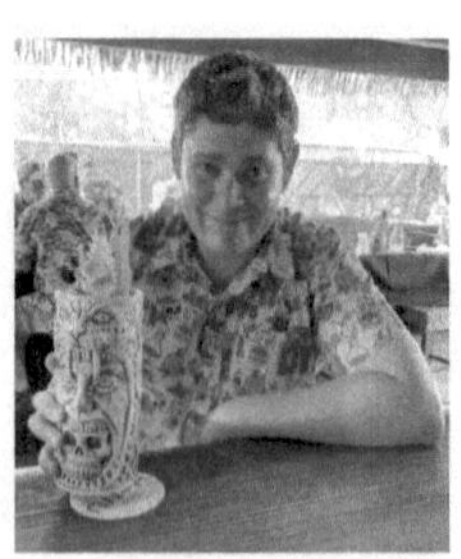

MJ Mars

MJ Mars is a geek, ghoul, and horror enthusiast living in Lancaster, UK. Her debut novel, The Suffering, was published by Wicked House in 2023. When she isn't writing, you'll find MJ playing pool, trying to skateboard (badly), or listening to rock music. She owes every success to her mis-spent youth.

Short story collection, We've Already Gone Too Far out now! Coming in 2025: The Fovea Experiments, a second novel to be published by Wicked House. MJ is currently working on a sequel to The Suffering.

Paul Taegel

Paul Taegel writes screenplays and other pulpy yarns. His original screenplay, *Vandal*, was produced in 2019. *The 2nd*, starring Ryan Philippe, was released in 2021 and made it to the top of Netflix's Top Action Films.. Paul grew up in Houston, TX, where his education began in the pages of *The Savage Sword of Conan,* the local UHF channel, and the glorious noise of Heavy Metal. He went on to earn a BA in English and Philosophy from Vanderbilt University and an MFA in Screenwriting from UCLA. Paul recently adapted Jeff Strand's epic horror-thriller novel, *ALLISON*. His original comic book series, *RIDGELINE*, is being published by Aftershock Comics. He lives with his wife and two kids in Colorado.

Matthew R. Davis

Matthew R. Davis is a Shirley Jackson Award-nominated author and musician living in Adelaide, South Australia, with over one hundred short stories and six books published to date. His latest is *The Cure On Track: Every Album, Every Song* (Sonicbond Publishing), with his next horror collection *Songs of Shadow, Words of Woe* (JournalStone) and his novelisation of the Australian indie film *Ribspreader* (with Dick Dale, Paroxysm Press) coming later in 2025. He began learning music at age fourteen and has played bass and sung in many acts, most notably the left-field heavy rock/metal bands Blood Red Renaissance and icecocoon. Find out more at matthewr-davisfiction.wordpress.com.

Kay Hanifen

Kay Hanifen was born on a Friday the 13th and once lived for three months in a haunted castle. So, obviously, she had to become a horror writer. Her work has appeared in over one hundred anthologies and magazines. Her first anthology as an editor, *Till the Yule Log Burns Out*, was published in 2024. Her first novel, *The Last Ballard*, debuted in 2025. When she's not consuming pop culture with the voraciousness of a vampire at a 24-hour blood bank, you can usually find her with her black cats or at kayhanifenauthor.wordpress.com.

RICHARD WALL

Richard Wall is a British author who turned to writing following a 22 -year career in the Royal Navy Submarine Service. Influenced by writers such as John Steinbeck, James Lee Burke and Andrew Vachss, Richard's stories reflect his life-long fascination with the dark underbelly of American culture, together with his love of Mississippi Delta Blues and classic American cars.

Richard has published three books - Fat Man Blues, Near Death, and Nicotine, Liquor, & Blasphemy - and is writing a collection of short stories with a blues theme.

Jay Bower

Jay Bower is a horror author living outside St. Louis, MO in the forest of Southern Illinois. He spends his time reading, writing, and convincing his wife the dark stories he writes do not involve her.

One time punk-rock skateboarder and heavy metal kid of the 80s, Jay approaches his work with the same indie attitude as those early punk bands.

He's the author of several dark novels and short stories. You can find him at jay-bower.com.

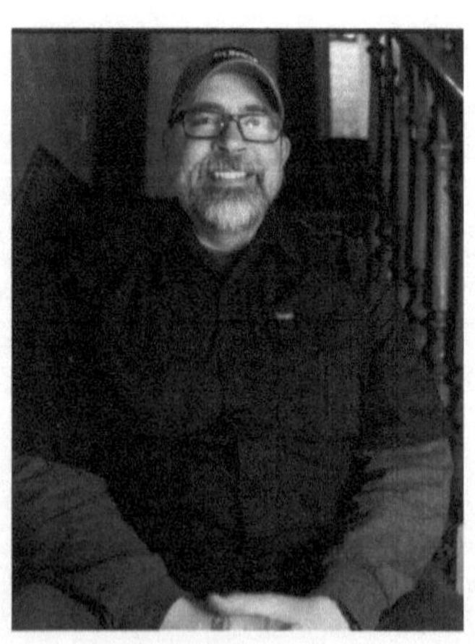

Jason Mecchi

Jason Mecchi grew up in Pennsylvania, which has been an inspiration for some of the stories that he has written. His debut short story collection, "The Pale Sky of Night" contains some of those Pennsylvania inspired stories. His debut novel will be published in 2025 as well as a new short story collection.

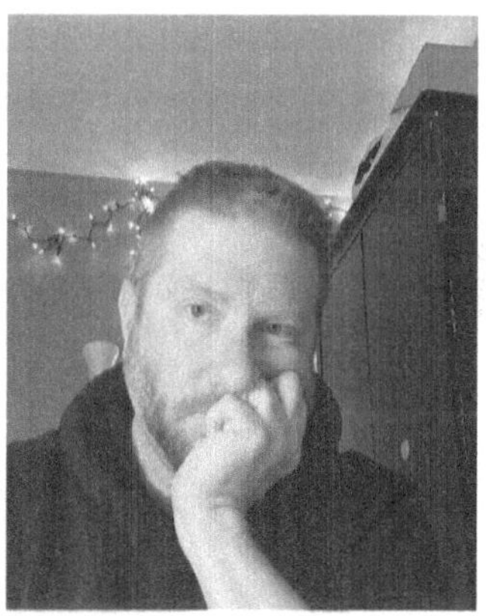

Joseph Murnane

Joseph Murnane lurks at the mouth of a cave off the banks of the Eno River in Durham, North Carolina, with four hellish animal companions and an eldritch queen of terrifying beauty. They say you can see him there just before dawn, but only out of the corner of your eye, and only if he wants to be seen. He can be reached via blood dance, or if the trials prove too difficult, email works too. jmurnanehorror@gmail.com